NO GREATER AGONY

Todd Allen

No Greater Agony

Todd Allen

Dark Dragon Publishing
Toronto, Ontario, Canada

No Greater Agony

ISBN: 978-1-928104-10-0
eISBN: 978-1-928104-11-7

Cover Illustration and Design ©
Back Cover Design © by WAV Design Studios

Dark Dragon Publishing
88 Charleswood Drive
Toronto, Ontario
M3H 1X6
CANADA
www.darkdragonpublishing.com
Printed in the United States of America.

For more information on Todd Allen
toddallenbooks.com/

For Maya.
Welcome to the family.

Acknowledgements

I would like to thank Karen Dales, Managing Editor at Dark Dragon Publishing, for her excellent work on this novel and for pushing me when I needed it. Seriously. Special thanks go out to Keith and Cheryl Johnson for reading early drafts of the story and for sharing their valuable insights; to Jeremy Gilmer for the long talks that always restore my passion for writing and to all my friends and family for being the best friends and family a guy could ask for.

Above all, I thank my wonderful wife, Michelle, for her unconditional, unwavering support. *You're the only reason I ever reach "The End".* And to my girl Maya for making every day the best day.

And, of course, I thank you, the reader. If you're ever near Wabasso Lake, look me up.

Prologue

1953

The Scoutmaster's whistle shrieked, setting off a stampede of young men. Over one hundred identical hiking boots trampled the dusty ground leading to the row of cabins. Ben was one of the first boys to reach them. He threw open the door of the furthermost one. Nathan entered at his heels. His pale and pimply face beamed. They would have their pick of the bunk beds on either side of the narrow structure.

Nathan was smaller than the other fifty-plus boys at camp and Ben figured he'd be the target of fifty-plus jokes a day. Despite his disadvantage, the kid never shied away from speaking his mind—especially in defense of the rules—as Ben had learned during the raucous bus ride from the city. As the other boys laughed and sang songs and threw paper airplanes, Nathan scolded and warned them of the dangers in distracting the driver.

Ben dumped his duffle on the floor next to the bottom bunk on the left side.

Scotty rushed in next and shoved Nathan into the wall. "You're takin' the top bunk, runt."

Ben had met Scotty on the bus. Scotty came from the lower west side of the city where it was said that kids were not so much raised up as they were dragged up. He shocked the other Scouts when he pulled a pack of cigarettes from his duffle upon arrival and lit up. He smoked lightly, cussed heavily, and combed his hair like James Dean.

Scotty turned and studied Ben's bunk. "Maybe I want that one," he muttered. He looked at the cabin's lone window beside the door. "Which way does the sun come up? Yeah. I want that one. Beat it, Benny."

Jeremy Fuller stepped inside the cabin. He nearly had to duck to keep from striking his buzz-cut on the doorframe. "That one's mine," he told Scotty, pointing at the bunk Ben had chosen.

Scotty put his hands up and nodded. He turned back to Nathan. "What are you waitin' for? Get up there, runt."

Ben picked up his bag as Jeremy went to stand beside him. The tallest Scout slapped a hand on his back. "It's all right. Take the bottom bunk. I like the top one better." He gave Ben a reassuring grin before climbing up to his bed.

Ben had known Jeremy for a few years. Everybody knew Jeremy. He was a standout in the classroom and on the football field, and as a Scout, he had no equal. He'd earned every merit badge he wanted, plus a bunch he didn't want, but they were there for the taking, so he took them. Ben, a year younger than Jeremy, didn't have a front row seat to his accomplishments, but he watched his legend grow from a distance. He did this with a small degree of head-shaking awe and with more than a small degree of envy. In Jeremy, people saw the brightest future.

Nothing of the sort could be said of Ben Campbell.

Ben did well enough in English class and always attained top marks in creative writing, but that was the extent of his scholastic talents. A slight kid, he didn't play competitive sports, preferring instead to spend his free time with his nose in a book. Arthur Conan Doyle and H.G. Wells were his favorites and in the early spring, he foresaw a summer vacation packed with good reading. That was until his mother handed down news that he was the Scout's newest recruit and he'd be shipped off to Camp Wabasso for eight weeks. She'd said the goal was to "get the cob webs blown off you". Ben knew it was merely a ploy to remove him from home during a time his mother admitted was a rough patch.

The Korean War was over. Ben's father had returned home safe and sound. Only he wasn't quite the same man as the one who had left Ben, his mom and his older sister before the fighting. The word that kept popping into Ben's head when he considered his father was *less*. Dad still talked, he just talked less. He still smiled, just less. He still laughed, just less. The one thing he did more of, was sleep. Ben's mother said he simply needed to get used to being home again, that this new, lesser version of Dad wouldn't be around for long. Ben wasn't so sure. The idea that post-war Dad wouldn't change back to pre-war Dad frightened Ben more than anything.

He had been frightened for nearly a year now. It wore on him, changed him, leaving him scarred somehow—not the kind of mark that everyone could see, but the other kids sensed it all the same. They sensed it in the way they sensed bed-wetters and cry-babies. They began to treat him different-ly. It seemed Ben had contracted Less Disease from his father. People talked to him less. They asked him to play ball less. They invited him to birthday parties less. Ben was getting used to *being* less.

Jeremy's father also fought in Korea. In fact, both of their fathers were honored with a neighbourhood barbeque upon their return. They seemed like the only two guys who didn't want to be there. Coming in a close second were their sons. That afternoon, Ben saw a familiar scar in Jeremy's face. He suffered from Less Disease, too.

Perhaps that's why Jeremy cut through the maze of boys and duffle bags earlier today and approached Ben with a hand-shake and a "good to see you again". Ben was beyond sur-prised. He didn't think people remembered him. Ever. But Jer-emy did. He even asked the Scoutmaster to make them cabin mates.

Having secured the bottom bunk, Ben went about making his bed. He unfastened the ties around his mattress and the bed unfurled. He froze. An unexpected item stared up at him.

The sight of it locked him up solid. In the middle of the bed-roll lay a stack of type-written and double-spaced pages, stapled in the upper left hand corner.

All sorts of thoughts raced through his head.

What is this? A story? What's it doing in the middle of a bedroll? My bedroll?

Ben scooped it up. Shielding his discovery from the view of the others, he studied it. Indeed, it was a story. Surely, one of the Scouts from last year's troop had brought it along, and instead of packing it up at the conclusion of camp, forgot it in the bedroll.

Or perhaps, someone hid it here.

He wondered if its owner went to such lengths because it was an especially racy story and if a troop leader was to find it, there'd be hell to pay. Was it the literary equivalent of those new *Playboy* magazines boys all over the country now stashed under their beds? The sharp bleat from the Scoutmaster's whistle outdoors told Ben he didn't have time to find out. It signaled the troop to reassemble outside the mess hall for orientation. Ben quickly tucked the story under his mattress. He would read it when the opportunity presented itself.

"Let's go," Jeremy said, jumping down from the top bunk. "We don't want to get in a jam on the first day."

Clouds gathered in the Appalachian foothills and by midday they rolled in to threaten the lake. While the troop toured the archery range, heavenly cannon fire boomed. The Scoutmaster, known to the majority of the troop only as Mr. K, decided to have them spend the rest of the day undertaking indoor activities in the large mess hall. The thunder receded sometime during the evening meal. Then the rains came in earnest. Many of the troop groaned at the prospect of sprinting back to their cabins in the downpour.

Standing in line at the mess hall entry, awaiting their turn to leave, Jeremy smiled at Ben. "Last one there's a rotten egg."

"Won't be me," Ben said, but when Mr. K opened the door for them, Jeremy bolted to a healthy lead.

Ben burst from the mess hall after him and soon closed the

gap. He had a pretty good idea Jeremy let him catch up to make a game of it. Overtaking him was a pipedream, Ben knew, as he sloshed through the ankle deep mud puddles along the trail while his long-legged friend vaulted those same puddles with ease. Ben's feet were soaked, his shorts were soaked and somehow, he couldn't stop laughing, nor could Jeremy as they slowed down at the cabin door. More surprising was the giddy laughter that issued from the trail behind them. Scotty, still at top speed, piled into them and they all tumbled into the cabin and fell in a heap between the bunks. The official rotten egg crossed the finish line next.

Nathan released a war cry as he dove onto the writhing tangle of arms and legs on the cabin floor. The race devolved into a spirited wrestling match, each boy fighting for breath more than fighting each other. An errant elbow caught Ben's cheek, but even as it started to smart, he could only laugh harder.

Long after the humour died off, the boys lay awake in their bunks, listening to the wind rattle the door and whistle through the gaps in their rudimentary summer home. Rain lashed the front wall, beating like drums in a marching band. Ben could feel the cabin shift during particularly strong gusts and it occurred to him that, if the place weighed a few pounds less, it might be carried away on the wind. Scotty seemed to share the uneasy thought, enough so as to gather his matches and light the lamp on the small table between their bunks.

Conversation commenced in a somewhat halting manner. Nerves left edges on the boy's voices. Nathan wondered aloud how long they should expect the rain to last. Jeremy ruminated that the next morning's hike was apt to be washed out. It was clear from his tone that he cared little about a cancelled hike, but preferred keeping up the chatter over listening to the storm. It struck Ben that he had just the thing for the occasion. He pulled the stapled pages from under his pillow.

"I got a story here," Ben said tentatively. "You fellas want to hear it?"

Across the narrow room, Scotty rolled onto his elbow,

while on the bunk above Nathan raised his head. In the weary kerosene lamplight, Ben could see that Nathan's hair was already matted. "Mr. K said it was lights-out," Nathan answered sharply. "That means it's time to sleep. We're not supposed to be talking, and we definitely shouldn't have that lamp lit."

"Oh shut up, kiss-ass," Scotty said. "I wouldn't mind hearing a story."

"Yeah, Ben, let's hear it," Jeremy said.

In the lamp glow, Ben could see the trace of anticipation in Scotty's face. He couldn't see Jeremy's expression in the bunk overtop, but he hoped it was the same.

Ben started to read aloud, and before long, it became clear that the story was intended to frighten its audience. It's quick pace drew him in, any apprehension he had of reading aloud quickly faded away. The only sounds were that of his voice and the violent storm.

The story ensnared the Scouts. They hung on its every word and it absolutely thrilled Ben. He read on with a vigor he was never able to summon when prompted to read in front of his classmates. As the story unfolded, the boys laughed during a funny part and gasped when the plot twisted. A yelp even escaped Nathan's mouth before he could slap a hand over it. They genuinely enjoyed it—no one more than Ben—until Mr. K made his boisterous entrance.

The door slammed against the wall, half thrown by the wind and half by the Scoutmaster who filled the doorway. Rainwater ran from the shoulders of his slicker and poured from the wide brim of his hat. Droplets steamed on the glass casing of his hoisted lantern and flecked from his bristling beard. "Get that lamp out, right this minute," he bellowed, loud enough for every boy in the other twelve cabins to hear. "Just because there's a storm, it doesn't mean the rules go out the window. You're Boy Scouts! Act like it!"

Scotty wasted little time in dousing the lamp.

Mr. K stared the boys down in their bunks for a good minute before closing the door behind him and returning to the driving rain.

Ben lay awake for some time, reveling in his story-telling ability. He replayed his cabin mate's reactions over and over in his head. They had been captivated by the tale and Ben knew, when Mr. K burst in and every one of them jolted with surprise, it wasn't the Scoutmaster they were thinking about. They had pictured the monster from the story.

The new day marked the return of the searing sun to Camp Wabasso. By lunchtime, the last of the stubborn raindrops had fallen from the tree limbs and the puddles were well on the way to becoming empty basins of cracked clay. Ben and his cabin mates huddled around a canoe on the slender spit of beach. A few groups of Scouts had already taken to the lake for the afternoon excursion. Their paddles slapped awkwardly on the water or banged against the boat rails as they whooped excitedly. The screech of the Scoutmaster's whistle reminded the paddlers to behave. Despite the promise of a fun outing, the cabin mates went through their safety checks at a snail's pace. Out of the earshot of the other Scouts, they took the opportunity for private conversation.

Jeremy passed Ben a lifejacket. His voice low, "I've been thinking about that story all day. I have to know what happens."

"Me, too," Scotty said from across their canoe.

Ben had been thinking about the story all day, as well. Although, what he focused on was how it had captured his friends' attention and his desire to capture it again. "I'm really glad you fellas liked it," Ben said.

Scotty leaned in. "Wait a minute, did you write that story, Benny?"

Ben held his breath.

A chorus of howls came from the lake. One of the canoes tipped and the Scouts it carried went sprawling into the water. The whistle sounded again. Most of the Scouts on the beach laughed and gave up sarcastic applause to the boys bobbing in their life jackets. With other pressing matters at hand, Ben's group gave the capsized canoe no more than a passing glance.

Jeremy shifted closer to Ben so he could hear the answer

to Scotty's question over the ruckus on the beach.

Ben's heart thumped half a dozen times before he said, "Yes, I did. I wrote it."

"Cool," Scotty said. He ran a hand over his pompadour hairdo, as he seemed to do whenever he uttered the highest compliment.

Jeremy said, "I knew it. You're smart, Benny. I could never come up with a whole story on my own. I can't even use a typewriter, let alone do that many pages."

Ben lowered his head, sheepishly. Deserved or not, the other boys' praise filled him with satisfaction.

The others studied Nathan, who laid the paddles in the bottom of the boat.

Nathan huffed. "They're right, Ben. It's good. You have a talent."

"That's nice, runt," Scotty exclaimed. He punctuated his statement with a jovial slap on Nathan's back that almost sent him to join the paddles.

Ben slowly exhaled, but his heart still knocked against his ribs. It continued to thump hard throughout the rest of the day's activities and into the evening. For the first time in his young life, he couldn't wait for lights out.

He could barely lie still as Mr. K looked over them, bedded-down for the night.

"I don't want another episode like we had last night," the Scoutmaster warned. To drive it home, he stared at each of them for several seconds while stroking his unruly beard. Finally, Mr. K took his lamp and departed the cabin.

In a hushed tone, Scotty said, "Are we in the clear?" He shook his matchbox to get his meaning across.

"You're going to get us all in hot water," Nathan hissed.

"I didn't ask you, runt," Scotty shot back.

From the top bunk, Jeremy whispered, "Give it a minute, Scotty. Mr. K will be on the lookout. Let's give him time to get bored and turn in."

Ben agonized as the minutes passed by. He pictured an hour glass in which the grains of sand dropped as slowly as pebbles to the bottom of a deep lake.

Finally, Jeremy's voice climbed out of whisper range. "It's time."

Scotty must have held the match head poised on the striker because Jeremy barely got the words out before it flashed to life. Lighting the lamp, Scotty grinned like a mad devil. "Have I been looking forward to this."

Even Nathan peered down at Ben from his bunk, unable to mask the interest on his pale face.

Ben pulled the pages from under his pillow. "All right, guys. Anyone remember where I left off?" he said, knowing exactly the place, though hoping to undersell his excitement.

Jeremy's voice sounded from overhead. "The wolf-man."

Scotty sniggered with anticipation.

Ben held the story up to the lamp light and turned through the pages until he found his place.

He cleared his throat.

"Right. Well. 'Young Bobby caught sight of it down by the riverbank. The full moon lit the place in a cold, blue light. It was strong enough that Bobby could see it clearly despite the fifty yards between them. He could see the silver-grey hair covering its entire body. He could see its long black claws at work. He could see its wicked eyes, the colour of Florida Oranges. And he could see the scraps of the Imperial gas station uniform it wore before it had changed under the moon, when it was still a man named Charlie Reid.

"'It was distracted, eating the fat salmon it had snatched from the river. It mashed the fish into its mouth like it hadn't eaten in days, like it could eat ten more. Bobby felt relatively safe behind the boughs of the pine tree. Sticking to the shadows, surely he was impossible to pick out of the tree line. In spite of that, Bobby's heart nearly stopped when the monster on the riverbank dropped the remains of the fish and threw its head back.

"'Then Bobby's heart started to pound. He realised what the beast was doing with its head cocked back and its wriggling muzzle pointed skyward. It was smelling the air. It caught wind of something that shouldn't be there—of some*one* that shouldn't be there.'"

Scott wheezed, "Oh shit."

"'Bobby tried to stay calm. He still had the trees and the river between him and it. He decided to back away slowly and head for the safety of home. When he got back there, he would have to convince his parents of what he had seen and with any luck his father would take him seriously enough to brace the door and load the rifle.

"'When Bobby took his first step backward, the dry twigs and leaves on the forest floor crunched underfoot. In the still night it sounded like the lash of a leather whip. Bobby's heart pounded harder. He looked back to the riverside to see if the beast had heard.

"'Those Florida Oranges were aimed right at him. Those eyes were like X-rays and they didn't need the moonlight to see Bobby's brown eyes or to count the freckles on his nose. Suddenly, the river wasn't between them anymore. The monster lunged, nearly crossing it in a single bound. It splashed down and coiled to leap again.'"

"Move, damn it," Jeremy whispered.

"'Bobby ran for home as hard as he possibly could. He didn't slow down, even as tree branches scratched his face. All he could think about was ending up like that salmon—torn open at the belly and eaten from the inside out. Well, that, but he also thought about the gate at the park entrance, because, if he could make it there, he had a chance to make it home in one piece. There was a street light over the gate. It lit up everything all the way to the sidewalk and from there, his house wasn't far away. With any luck, he thought, that thing would want to keep out of sight and leave the sidewalk to him.

"'The wolf-man didn't care about lights and sidewalks or about being seen by people. All it cared about was eating. It was the night of the full moon and more than anything, it wanted human blood. That was its one and only thought as it cleared the river and swept past the pine tree where Bobby had stood only seconds ago. Two more huge strides threw him from the thicket of trees, just in time to see his prey pass between the park gates.

"'Bobby was never so happy to see a streetlight. There had been a time he hated the sight of them. Until recently, a lit streetlight had meant the arrival of his mother's imposed curfew. It had meant it was time for him to go in for the night, but his parents had rewarded him for showing grown up behavior and now let him stay out past dark. This was the result—racing home with a monster at his heels. Bobby didn't feel very grown up, with his heart lodged in his throat.

"'As he reached the sidewalk, he glanced at his neighbours' houses. Their windows were lit, their cars were parked in their driveways. Mr. Drummond had left his lawnmower in his yard again. Sammy Pruitt's soccer ball waited for him by his front door. These visions of normal, routine life made the idea of the wolf-man seem utterly unbelievable. But Bobby knew what he saw and as if he needed a reminder of the danger he was in, he heard noises coming from the shadows around the houses. A trashcan overturned. A cat screeched. Worst of all, he heard the scritch-scratch of the monster's claws as it crossed over asphalt driveways at his flank. Worse yet, the sounds were getting ahead of him. Bobby feared the thing would snag him before he even got close to home— before he saw his mom and dad again, maybe for the last time.

"'He saw the monster. It emerged from behind Mrs. McAllister's old DeSoto and in a single stride, it was on the sidewalk thirty feet ahead of him. Bobby stopped short. The wolf-man stopped too, blocking the way. Drool seeped from the corners of its jagged mouth as it anticipated its next meal.

"'It yanked the final scraps of shirt off its body, leaving it only in trousers, torn to ribbons up to the knees to accommodate new bulging calf muscles. Its orange eyes turned on Bobby. Bobby could actually feel them poking his chest like knives. There was hate in those eyes, and something else, too. Confidence. The wolf-man knew the boy couldn't possibly get away and so it did something completely out of character—it let the boy come to him.'"

11

"Why doesn't he run?" Scotty said, bumping his forehead with the heel of his hand.

"Just listen," Jeremy scolded.

Ben read on. "'Bobby saw it waiting for him to try to get past, but he didn't *need* to get past it. He peeked to his left and saw his bicycle leaning against the front steps to his house.

"'A dog barked.

"'The wolf-man whipped its head in the direction of the animal.

"'Bobby made a break for his front door.

"'The wolf-man saw him go and bolted after, laying in a course that would have them meet at the steps.

"'Bobby didn't dare look back. He focused on the door and nothing else.'"

"Jesus Christ, hurry you little bastard," Scotty said, sitting up in his bed.

"Ssshhh," Nathan hissed, risking the wrath of the scrappy west-side kid.

"Sorry," Scotty said, and whispered for Ben to keep going.

Ben continued. "'Just as the wolf-man reached for Bobby's shoulder, Bobby clutched the doorknob and twisted it. The *clunk* of the latch prompted the monster to veer off and it lunged for the corner of the house. Bobby yanked open the door and threw himself inside before banging it shut.

"'"What did I tell you about slamming that door?" his father hollered, as he rose from his armchair in the adjoining living room.

"'Bobby's mother rushed in from the kitchen, drying her hands on her apron. "What is all the ruckus out here?" she said.

"'Bobby didn't answer right away, partly because he didn't have the breath to talk and partly because the only thing he needed to do right then was scramble to his feet and lock the door.

"'"Explain yourself, young man," his father demanded.

"'Bobby got his wind. He wanted to blurt out that he had seen a monster that it had chased him home, but the cross expressions on his parent's faces told him his wild story would not be well received. So he said, "I was chased…by a *man*."

"'Frowning, his father asked, "*Chased? By who?*"

"'Bobby thought for a second and told him, "Charlie Reid, from the gas station."

""'Oh my God," his mother said. "I always knew he wasn't quite right."

""'Did he touch you, son?"

""'No. I ran away before he could catch me. But he's right outside. Can you get the gun, Dad?"

""'No, no. We are going to call the police and let them deal with it."

""'But, Dad—"

""'I'll call the station house," his mother said and started toward the kitchen.

"'Bobby's father reached for the door handle.

""'What are you doing?" Bobby said.

""'I'm going to have a chat with Charlie Reid, that's what."

"'Bobby gripped his father's arm, holding him back. He couldn't let him walk out there unarmed with that wolf-man stalking about. "You can't go out there," he said.

""'Why not?"

""'He's still out there."

""'He's no threat to me."

""'But, Dad…"

"'His father's expression changed again. He looked frustrated. "Bobby, are you telling the truth about Charlie Reid? Did he really chase you?"

"'Bobby went quiet. If he couldn't get his father to believe a man chased him, how could he make him believe a monster did? He thought hard for the right words to say.

"'Suddenly, it didn't matter. A knock at the door broke the silence. A single, loud knock—more a thump really, and it gave Bobby and his father a start.

"'His dad quickly composed himself and said, "Charlie, is that you out there? Been drinking again, eh?"

"'The silence crowded in as they waited for an answer.

"'His father moved to grip the doorknob. It rattled violent- ly as the door sustained another, heavier blow. Bobby heard the splitting of wood. Plaster dust from the ceiling sprinkled his shoulders. They both took an instinctive step back from the door. Bobby's mother returned to the entry, her eyes bulg- ing. "What in the world…"

""'Think I *will* get the rifle out." Bobby's father went to the hall closet. From there, he called to his wife, "The shells are in the junk drawer in the kitchen."

""'I'll get 'em," she replied, barely audible.

"'Bobby went with her to the kitchen, feeling like he couldn't let her out of his sight with that monster at their door, but as they rounded the corner, she screamed louder than Bobby had ever thought her capable. In an instant, he saw the cause. At the window, a dusky hand coated in shaggy grey growth slapped at the glass and dragged curved nails across its surface. Fear grabbed him at his core and any ideas he had of protecting his mother vanished. The glass screeched under the pressure of the razor nails and before Bobby could add his shriek to that of his mother's, the claws were gone, leaving only four long etches in the window.

""'What in hell?" his father yelled. He charged into the kitchen, rifle in hand.

"'His mother looked at him, her skin snow white. "*Bear!* It's a bear. I saw it in the window!"

"'Before his father could voice his doubts, a cavernous thud sounded overhead. A scratching sound followed as it traveled the length of the roof.

"'Bobby swallowed hard. *It's on the roof.* He turned to his father for courage.

"'His father aimed his gaze upward, open-mouthed and mumbled, "Bears don't do that—" Another crash at the end of the house cut him off. "You called the police, right?"

"'Bobby's mother shook her head. "No…the noise at the door. I got…no. I'll call now."

""'There's no time. Get the shells."

"'A fresh wave of dread terror ran through Bobby. *No time? Before what happens?* As the answer came, it sent another colder wave through him. A smash from the living room was followed by the sound of broken glass scattering across the floor.

""'It broke the window," Bobby gasped.

"'His father snapped his gaze in Bobby's direction. It seemed like he was about to ask, *what do you mean, it?* Instead, he said, "Go to your room and brace the door." He pulled Bobby's mother by her arm and told her to go with their son. She practically dragged Bobby down the hallway toward his room while his father headed for the living room with his empty rifle.

"'When they reached Bobby's room, his mother pushed him inside. "Don't come out, no matter what." She hurried off to help her husband.

"'Bobby stood there, facing his door, regretting that he didn't warn his parents of what really pursued him here. They thought they were going to find Charlie Reid breaking into the house. They thought he would see the gun and run off, but the thing that used to be Charlie Reid wouldn't run from anything tonight.

"'Bobby heard his father's raised voice beyond the door, but an animal growl that sounded like rolling thunder drowned it out. Only the pitch of his mother's scream cut through it.

"'Then there was silence. Bobby stood perfectly still, fighting the urge to go to them. A footstep sounded in the hall. His breathing began to run wild. Beyond his door, the floor creaked as someone drew near. He clamped a hand over his mouth to keep quiet, but he still heard breathing. It came from outside the door—a hurried inrush and expulsion of breath, like a dog sniffing. Next came a scrape across the surface of the door that reminded him of blades on a cutting board. Bobby braced himself, then—'"

Thump.

Jeremy, Scotty, Nathan—even Ben—yelped as something

struck their cabin door.

It took a moment before each boy realised he'd just been the victim of a practical joke. Someone—the smart money being on Mr. K—had been listening to Ben's story and delivered a well-timed knock in hopes of causing a scare. He succeeded in spades. The cabin mates exchanged embarrassed looks and began a round of shameful laughter. Not Ben, though. He didn't think Mr. K had a sense of humor when it came to Scouts who broke the rules, especially for the second night in a row. And why didn't he come in by now to share in the aftermath of the joke?

Ben's thought was interrupted by another slam at the door, this one harder than the first.

The laughter between the boys immediately died. Jeremy cleared his throat. "Mr. K, is that you?"

The boys craned their ears for an answer. A moment later, it came.

A low, rumbling growl.

The boys bolted upright in their beds. Jeremy jumped down from his bunk and Ben got up to stand beside him, or perhaps somewhat behind him.

Scotty got up, too, saying, "Oh, somebody's goofing on us." He turned to the door and shouted, "Who's out there?"

A pale, silver-haired appendage slapped the window beside the door and dragged long black claws across the pane.

Scotty wailed and threw himself backwards. He fell onto Ben and the two of them nearly toppled the lamp on the nightstand. Jeremy, who always seemed to have an answer to every dilemma, stood frozen in place, while bestial talons sliced grooves in the cabin window.

By the time Ben gathered his footing and looked again, the claws were gone. "Jeremy," he said, "What was that?"

The older boy had no response. He didn't move an inch.

Ben braced himself for another attack on the door. Instead, it came from behind him, at the rear wall. The impact shook the cabin. Ben spun and jumped away from the wall.

Now Jeremy moved. He grabbed Ben by his collar and

yelled, "What is this, Ben? What's happening? It's just like your story!"

Speechless, Ben shook his head. He turned his dumbfound expression to the others. Scotty glared back. Nathan, who stayed in his bunk, pulled his covers over his head. "I…I don't know," Ben said. "I don't know what is happening!"

"Did you plan this? It's a joke, right?" Jeremy demanded.

Ben's face twisted with anguish. "Honest to God, I don't know what's happening."

There came a thud overhead.

Then another.

"It's on the roof!" Scotty said.

Loud knocks at the door could be seen as a prankster's ploy, but jumping on the cabin roof was excessive. That was nobody's idea of a joke. Jeremy, watching the creaking ceiling, released Ben. "What do we do?"

"I'll tell ya what," Scotty said, setting his jaw. "I'm gonna run for it." He went to the door, and despite the fact he was in underpants and barefoot, he pulled it open and broke into a sprint.

"Scotty, wait!" Jeremy yelled, but Scotty had already gone, running into the black of night. All Jeremy could do was fling the door closed behind him. He turned his panicked expression on Ben.

Footfalls sounded on the roof. They pounded toward the front of the cabin and then came a scrape as the feet launched. Silence followed. Nathan peeked over his blanket. Ben and Jeremy held each other in a trembling stare. They heard a rustling sound, then a scream.

Jeremy's eyes widened.

Ben clutched fistfuls of his hair and raised his head toward the ceiling. "Help us! Somebody! Help!"

Jeremy joined in. The cabins at Camp Wabasso stood close together. The other Scouts would certainly hear their plea and bring the grown-ups.

Nathan added his voice to the chorus.

Their calls for aid were cut off. The window imploded.

Scotty flew headlong into the cabin and landed belly-up. Blood soaked his James Dean hair and ran down his face in rivers. Gaping red slashes marked his chest and abdomen. His head rolled to the side, bulging eyes seeing nothing.

The chorus fired up anew, only the cabin mates no longer yelled for help, but gave vent to the terror boiling over in each of them. In the course of retreating from the window, the boys struck the table and this time the lamp did tip. It rolled. It cleared the table edge. It smashed on the floor and splashed fuel on to the bottom bunks, igniting them in seconds. In a few more seconds, flames climbed the walls. A toxic cloud of smoke gathered in the rafters.

Jeremy lunged to the cabin door. "We have to get out—take our chances out there," he said, fanning the smoke from his face. "We'll run for it. It can't get us both."

Ben reached up for Nathan's foot and tugged. "Nathan, come on. You gotta get down." Too frightened to move, he remained curled under his blanket even as the flames started to lick at his bedclothes.

"Nathan, come on!" Shielding his face from the fire, Ben moved closer to the bunk. He would drag Nathan outside if he had to, but before he could get a good grip on his small friend, he felt a hand clamp down on his shoulder.

Jeremy yanked Ben back from the flames and toward the door. Taking a line from Ben's story, Jeremy said, "There's no time."

Ben saw in Jeremy's face something of the killer instinct that set him apart from the other boys. His eyes were cold, heartless. He would save himself even if it meant Nathan had to burn.

Ben drew a breath of mostly smoke and choked on it. The poisonous mouthful was enough to convince him that Jeremy was right. He swallowed hard and nodded.

"You ready?"

Ben nodded again.

"You mean it, Ben?" Jeremy's brow stiffened. "You really don't know what's going on?"

Tears welled in Ben's eyes. All he kept thinking was, *I wish I never found that damned story.* Unable to gather his voice, he simply shook his head.

A scream erupted from Nathan, as he thrashed in his bed, flames eating his blanket.

Jeremy gripped the handle and pulled on the door knob. "Good luck."

It didn't open.

He pulled on the handle again. It didn't budge.

Ben grabbed a handhold, too, and both boys put everything they had into it.

The door refused to move. Something held it closed from the outside.

Jeremy roared in frustration. He raced toward the window. He threw one leg over the sill and was about to jump outside when claws, painted red with Scotty's lifeblood, slashed at him.

Jeremy stumbled back inside. Turning toward Ben, he revealed his open throat, soaking Ben's face with arterial spray.

Ben screamed and fell backward. Jeremy landed on top of him, squeezing the gashes in futility.

Ben fought his way from under his writhing friend. He scrambled to his feet in time to dodge the flaming heap that had been Nathan, falling from the bunk. The smoke reeked of burnt hair and cooked meat as it billowed off the boy.

Flames reached for Ben's undershirt. He frantically slapped at them.

Jeremy's lifeless hands loosened their grip on his throat.

Ben threw himself toward the door. He pressed his face to the pinched gap around it, desperately seeking the scraps of clean air leaking into the space. Behind him, the fire spoke in snaps and crackles. It even sizzled as it consumed the flesh of his cabin mates. The ghastly sound threw Ben's terror into another gear. He grabbed the door handle and yanked again.

Useless.

Whoever or whatever held the door, it would not let it move in the slightest. As if to declare its identity, his attacker

released a long mournful howl.
 Ben did, too.

Chapter One

2012

If by some stretch, Rural Route 10 could have been considered the beaten path, Jack was well off it. The twisting country byway he'd taken hours ago had deteriorated from asphalt to gravel, and finally, from gravel to dirt. He had been told more than once that he needed a change of scenery, that if he got out of his confining home office for a while, his work would start flowing freely again. This time he took the advice without protest. He decided to follow that old sports axiom that said, sometimes, a team on a losing streak, needs a road trip to get back in the win column.

Ten minutes north of the city, Jack had felt the pressures of home sloughing off his shoulders, though after negotiating the foreign terrain for so long, a twinge of angst began to creep back in. What would become of this steadily shrinking road in another few miles? He'd followed his directions closely, but the way did not *feel* right. Ominous trees crowded the road, stealing away the summer sky and much of Jack's nerve.

The phone rang. He flinched.

Jack retrieved it from the Buick's console and read the name on its screen. *Ted Marsh*. Jack let it ring.

He had also been told that cell service out this way would be spotty at best and he decided to use that tidbit as an excuse for ignoring his agent's call. Besides, what would he tell Teddy

-baby that he hadn't already said a dozen times before? *I need more time. I need an extension. I need another extension.*

But, never tell him why, Jack thought. *Don't you ever say it. Never ever use that dirty word with him—that nasty B word. Saying it aloud would only strengthen its hold.* He looked up at the encroaching trees, their limbs tangling overhead, and his anxiety grew.

The phone chirped, signaling a new voice message.

Jack eyed the phone, debating.

He picked it up and clumsily entered his code, keeping watch of the road.

Moments later, he heard the voice of Ted Marsh. "Jackie-baby, how goes it? I take it you're there already and you probably figured out your phone has more use as a paperweight, am I right?" Ted's recorded voice shed a chuckle as phony as the van Gough hanging in his waiting room. "Anyway, I'm sorry I missed you, but I just wanted to say good luck. I know things haven't been easy on you lately and the pressure that comes with this business can be a real bitch—"

Jack grinned at the sentiment. It was a refreshing change from the script Ted had been working from of late. In fact, Ted had been exerting more than his share of the aforementioned pressure.

"—but I hope you understand how much is riding on what you can accomplish in the next few weeks. I can't stress enough how important this is for *both* of our careers."

"Now there's the Ted I know," Jack said, his grin dying.

"And, I have to tell you, it wasn't easy to get you into this retreat. It's very exclusive, as you know. I had to call in some big favors and, I shouldn't have to tell you by now, in this business, favors are money. But I did it for you Jackie. I believe in you. I know you have another bestseller in the works. But, you really have to deliver on it this time. Two deadlines, Jackie, two, have gone by and I'm running out of things to tell the publisher."

Jack glanced at the laptop bag on the seat beside him and any feeling he had of escaping his troubles vanished. The familiar pang settled into the centre of his chest. He felt it swell and threaten to synch off his oxygen.

Ted's digitized voice changed to one of noticeably ingenuous cheer. "Anyway, Jackie, I know you will make the most of your time at the lake. Everyone who works there does. Hundreds of writers have finished difficult projects there over the years. There must be something in the water that gets those creative juices flowing or something. That's for you artist-types to understand. I just know it will be no different for you, and in a few weeks, we'll be able to look back on this as a triumph."

Jack wasn't so sure. He keyed the phone off and set it back in the dash.

The road ahead disappeared around a subtle bend. Jack thought about that *B* word again and how it would, in all likelihood, keep him from achieving any sort of triumph. It had become so strong of late, he would not have been surprised to round the bend and find it had manifested into a real life roadblock. Or perhaps it would take the form of a moose—a great lumbering beast in the road, poised to absorb his Buick and flatten its roof.

Jack tightened his grip on the wheel. The road began to straighten and as it did, he did not find any obstruction before him, rather a sign. The painted wooden marker partially recessed into the greenery reported, *10 miles to Wabasso Lake*.

Jack stopped the car at the gated entry. Twin pillars of natural stone and mortar supported the tall wrought iron gates. Jack spied an understated bronze plaque on the pillar to his left. The sign, at eye level to drivers, told Jack he had reached his destination. Etched at the bottom of the plaque were the small letters, EST. 1933. He dug his phone out of the console in the dash, got out and approached the gate. A tug confirmed the entry was locked. He had a contact number in his directory, only when he attempted to call it, found that his phone had no signal, as promised.

There was no fencing on either side of the pillars. Jack supposed he could cut around, walk to the retreat and come back with a staff member to get his car.

No sooner had he made up his mind than he heard a brief buzzing sound. The gate offered a metallic *clink* and began slowly sweeping inward.

Hmm, he thought. *Nice touch. Exclusive indeed.*

Back behind the wheel, Jack eased the Buick through the entry and down a gravel lane, lined on either side by nicely groomed trees. The birch and oaken giants stepped back along the driveway and allowed a squared evergreen hedge to thrive at their feet. About a hundred yards inside, the lake came into view, sparkling in the midday sun.

Jack had always been the indoor sort, but he imagined his boys would have loved the sight. Brian and Thomas likely would have been jumping from the car in a race to be the first one in. With one glance at Wabasso, Jack knew that it was a grown up's lake, not for kids to play in, but to be appreciated from afar, over a cigar and a brandy.

A rustic structure appeared to the left. The sign over its door read, OFFICE and Jack pulled into the adjoining parking lot. He found a place for his well-used ride, leaving space between it and the luxury sedan on one side and a red convertible roadster on the other. He shut off the motor. It gurgled as though to declare it couldn't remember its last tune up.

What am I even doing here? Jack thought as he eyed the neighbouring cars. The only car in the lot he wouldn't need to sell his house to afford was a battered grey pickup parked off to the side. Jack took little comfort in its presence when the lettering on its door told him it was property of the retreat.

It's not too late. You don't even have to get out of the car. You can go back.

He knew that wasn't true. The way back was blocked.

He reached under the dash and pressed the trunk release mechanism. It gave an encouraging *thunk*, but when he got out, Jack saw that the lid had failed to open, as it did with increasing regularity. He put two fingers under the lip of the trunk and lifted.

Nothing happened. He looked around.

The windows of the office were empty, the lake, the beach, void of people as well. He gripped the trunk and yanked on it. The whole car swayed, though the result was the same. He eyed the performance car to his right and the luxury sedan to his left. They seemed to mock him.

"Don't make me do it," he pleaded with the Buick. "If anyone sees, I'll die of embarrassment."

The Buick held its trunk fast.

Jack checked again for potential witnesses then he made a fist and thumped the lid, Fonzie-style. The cavernous trunk emitted a loud *bumpf* and the lid popped open. Jack grabbed his bag from it, shouldered it and closed the lid as quickly as he could. He retrieved his laptop from the front passenger seat and distanced himself from the old Buick not a moment too soon.

On the short path to the office, he started to feel more comfortable. He dusted the sleeves of his custom tailored sports coat and smoothed his matching woolen Vee neck. His designer blue jeans fit perfectly and he felt his alligator skin shoes would make even a homeless man look pretty darned good. Yes, top it all off with a fresh trim and a clean shave and he was all dressed up for the dance—or at the very least, ready to meet the other patrons of the exclusive retreat on even ground.

Jack smiled on first sight of the quaint office interior. It could have been lifted from the pages of an outdoor catalogue. Everything was wooden, organic. Untreated pine boards covered the walls. Stained timbers comprised the flooring. Decades of foot traffic had scuffed a pale pathway in the otherwise dark surface. Most foot traffic seemed to lead to the long front desk across from the front door. A small pot belly woodstove occupied the corner left of the door. Jack smelled the acrid scent of cold ashes. A few feet beside it, stood a bookcase filled with hardcovers. Next to it, an identical case bore only enough books to populate a shelf and a half. As he scanned the titles, Jack grew dismayed to find that his genre was absent. There wasn't a King, a Straub, a Laymon or even a Koontz.

"You must be Mr. Bishop," came a voice behind him.

Jack turned to the front desk where a bearded man with longish, dirty blonde hair stood smiling. He must have entered from the doorway behind the desk. The door stood ajar and Jack could see the smoke of another woodstove wafting from inside.

"Yes," Jack said. He went to the desk and presented his hand.

The man, dressed in a worn poncho, appeared as though he had just woken. He gripped Jack's hand in an overhand fashion as if to arm wrestle him and gave it a firm squeeze. "All right," he said. "We've been expecting you. I'm the caretaker. Walter Kubanowski is my name, but you can call me Kubby. Welcome to Wabasso Lake."

"Thanks, it's really great to be here...*Kubby*," Jack said, taking his hand back. "Oh and please, call me Jack."

"Jack, cool. Great to meet ya," said Kubby. He opened a ledger on the countertop and turned it toward Jack. He pointed a finger at the most recent entry. "Okay, here's Jack Bishop's stay, beginning on June 28th and lasting... indefinitely," he said. "Just sign here."

Jack took the pen from the gutter of the book and signed.

"All right," Kubby said, holding up his hand. "It's official. You're in."

Jack realised that Kubby sought a high five to celebrate the occasion. He indulged his host and after they awkwardly smacked hands, Jack decided the smoke coming from the back room was not the result of wood burning. The distinct odor and Kubby's bleary, red rimmed eyes attested to that.

"Let me show you to your cabin," Kubby said. He took a key from a pegboard on the wall and walked out from behind the counter. He wore faded jeans torn at both knees and had nothing on his feet. "Can I take your bag?"

"No, thanks," Jack said, and as Kubby went out the door,

he asked, "Don't you want to put on some shoes?"

"Nah," Kubby said, stepping down in the dirt. "If I put 'em on I'd only have to take 'em off later."

Jack followed along.

They continued down the road past the parking lot and toward the lake. They turned right, down a path, before reaching the beach. "How many staff works at the resort?" Jack asked.

"Just me."

"Really?" Jack said. *Oh dear God.*

"Yeah, I got six guests to take care of." Kubby looked back over his shoulder. The makings of a proud grin tugged at the corner of his mouth.

"Oh, I was under the impression, the place would be, umm, full."

"Yeah, it is. We have a full house." Kubby stopped and regarded Jack, full grin engaged. "Now that you're here, you're number six."

Jack felt another high-five coming on so he preserved a healthy distance from the caretaker. "I thought it would be a little...bigger. I mean, you seem to have a lot of property here."

"Sure, sure." Kubby nodded and started down the path again. "The retreat owns the whole lake and all the land around it, but the ownership likes to keep the operation small. You know, quaint. This place is for writers to come and work in peace and quiet. There're no phones except for the one outside the mess hall down here. We don't have a lot of electricity—just enough to run the kitchen and office and some lights, and plugs in the cabins. We make our own power with a generator. I can show you later. It's pretty cool. It's in like an underground bunker to keep the racket down, you know."

The path opened to the right. There, behind a crop of birch trees stood another wooden structure, slightly bigger than the office.

"Is this my cabin?" Jack asked.

"Nah," Kubby replied with a measure of humor. "This is

the mess hall. It's got a full kitchen you can use anytime. I do most of the cooking around here, so if you want something in particular, you have to let me know the day before in case I have to go to town to pick something up. But I know you writer types don't really keep a set schedule, so you can feed yourself whenever you like."

Jack had not envisioned cooking for himself. Teddy-baby told him he was going to a resort and the very word *resort* did not imply self-serve. As they walked around the corner of the rough building, Jack peeked through the dingy windows, wondering if it was actually clean enough to eat in.

"Oh, and before I forget, there's a first aid kit in the mess hall, if you need it. I have one in the office, too, but this one's closer to your cabin. Oh yeah, and that's the only guest phone right there," Kubby said pointing at the small, three-sided booth beside the front steps.

Beyond the mess hall, the path went closer to the beach and smaller trails broke away to the right in a few places. "Those paths lead to your neighbours," Kubby said quietly. "I probably don't have to say it, but our biggest rule around here is *never*, for any reason, go to someone else's cabin uninvited. Some writers, maybe you, too, totally freak out if they're interrupted when they're working. So try to be, you know, *cool* about that."

"That won't be a problem."

"Great. Here we are: Cabin Six," Kubby said.

He led Jack down one of the side paths and a few yards in, a modest structure tucked amid the alders and birches came into view. Jack paused on the path to take it in. The cabin, while small, appeared to have been recently freshened with a coat of white paint. Stark black shingles covered its peaked roof. The front door bore a stenciled number six, and situated to either side of it were paneled windows. Kubby went up the few steps to the door, unlocked it, and ushered Jack inside.

Jack set his bags down and assessed his new, stress-free, work environment. The cabin was Buddhist simple. It housed only the bare essentials: a plain table pushed against a windowless wall, an unremarkable wooden chair, a one man cot, an empty four foot shelf for writing supplies and a closet to hang clothing. As Kubby warned, electricity was sparse. In the centre of the ceiling a small globe light fixture hung and beside the table was the cabin's only receptacle. Jack took a deep breath. He could work here. He felt it in his bones. There would be no distracting phone calls, no drop in visitors, no bullshit. There was no room for it.

"This will do nicely," he said.

"The last tenant was Preston Furlong," Kubby boasted.

"I see. What has he written?"

"Poetry, yeah, some of the best of our time. Like some really far out shit. I can loan you a copy of his first collection. It would definitely get your brain cells buzzing. Does for me, anyhow."

Jack went to the table and pressed down on the top to test its strength. "Thanks, but I think I'll be pretty busy with my own work.

"What sort of stuff do you write?"

"Thrillers."

"Wow, right on." Kubby smiled, but not with his eyes. From his reaction, Jack gathered Kubby didn't have much interest in the genre.

Scratching the back of his head, Jack added, "Well... thriller, I should say. I'm working on my second novel."

"Ah."

"It's been kind of a challenge."

Kubby perked up. "Yeah? You're pushing your boundaries, huh? That's good, man. Keep denying that horizon."

Jack wasn't entirely sure what the caretaker was getting at. "I'm...I'm actually a little behind schedule, and I just want to concentrate on finishing my draft."

"Yeah, you're in the right place." Kubby proclaimed.

"I think so, too." Jack said with a little less conviction.

"Cool, cool," Kubby said, surveying the room. He brought his hands up to his face and drummed on his hairy cheeks. "What am I forgetting? There's always something. *Right*, umm, the shower house is behind the mess hall. There's a path. *Shit,* I should have shown you on the way by."

"That's fine. I'm sure I'll be able to find it." Jack took a cursory glance out the window.

"Yeah, that reminds me, try to keep your showers short, if you can, 'cause hot water is kind of a precious commodity around here." Kubby took a step toward the door. "There are clean towels in the closet. You can leave your dirty ones in the shower house. I pick 'em up every day."

"Will do." Jack followed Kubby to the door, eager to have the cabin to himself.

"I change the bed sheets on Wednesdays, too."

"Sure," Jack said, holding the door open. As Kubby passed by, Jack caught a whiff of his weathered poncho and it put him in mind of college afternoons and Led Zepplin records.

On the steps, Kubby stopped again. He scratched his head and said, "There are some cool hiking trails, if you keep going on the path past here. It's mostly up hill, but you get a really nice view of the lake up there."

"Great. I just might check it out sometime." Jack resisted the urge to remind his new acquaintance that the hike back would actually be downhill.

"Speaking of the lake, there are canoes down by the beach. Feel free to go for a paddle. All I ask is make sure they're upside down when you put 'em back so they won't fill with rain water. Oh, and if you go across the lake, don't go ashore. Our insurance policy doesn't cover guests over there if anything were to happen."

Jack decided to stop responding. He felt it only reminded the caretaker of more things to tell him.

"Well, okay, Jack, it's close to noon. Pop over to the mess for lunch, if you want." It seemed like he was finally leaving. "I'm making sandwiches." He stepped his bare feet down in the dirt and started for the path. "Roast beef and chicken," he said as he waved.

Jack waved from his doorway.

Once he shut himself inside the cabin, Jack could not help

but smile. He found Kubby pleasant enough, but he could see how the hippy's spacey demeanor and forgetful nature would grate on his nerves before long. *They don't call it dope 'cause it makes you smart.*

He spent a few minutes getting settled in. He hung some of his clothing in the closet, the rest he situated on the shelf. Next he set his laptop on the table and plugged it in to charge. Finally, he produced an unframed photograph from his laptop bag. In it, Brian and Thomas displayed incomplete sets of teeth. They were on the beach at New River, stretched out on colourful towels. Jack unfolded the edge of the picture to reveal a blonde woman next to Thomas. He eyed her briefly before folding her out of sight again. He stuck the photograph to the unpainted pineboard wall over his desk with a thumbtack from his office supplies.

He was ready to work.

A tiny green LED on the laptop blinked when he pressed the power button. He sat in the wooden chair. It was surprisingly more comfortable than it looked. The computer proceeded to tick and emit soft buzzing sounds as it booted up. Jack wondered if those sounds were normal. He had never noticed the subtle noises before, but he had never been in a place this quiet before, either. He began to see that, here, one could truly be alone with their thoughts, and he wondered if that was such a good thing.

The desktop illuminated onscreen: a serene river was the background *du jour*. Jack moved the pointer to an icon labeled *WORK*, which he opened to display a lone document inside. He double clicked the file, inspirationally named *BOOK2*, and waited for it to load. The screen populated. It showed one short paragraph ending with an incomplete sentence. The cursor blinked at the end of the text. Jack read the last few lines leading up to it.

"'It was under that old hangin' tree, Billy's grandfather stopped him. The old man laid a wide farmer's mitt on the boy's head. It had swelled knuckles that had been broken and rebroken in countless wars waged with other hard men. "Son," the man said. The boy looked up at him, his lower lip showing the slightest of tremors. "You're old enough to know," the man continued. "The true measure of a man don't come in inches and feet or pounds and ounces." He stared at the boy. "It don't even come in battles won and lost. It comes""

It ended there.

"It comes..." Jack said aloud. He bit his bottom lip and winced as he searched the depths of his intellect for the right words. He read the paragraph again, quickly this time, as if he hoped momentum would carry him into new, undiscovered territory.

"It comes..." he said. He waited and waited.

"*Shit sakes.* Where does it come from?"

Jack eyed the cursor. It blinked in answer. He released a long breath and drew another. He closed his eyes and tried to gather his thoughts. One particular thought, however, could not be herded. It ran loose on the perimeter of his reasoning—a wild thought, spreading unrest throughout the rest of the flock, dashing this way and that. It drew Jack's focus until it was front and foremost and nothing else mattered—that untamed letter B.

"No," he said aloud, opening his eyes to the screen. The cursor blinked. His heart thumped in rhythm to it. It was something else he had never noticed before and now he could not fathom how he had missed it. The cursor blinked in sync with his heartbeat, pulsing in his ears.

Man, this place is quiet.

Alone with my thoughts.

Alone.

Jack abruptly pushed his chair back from the desk. He slapped a hand over his mouth and went to stand by the window. Outside the sun dappled lake peeked between the trees. Leaves fluttered on an easy breeze.

A red streak cut across the greenery. A cardinal found a perch on the limb of a young maple a few yards from Jack's window.

Well, not entirely alone.

The bird preened its breast feathers, then it seemed to spy Jack on the other side of the glass. Its tiny black eyes fixed on him. It sang. Two long whistles followed by shorter, looping bursts.

"Howdy, neighbour," Jack said.

The cardinal lingered on the branch a few more seconds before taking wing. Jack watched him flutter off, a little saddened the encounter ended so quickly, a little more so that he lost a welcomed distraction.

Maybe I should eat something. The idea of one of Kubby's roast beef sandwiches made his stomach rumble. *Yes. I can't work on an empty stomach. I'll eat and then do some work this afternoon. I'm fine. Just hungry. No problem. And no fucking B word.*

He went back to the desk to close his laptop. Before he did, he glimpsed the heading on the page and felt his chest tighten again.

Chapter 1, it read.

Chapter Two

Jack followed the path back to the mess hall. When he approached the door, he heard the murmur of voices within. He paused, his feelings akin to a child's on the first day of school—more nerves than excitement. There were real writers in there, writers who had likely completed important works. They would not have been admitted to Wabasso Lake, otherwise. They probably did not need pushy agents pulling strings to get them in. They *earned* their way. Maybe they would be able to sense that he had not. Maybe they would smell the incompetence on him. Or worse yet, his *real* problem.

Don't be ridiculous, he told himself. *They're only people. When you get down to it, they're just like me.* He took a breath and opened the door. *They just drive nicer cars.*

The dining area dominated most of the space inside. It held three rows of long, rudimentary wooden tables with benches. It reminded Jack of a grade school cafeteria. Seated at the first table was a solitary man, reading from a laptop screen with a half-eaten sandwich on a plate off to the side. He appeared to be in his fifties with long, but thinning grey hair pulled into a ponytail. His thick, black rimmed glasses exaggerated his eyes. Jack said hello, and the man looked up briefly before returning his attention to the screen.

Three others conversed over sandwiches at the far table, nearest the kitchen. One of them watched Jack as he entered the hall. She smiled and his nerves fluttered again. She couldn't have been smiling at him, he decided. Lustrous red hair tumbled off her shoulders as she shifted in her seat. Her green eyes, so bright and engaging, seemed to dim everything else around her. He caught himself beginning to stare and averted his gaze.

The man seated across from her was in the midst of telling a story. His voice bellowed. "So, Albert Billings was in attendance as well, that sot. And when I saw him, I said, 'Well if it isn't the man of a thousand, thousand adjectives.'

"He said, 'Warren, old boy, don't you mean the man of a *million* adjectives?'

"To which I said, 'There you go again! My God man, you are unstoppable.'"

That earned him a titter from his lunch mates.

As Jack walked further inside, past the second row of tables, he found Kubby manning the kitchen behind a long serving counter to his right.

"There he is," Kubby said, when he noticed Jack. "It's the new guy. You look like a hungry man. What'll it be, roast beef or chicken?"

"Surprise me."

Kubby gave a thumbs up. "Yeah, you got it."

"Over here, *new guy*," the woman with the green eyes said. "Come, join us."

Jack went to the table to introduce himself to her and her two companions. "Hi, I'm—"

"Jack Bishop, right?" she said, leaning forward and resting her folded arms on the table. She studied him briefly before her smile returned. "I'm Kate."

Jack felt a cold sweat break on the nape of his neck. "A pleasure," he said, giving an tremulous smile. Unsure where to lay his gaze, it drifted over the table to the plates of bread crusts and balled up paper napkins.

"This is Ralph Deakins," Kate said, tilting her head toward

the fiftyish man beside her. He sported a too-black-to-be-natural bowl cut and possessed a plump build.

Jack shook his hand. Mr. Deakins seemed less enthusiastic to make his acquaintance.

"And this is Warren Hellickson," she said, gesturing toward the story-teller opposite.

"Hiya, Jack," Warren said, exchanging grips. "What brings you to town?"

"Umm, well…"

"That's a joke."

"Have a seat, Jack," Kate said. She gestured at the open place next to Warren. He sat. "Don't pay any attention to Pierre over there." She nodded at the man sitting alone by the door. "He can be a bit of a cold fish with everyone."

"He's actually here to *work*. Go figure," Warren put in. His thick hair, swept back from his forehead, showed more silver than black and his heavily lidded eyes suggested an incessant boredom with his surroundings.

"We *all* are," Kate said. "Just not in the mess hall." She turned to Jack. "It's kind of an unspoken rule that the mess is for dining and socializing only."

Kubby appeared at the table. He set a plate and tumbler filled with water down in front of Jack. The sandwich, roast beef on whole wheat with mustard, stoked his appetite. "Looks good, Kubby. Thanks."

"If it works for ya, I can make another," Kubby said, and then asked if anyone at the table wanted seconds. With no takers, he returned to the kitchen.

"I don't know what *you* hope to achieve here—" Ralph droned.

Jack held his breath.

"—but I can assure you, Jack, you *will* lose weight."

The others chuckled at Ralph's wit and with that, Jack's angst abated.

"Are you the sort of writer who talks about his books while they're in progress, Jack?" Kate asked.

He dreaded the idea of trying to articulate his work to other, more established writers, of opening the door to their judgment, or even worse, their silence. Whether she knew it or not, Kate was mercifully letting him off the hook. "No, no, I prefer not to," Jack said between bites. "I guess, I'm a little superstitious that way."

"Well, I can't wait for you to finish," she said. "I simply loved *The Long Night*."

Jack felt like he was about to fall victim to a cruel joke. "Really? You read it?"

"Oh, yes." Kate's eyes grew larger. "It positively scared the wits out of me."

"I'm afraid I'm at a disadvantage," Ralph said.

"Jack here writes thrillers," Warren said. "Or do you prefer *horrors*, Jack?"

Jack swallowed his mouthful. It scraped its way down his throat. "I can tell you my agent prefers to call them thrillers. He says it opens a broader market."

"Right. Either way, Ralph," Warren went on, "it's more exciting than that political fiction you grind out and far more so than my verse. Tell me, Jack, do you reciprocate Kate's appreciation of literature."

"Warren..." Kate scolded.

Jack felt his cheeks flush. "I guess it's my turn to be at a disadvantage."

"Don't be silly," Kate said. "I don't think my novels would suit your appetites."

"No, I don't imagine," Warren put in. A sly grin spread on his face. "Jack probably needs more fiendish villains than scorned housewives and philandering husbands."

Ralph snorted derisively. He regained his composure. "Whatever drew you to write *horrors*, anyway?"

Jack put his sandwich down. His appetite quickly diminished. Getting accepted by these seasoned writers had turned out to be wishful thinking. He should have seen this coming. He wanted to excuse himself from the table and retreat to his cabin. He looked at Kate. There was a sort of sympathy in her eyes, but something else, too. She, perhaps more than the others, wanted to hear his answer, and before Jack realised what he was doing, he formulated one. "Well, Ralph," he started, "I think the horror genre has an undeserved reputation for being all about blood and gore. True, there is some of that, but the genre isn't *about* that at the core."

"I suppose some might say—present company excluded, of course—that it's, well, a tad immature," Warren said.

"I don't see how it could be considered immature to explore human nature as human values are broken down in the face of a threat. In fact, as a society, I think we *need* to consider the worst case scenarios, and to do that, we need the horror genre. It makes for the perfect weapons test field. All the missiles and bombs are fake so we can examine our fears and how they ultimately affect human behavior in a safe environment.

"And there's an antiquated notion that horrors are always morality plays. That's simply not true. They're not about good versus evil, anymore. They've really moved past that to the present day idea that evil isn't black or white, but quite often, an ambiguous grey. It's about whatever you happen to have on any given day versus some looming threat. Sometimes, what you have isn't good enough. And you lose."

"Or die," Warren said.

"Die. Yes."

"In blood curdling screams, in the monster's clutches," Ralph added in his best attempt at a Vincent Price impersonation—brow absurdly raised, mouth gaping and downturned.

Jack smiled wryly. "That's interesting, Ralph. When I think of the classic horror monsters—your vampires, werewolves and the sort—I don't see fangs and fur." He paused and leaned forward. "I see famine, poverty, disease—the real troubles of the world. And I think it's a good thing people can pick up a book and face fictional terrors. Then the real ones don't seem so overwhelming when we inevitably encounter them in daily life. The best horrors still work on these base levels. They have a way of making us face what we *truly* fear."

"What do you recommend I read if I'm afraid of economic collapse?" Warren asked, making Ralph snort again. "I just bought a boat."

Jack ignored Warren's wit. "I've found that the people who don't dare to look into the dark places are usually the ones with something to hide. Maybe when they search their dark corners, they don't like what they find out about themselves. After all, you can learn a lot about who you are when you're truly scared."

"Here, here," said Kate.

"And, personally, I don't want to live in a world without monsters, real or imagined. If we did, how could any of us appreciate innocence and beauty when we discover it?"

Kate tilted her head at the sentiment. Ralph rolled his eyes.

"Ralph you asked, what drew me to write horrors? Well, maybe it's because I get to explore these themes, these fears. And as I do, sometimes I get to examine something about the human condition. But don't forget, I also get to brutally *kill* as many unsavoury characters as I like." Jack grinned at Warren and Ralph. "And that's just plain fun."

Warren cocked an eyebrow.

Kubby's laughter drew everyone's attention. He was leaning over the counter, listening in on the conversation. "Nicely said, Jack-man," he put in. Warren's eyes narrowed and Kubby retreated to the kitchen.

Jack bit into his sandwich. "This is good. Did you try the roast beef?" he asked Kate.

She smiled and shook her head.

Jack and Kate stepped from the mess hall into the radiant summer afternoon. "Well, that got a little awkward in there," Kate said in a hushed voice. "Let me apologize for those two. They're not always that rude."

"I'm sure they're nice guys when you get to know them," Jack said.

Kate frowned as she reconsidered. "Actually, come to think of it, they *are* pretty rude most of the time. Sorry, nonetheless."

He followed Kate down the steps and strolled beside her as they found the trail leading back to the cabins. Jack's heart still pounded from his confrontation with Warren and Ralph. He took a few deep breaths to settle himself. For the first time, he noticed the natural perfumes on the air. The blending scents of wild Lupines, Star Daisies and Honeysuckle came all at once. He took another breath and wondered how he hadn't detected this pristine country air as soon as he had gotten out of his car. Perhaps he was still shaking off the effects of city air, tainted by car exhaust and industry. This was what air was meant to taste like.

Kate couldn't hold back her laughter. "Obviously, they're not used to being talked to like that," she said. "The look on their faces..." She attempted to raise her brow the way Warren had and laughed some more.

"I don't know what got into me," Jack said, throwing his hands up. "It was like an out of body experience. I didn't like what they had to say, the next thing I know I'm shooting my mouth off."

"Well, I think it was impressive how you defended yourself." Her register dropped. "The nerve—calling your work immature. Warren writes poetry about the personalities of sea shells, for God's sake. Makes me wonder what they say about my novels when my back is turned."

"It's probably not worth thinking about," Jack put in.

The path brought them to the edge of the beach before it veered off into the trees. Kate loosed an audible sigh when she took in the lake, its surface ablaze with midday sun. "It still gets me every time," she explained.

Jack smiled at her. He estimated her age to be around thirty, a few years his junior, but when she tilted her heart shaped face a certain way and the smattering of freckles that bridged her nose became more apparent, he wondered if she was considerably younger. He felt himself getting lost, staring at her red tresses reflecting the fire of the sun.

He snapped out of his deepening trance as they started in

the direction of the cabins.

"So how do you like it here?" she asked.

A group of Monarch butterflies crossed their path to flit about the wildflowers. "It's quite a place. Kubby said the retreat owns the whole lake. It must be worth a fortune."

Kate studied at him as though she didn't fully get his meaning. "It is paradise," she said.

"Oh, for sure." They strolled between the birches and Jack caught the scent of the hyacinths lining the pathway. "There aren't many places like this around, you know, that are still pretty much untouched."

"Jack, there aren't *any* places quite like this." Kate said evenly, eyes trained on the unfolding trail.

Jack considered the intensity of her response a bit unusual, but chalked it up to her being a big Wabasso fan. He could see himself becoming a fan of the retreat, too, if it actually helped him to accomplish some writing.

Hell, I'd learn to love doing hard time, if I could write in jail, he thought. Anything would be better than living with the B word. He felt a pit of despair opening beneath him and quickly changed the subject before he fell in. "How many books have you written here?"

"Hmm..." Kate squinted as she weighed her response. "Twelve, I think. Maybe thirteen."

Jack fought to keep his mouth from dropping open. "Thirteen? *Holy...*that's a lot of resort time."

Kate did not fail to catch Jack's reaction and it prompted a grin. "I know. Wabasso has given me so much, I feel like I owe it a huge debt."

"I hope the place is as generous with me. Of course, my ex -wife will get half of whatever it gives me."

"I have an ex, too. Been there, done that. Got the tee shirt and lost it in the divorce." Her tone lowered. "I don't know what I was thinking."

"Me neither, but I think everyone should get married at least once." Jack's attempt at injecting some levity into their conversation actually stung him more than he expected. They both shed a humorless chuckle that left each of them solemnly reflecting on days past.

When the silence threatened to become awkward, Kate broke it by saying, "So you're here to finish your *second* book?"

"That's right," Jack said flatly.

She must have detected new apprehension in his voice. "A lot of gossip gets around the dinner table here. I suppose, it's because there isn't much else for us to talk about. I don't mean to pry."

"It's okay." He exhaled loudly. "This is just sort of new to me."

She gave him a coy, sidelong look. "I liked your argument in favor of the horror novel. I really do like them, you know. I just don't always like how they depict women. The girl is usually some whimpering piece of arm-candy who can't defend herself."

"Oh, I don't know. I think you might be overlooking the importance of the damsel in distress. It is another metaphor, after all—one you sort of need in any horror story."

Shoving playfully on Jack's arm, she said, "That sounds like something you cooked up for Warren and Ralph."

Jack shrugged. "It might have come out eventually, if I had kept on my tirade. Glad I held something back. I didn't want to get into it with them."

Kate stopped on the path prompting Jack to follow suit. She squared her shoulders and placed her hands on her hips. "So, get into it with me, then." An impish smile played on her lips.

Her direct challenge threw Jack off balance. "Okay...well, let's see." He grinned nervously and cleared his throat. "Umm, I think you see the best depiction of the *damsel* in those old horror movie posters. I loved them as a kid. In fact, the walls of my office are plastered with them. They're great 'cause they include all the main elements for a good horror story—even if the movies themselves were terrible. They usually show some heroic, cleft-chinned man shielding a pretty girl from a vampire or zombie or something. They remind me that every horror novel requires three basic elements. There's the main character, who readers will hopefully relate to, the damsel who needs rescuing and, of course, the villain."

"I see." Her eyes narrowed. "So you think female characters ought to be defenseless screamers who need a man to protect them from danger?"

Jack shook his head. "She is a metaphor, remember? Just like the monster."

Kate chewed on that a moment. Starting to walk again, she said, "Okay. I'm listening."

Jack took a few hurried steps to catch up to her. "She's the opposite of the monster. She can represent beauty or innocence...love. She is whatever the main character is willing to risk his life to save. She is what he simply can't live without. Of course, today, the damsel isn't always a woman. It might be a man or a child or a dear friend or perhaps something a little more abstract like one's freedom or identity. However it is represented, it's crucial for building fear, because, you can't really have fear without the threat of losing something you love."

Kate regarded him for a long moment. "Okay, that's not bad."

Jack thought she wanted to say something else and stopped herself.

She slowed her pace. "Well, this is me," she said, nodding at a pathway cutting through the trees to their right. Jack glimpsed a small cabin tucked secretively amid the greenery at the end of the path. The perfect place for a writer to be alone with her thoughts. "Time to get back to work."

"Yeah, same here," Jack said. "Gotta get some stuff down while it's still percolating."

She studied him, cocked her head slightly and turned toward her cabin. She went a few steps before stopping and turning back. "You're *supposed* to be here, you know."

Jack felt his blood thin. He wondered if Kate's vision could penetrate his flesh and bones and see the fears massing in his core. *Does she know why I'm really here? Does she know my problem?*

Her expression softened. "Just…let the place work for you."

"I'm not sure I understand what you mean."

She considered him. "I won't bore you with what I think of this place. Take some time and form your own relationship with Wabasso. Just remember, it has a way of giving you what you need most. So let it."

"Umm, yeah, that's great because what I need is to buckle-down and get some work done." Jack gave a snicker completely devoid of sincerity. He eyed the path leading to his own cabin. The sunlight seemed a little dimmer down that way. "Thanks for the advice."

She offered him a smile and watched as he started down the path.

He hoped he didn't appear as unnerved as he felt.

Magazine article published in the *Mill Street Literary Review*, May 2012, edition:

What Happened to Tanner Black?
by William Jessop

What Happened to Tanner Black?

He died is the short answer.

The slightly longer one is that he suffered a heart attack, and after a prolonged stay in hospital, succumbed to complications—i.e.: pneumonia. Either way he's gone. That much is indisputable. What I want to know is what happened to Tanner Black, the author, and why did his writing career meet a demise long before the man? For his considerable fan base (a number in which I loyally rank), the answers have never been satisfying.

For the rest of you, let me take a slight detour from my usual course as *Mill Street* literary critic so I can explain a little about Mr. Black.

He was the author of a successful series of detective novels that spanned three decades. His works did not rank among the highest earners of our time, but they did set benchmarks for crime novels of the hard boiled variety. Ultimately, they were just plain fun to read.

Black was one of the first writers to focus on the villain as intently as he did the lawmen who dogged him. This radical approach, earned him the adoration of fans worldwide. Year after year we joined in the hunt for his knife wielding sociopath with bursting anticipation, wondering if this time the rumors were true and he would finally be brought to justice, or how he would wriggle free of a seemingly airtight trap. Year after year we waited with bated breath. That is until two years ago, when among the relentless chatter of online posters, bloggers and tweeters, a short press release graced the web:

Lightning Storm Press would like to congratulate Tanner Jameson Black on the news of his retirement. It is our utmost wish that he reflects on his stellar career with fondness and pride, and that he enjoy continued success in all his future endeavors.

I was shocked and horrified. Like many other vocal fans, I went through a stage of denial, calling the statement a hoax with an aim to build buzz around an upcoming release. Then his website—TannerBlackBooks.com—was taken down. I began to worry. The man, himself, remained quiet, but the rumor mill was just getting started. News emerged that work on the latest installment of his slasher series had not gone well.

Then reason for hope arrived. Word circulated that Black was coming out of retirement to complete his current novel. Just as quickly, that hope vanished when his agent released the following statement:

It is with tremendous regret that I inform you of the passing of Tanner Jameson Black. He was a consummate professional and a dear friend. He left this world a better place than the one he found. The loss his passing represents to the writing community will be immeasurable for quite some time.

No one is quite sure why he retired before completing his series. Some say he suffered from a profound writer's block. Others maintain that illness simply kept him from working. I do not think that was the case.

I had the good fortune to meet Black at a book signing a few years back. When the line finally spat me out an hour and a half into the event, I was not met with a man at all fatigued by the process. Rather, I met a bright eyed and witty man in his late-fifties who seemed as pleased to meet fan number 192 as he was to meet fan number one. He shook my hand and on top of asking my name for the autograph, asked where I was from and commented on the superb fly fishing river on the outskirts of my hometown.

This encounter replayed in my head several times in the days following his death. What makes a vibrant man in his writing prime simply walk away from the craft he loved?

The stubborn question returned to me again and again. It arose while I was at work, in line at the grocery store, on the bus. Finally, I put pen to paper and submitted my burning question to Black's agency. They were good enough to respond in kind a few weeks later, but not with the informative letter I had hoped for—one that would explain my favorite author's unpopular choice. Rather, the letter amounted to a literal dressing down—a reminder of the role of the literary fan and how I lacked an appreciation for it. The letter also schooled me on the writer/agent relationship and how it is primarily built on trust and discretion. In short, my questions were best kept to myself. It seemed I had struck a nerve. What is worse, it only served to deepen my curiosity. More than ever before I was determined to get the answers I so craved. Follow me in this column in the coming months, loyal readers, as I endeavor to find out exactly what happened to Tanner Black.

Chapter Three

Jack sat on the plain wooden chair in front of the writing desk. He opened the laptop and, as he did, closed his eyes. Soft buzzing and ticking emanated from the machine while it prepared for its role in the creation process. He did his best to ignore it. Instead, he focused his thoughts to task and exactly what it was he wanted to say. When he opened his eyes, Billy and his grandfather would be there on the screen, under the old hangin' tree. They would stare back at him in silence, waiting for his take on how to get the *true measure of a man*. The laptop ceased its electronic chattering as though it too waited with bated breath for Jack to continue telling his tale.

He opened his eyes to the mostly blank screen.

The cursor sat at the end of the row of text, blinking at him.

Jack drew a breath and it rattled in his chest—the first vague sign of approaching panic. He slowly released it and started, as was becoming his habit, by reading his paragraph from the beginning. He ran through the words quickly, reached the end, and started through them again from the start, faster still. He began to picture the final sentence as a piece of broken train track. He felt, if he hit the track with enough speed and enough momentum, he would launch from its tattered end, leaving this slight hiccup in production far,

48

far behind. With his practice runs over, he read his paragraph once more, word by word, momentum carrying him forward until he reached the end of the fractured sentence and…

Nothing.

Jack's train of thought toppled from the broken track car after car until it hit the gorge below.

He leaned back in his chair and rubbed his face with the heels of his hands. He looked up at the cabin wall and the small photograph tacked to it. Brian and Thomas looked back at him. They, too, seemed to be waiting. Possibly, they wanted to know the *true measure of a man.*

Jack pushed his chair back and stood up all in one motion, his breathing shallow. The room began to turn. He pawed at his chest futilely, trying to get it to process air properly. Weakened, he dropped himself ungracefully onto the cot. Its springs squealed as it took his weight. He rubbed his forehead, now damp with sweat.

Maybe I should start somewhere else, he thought. *This is a tricky exchange between Billy and his grandfather. It's difficult to write, even on a good day. And, not every writer starts at the beginning of the book. Hell, some start at the end and work their way back.*

Right?

He buried his face in his hands and groaned. It didn't matter where he started. Wherever he decided to lay down words, one after the other, he would inevitably run into that awful *B* word. It was out there, lurking in the dark, waiting to catch him, and with its ugly black mitts, grasp him and never let him go. It might appear on page one. It might rise up at the end of chapter five. It might jump out to prevent him from reaching the climax. It would always be there, that dreadful…

"*Block*," Jack mumbled into his hands. "I'm blocked…have been for months."

He wanted to cry. Simply admitting he suffered from writer's block was almost more than he could bear. He felt some vital machinery deep within him overheat and grind to a halt. When he opened his mouth, he expected smoke to spew from his broken down inner workings. Instead, another moan escaped, this more desperate, sorrowful. It surprised Jack, how little it sounded like him.

On the cabin wall, Brian and Thomas continued to watch.

What would they think of their old man, if they could see him now? Jack thought. *Their father, bestselling author, who had become weekend dad, who became see-you-after-the-summer dad, was now gasping for air at the mere thought of writing a single syllable.*

He was supposed to be a provider to those boys. They depended on him. Teddy depended on him, too, in whatever way agents depend on their clients. The publishers who gambled on him waited for a new Jack Bishop to sell before the holidays. Jack let them all down. The cabin began to shrink. It grew warmer, the air, mustier.

Jack sprung from the cot and stumbled to the door on drunken legs. He opened it to the brilliant day beyond and dropped heavily on his rear end on the front steps. He tightly squinted his eyes as he sat there and searched for his lost composure. He reclined on the steps in an effort to appear casual should anyone happen by—like he was taking a break from work and came outside to get a bit of air. He wondered what Warren and Ralph would do if they saw him like this. Would they offer assistance, or would they be too busy laughing?

Jack assumed the latter.

He first noticed the soft breeze off the lake when it tickled the back of his neck where the sweat was thickest. Then he felt it fan his hair. Then he smelled it—the rich mingling of earth and blossom. The pressure in his chest abated and he drew a clean breath. He felt as though Wabasso had opened a relief valve somewhere within him and the dangerous gases bled off.

Jack waited for the panic attack to subside. His heart rate returning to normal, his breathing became regular. He wasn't sure if he had the lake to thank for that, or if it was simply getting out of the dank cabin air that helped. He just let it happen.

Then he remembered something Kate said. *Wabasso has a way of giving you what you need most.*

And just when I needed relief.

Jack gazed at the lake, a shimmering sea of diamonds. It stung his eyes, but he couldn't bring himself to look away. Thoughts of writing and overcoming blocks ebbed along with the grip of his most recent panic attack.

When you're in the presence of something so beautiful, how can you think of anything else?

Jack slowly walked up the path leading away from the retreat. It was a semi-conscious decision. He wanted nothing more than to stay outside and take in the gorgeous sights of the lake. He just didn't want to do it within view of the other guests.

That left the hiking trail Kubby had told Jack about. He'd reported that it winds around the lake and climbs to yield a fantastic view at the top. That sounded like the perfect place for him to clear his head before returning to his cabin. *And, who knows,* he thought, *maybe some exercise will start those creative juices flowing again.*

Exercise, after all, was one of the tips for overcoming a block he had heard a few years ago. Back then, he paid little attention when old Mac stopped routinely attending meetings of their small writers group. In a bid to help, one of the other members brought the list of ten tips to share with Mac. Jack, at the time, churned out a thousand words most days and hardly listened to the discussion. He did, however, recall that the list recommended implementing a work schedule. It also suggested setting personal deadlines and it said something about examining the underlying issues behind the block. Jack felt his chest tighten. He stopped on the trail and took a deep breath. In moments, Wabasso's natural perfume began to soothe him.

The path came close to the lake before cutting into densely wooded terrain again. Jack glanced down at his expensive jeans and alligator skin shoes. He shrugged and kept going. Inappropriate hiking attire or not, he wasn't willing to return to the cabin to change.

The trees began to crowd the trail and wedge out the sunlight more and more as Jack made his way. He marveled at the silence amid the closing trees. They seemed to block even sound waves from penetrating their midst. The ground took on a steady incline. It must have been the 'mostly uphill' part that Kubby had warned of. In places, Jack found himself stepping on the tree roots that crisscrossed the path as though they were stairs. He continued on, pausing only when he broke through an enormous spider web spanning the path. He brushed the fine threads off his sleeves and kept climbing.

The path continued upward for several minutes. The forest floor became a carpet of dead pine needles and bits of dried leaves. Very little underbrush grew amid the tall trees. Jack figured smaller plants wouldn't get enough sunlight to survive in these conditions. Everywhere trunks stretched from the ground like great pillars bracing the canopy of green overhead. He wondered why he didn't see any fallen trees. He was no outdoorsman, but he would have imagined the odd dead tree lying here and there. Perhaps that's why he didn't hear the sounds of wildlife. Maybe animals didn't live around places where there were no fallen trees to make their homes in.

Jack crested the path where it rose and bent around a rather ancient tree that he guessed was either an oak or an elm—he couldn't tell. Its foliage was long since dead. He carefully picked his way around the tree and found a clearing on the other side.

As he stepped out of the tree cover, a blue sky patched with cottony clouds opened wide above him. Underfoot, clumps of bristly grass mottled the otherwise bare, grey rock. The trail had dirtied his shoes and his sweater still bore traces of spider webbing, but for the moment he focused squarely on the view before him.

The clearing extended a few yards and terminated at the edge of a bluff. Wabasso Lake spread out below, a pool of radiance wreathed in lush forest. On its southern rim were the meager structures that made up the retreat. The black roofs of the rudimentary cabins poked between trees one after the other in a line. In plainer view were Kubby's office, the mess hall and shower house behind it, all appearing much like match boxes from this distance.

The incline had been steady during his hike up here, but Jack was still surprised at how high he had climbed. The sharp slope under the rocky crag fell to the lakeside for a hundred feet at least. Admittedly, he was never a fan of heights and yet he eagerly edged his way to the lip of the bluff. He simply had to get a better view of that sparkling sheet of sapphires most people banally called a lake.

Jack clutched the spiny branch of one of the pine trees that had managed enough of a toe hold on the rocky terrain to lay roots. He used the pine to balance himself and assessed the drop before him. Doubtless, it would be a fatal fall. It wasn't so much a sheer drop, but if one were to go over, he wouldn't stop tumbling on bare rock until he hit the water. For some reason, that didn't trouble Jack in the slightest.

He gulped a deep breath and tasted the fresh scent of the water, strong, even from so far above. It conjured images of his boys swimming at the public beaches back home. He sampled the air again and the pine he entrusted with his balance took him back to the Christmas mornings of childhood. The few clouds lazing across the sky appeared close enough to touch. Jack's gaze fell to Wabasso again. A string of ducks paddled close to the northern beach, barely discernible from this distance, and yet, there they were, plain as day. Wabasso wanted him to see everything, it wanted him to smell everything, it wanted to share all of its secrets with him.

Jack scanned Wabasso's far side and what he saw interrupted his joyous moment. There, amid the trees on the north side—the side Kubby had declared off limits to guests—stood some sort of building. The mere corner of the structure peeked from behind a stand of evergreen. Its straight lines became more apparent as Jack stared. He wondered what it could be. Perhaps some disused accommodation from an older incarnation of the retreat? If that was the case, the building hinted at greater luxury than his small cabin provided. Jack figured it had to be at least two stories tall in order to peek over the shoulders of those pines.

He checked his footing on the crag and baby stepped forward to widen the angle of his perspective. The idea of a structure that size, on the otherwise vacant shore, piqued his curiosity. *Maybe it is the retreat owner's home and they don't care to socialize with the guests. That would explain Kubby's flimsy excuse of insufficient insurance coverage. Then again, maybe he was telling the truth and the building was condemned and the insurance policy really wouldn't cover guests who injured themselves in the derelict structure.*

Jack allowed himself another few inches to the edge of the bluff, and then looked to the north side again. He lost sight of the building. He scanned the thick weave of leaves and limbs for trace of it. He saw no ruler-straight roof lines, no geometric shapes. The only lines remotely close to symmetrical were the rising trunks of spruce and pine. He was so confounded by the vanishing structure that he didn't register the rattling of lose pebbles as they squirted from underfoot and tumbled over the bluff. Tightening his grip on the pine bough, he leaned out further in search of the building that had been in plain view only a moment ago.

Now, where the hell did—

Jack's thought disintegrated in a blinding flash of panic.

He slipped.

The world rocked violently. He felt the prickly pine branch tear his palm before it pulled from his grip. He felt the rocks bite into his knee and hip. Then the worst sensation struck him, that nauseating feeling of being at the mercy of gravity. He flailed his arms as he slid over the edge of the bluff. His right hand pawed uselessly at the bare rocks. His left slapped desperately at the pine tree. He tried to dig in his heels and failed. A new thought spread through his mind like chain lightning.

I'm going to die.

He saw his boys, their faces streaked with tears. He saw them looking back at him through the rear window of the silver minivan as she drove them away.

Utter dread had frozen him at the core, but in a fraction of a second, a new emotion took hold.

She didn't even look back.

White hot rage flared.

A pine bough came into his grasp. He squeezed it tightly, barely registering the pain of its quills digging into his palm. He rolled over on his belly and clutched the branch with both hands. Using his feet, he tried to push himself upward, but his smooth alligator skin shoes denied him any purchase on the bald rock. Jack gritted his teeth and kicked off the expensive loafers, right and then left. Then he fought his way up, knees and toes finding divots on the rock. Hand over hand, he worked up the bough until he was able to hook an arm around the pine's trunk. His energy all but depleted, Jack clawed his ascent until he could finally drag his legs atop the bluff.

Fresh sparks of pain reported in from various body parts. Jack quickly assessed his injuries. A bloody cross work of cuts marked both palms. He rubbed them on his chest to rid them of clinging pine needles. The knee was torn out of his pant leg and a nasty scrape seeped blood beneath. More blood saturated the toe of his left sock and he pictured nails lifting off as he had wildly kicked at unyielding rock for a toehold.

He lay back on the ground, breathing hard, the full extent of his near death beginning to settle in. His face twisted and he wiped at the wetness in his eyes. A steady ache began to pulse from the hip that bore the brunt of his fall. He knew only more pain awaited him as he considered the prospect of a barefoot hike back to the retreat. For now he rested, facing the sky and dragging in deep breaths of panic-soured air. Wabasso's sweet, natural perfumes abandoned him.

Chapter Four

H oly shit, dude!" Kubby gaped from the other side of the office counter. "What the hell happened to you?" Jack limped through the doorway. He raised his bloody hands in a placating gesture. "I had a little accident," he said. "I'm okay. It's really no big deal."

"Your hands..." Kubby trailed off as he studied his guest from top to bottom. "Where are your shoes?"

Jack's gaze shifted about the place. "I, well, I lost 'em."

Kubby's brow furrowed.

With his face reddening from the sheer embarrassment of the situation, Jack gave a sheepish grin. "I...umm, went for a bit of a tumble on the trail." When the caretaker continued to gawk in amazement, he added, "Umm, you said earlier there's a first aid kit here?"

"Yeah...oh, *yeah*. Come around here," Kubby said. His stupor finally broken, he moved to offer Jack a helping hand. "We'll get you all fixed up."

Jack gripped Kubby's shoulder for support and stepped tenderly around the counter. He noticed Kubby looking at the floor behind them as they went. Jack had left red blotches on the hardwood from one sodden sock. "Sorry about that," he said.

"Hey, don't worry about it." Kubby steered Jack through another door. "Just take a seat in there. I'll get the kit."

Jack went inside what he figured to be Kubby's quarters. It was a meek living space. He sat down in the room's only chair. Upholstered in orange-dyed leather, it reminded Jack of a seventies era desk chair. A small window admitted the late afternoon light. Under it, a set of shelves held a portable stereo and about a dozen CDs. It was also home to a few thick volumes that Jack imagined the caretaker prized above the others shelved at the front of the office. Jack didn't recognize any of the names on their spines. It served a sharp reminder that he really was an outsider among the more literary minded.

What must have been Kubby's entire wardrobe was folded and heaped on the floor in the corner. From a lineup of hooks on the wall, hung his poncho, a green plastic raincoat and a wide brimmed straw hat. Against the opposite wall waited Wabasso's customary single man cot, topped with a tangle of threadbare blankets. Jack couldn't decide if Kubby led a charming, simple existence or if he simply lived hard.

"Okay," Kubby said, entering with a towel slung over his shoulder and carrying a bottle of water and a green metal box bearing a red cross. "Let's get you patched up." He sat on the edge of the cot and placed the towel on the floor between them. Then he unlatched the kit and opened it on the bed. Jack noted the small brown bottle of rubbing alcohol amid the gauze and bandages and knew he had more pain on the way.

"Thanks for helping me out like this," Jack offered.

"Oh, no problamo. I feel so bad that I didn't warn you about the trail. It can be pretty tricky country up through there. There's all kinds of roots and stuff to trip on." Kubby scratched at his beard. "So where do you want to start? That knee is leaking pretty good."

"Yeah. It hurts like a bugger."

"I'll bet." Kubby reached for Jack's leg and paused. "Hey, do you want to drop-trow or should I just rip the pant leg?"

"They're already ruined. Tear away."

Kubby lifted up Jack's foot by the heel, making him wince as his leg straightened. The caretaker rested Jack's foot on the cot between his own legs. With it inches from Kubby's crotch,

Jack scanned the room in search of a distracting conversation topic.

"You know, it's kind of funny," Jack said, his gaze drifting over the walls. "You tell your kids to be careful when they're playing outside and you worry about them, but they never seem to come home in this condition."

"Yeah, I'm sorry about all this," Kubby reiterated. He grabbed two fistfuls of denim and ripped Jack's pant leg wide open at the knee. The jarring effect had Jack biting his lip. "I really should have warned you about that trail."

Once Jack got past this new hurt he said, "Well, to be honest, I didn't really fall on the trail."

"Yeah?" Kubby inspected the gashed knee.

Jack's gaze shifted to the window and settled on the trees beyond, branches nodding with the breeze. "I went up the trail without even stumbling." Jack heard the rustling of plastic wrappers as Kubby went into the kit for something.

"Yeah? Umm, I have to clean this, Jack. I'm afraid it's gonna sting."

"Go ahead," Jack said, watching the trees, drawing comfort from their subtle swaying. He heard the contents of the brown bottle sloshing and waited for his knee to catch fire. Kubby pressed a wet cotton swab to the wound and at first it felt cool. The sensation was short lived. Kubby undersold the situation when he said *sting*. Jack gasped as what felt like a red hot branding iron pressed to his knee. He squinted hard, sucked in air and sat straight up in the chair as his every muscle tensed in unison.

"That should do it," Kubby said, and Jack felt the swab lift from his knee though the burning sensation lingered. "I don't think it's gonna need stitches."

Jack's eyes shot open. He hadn't considered that. He pictured Kubby sewing the split in his knee closed and a shiver travelled the length of his spine. "No, I don't think it needs stitches, either," he blurted.

"Yeah, I'll just dress it with gauze and wrap it good."

Jack turned to the window again in anticipation of more

discomfort. The trees waved hello. Kubby opened more wrappers from the kit.

"Like I was saying, I didn't have my little accident on the trail," Jack continued, as much to distract himself as to tell the tale.

"Right." Kubby applied pressure on the wound as he fixed his bandage and began tightly wrapping it.

"I made it to the top—where there's that sort of lookout place."

"Yeah, all the way to the top, eh?" Kubby said, focusing squarely on his task.

"Oh, I nearly forgot. I was looking across the lake and something caught my eye. There was a building of some sort, half hidden in the trees."

"The mess hall?" the caretaker asked absently.

"No, it was on the *other* side of the lake."

Kubby stopped wrapping Jack's leg.

Jack turned from the window and found the caretaker staring at him, his brow furrowed once more. "That's impossible," Kubby said, a new intensity entered his voice. "There's nothing over there."

Jack paused. Kubby's defensive reaction threw him a little. "Yes, I remembered you telling me that. That's why I thought it was so strange—"

Kubby cut him off. "We're not even allowed to go over there. The owners said."

It seemed the far shore was so taboo a topic, the caretaker couldn't tolerate the mere mention of it. The moment threatened to turn awkward. Jack hoped continuing his tale would lighten the mood. "Right, well, I went to the edge of that bluff, you know? And, I tried to get a better look at whatever that building was."

Kubby dropped his gaze and muttered, "We don't have insurance coverage over there."

Jack forged ahead. "Anyway, I was holding on to this pine tree for balance and I stepped out."

Rather than voicing another protest, Kubby said, "What

did you see?" His eyes peeled wide and locked on Jack's again.

Jack pictured the straight edges that simply had to be those of a roofline and wall—they were there one second and gone the next.

"*Nothing*," he said. "There was nothing there."

"Nothing," Kubby breathed. He seemed genuinely relieved by the report. He even smiled as he went back to wrapping the wound.

"That's when I slipped and nearly fell to my death," Jack said, gesturing at his injured knee.

That brought Kubby's work to a halt again. "*Over the cliff?* You gotta be shitting me."

"I wish I was. A pine tree saved my life," Jack said, showing his upturned hands and the numerous cuts the pine bough left him with.

Kubby studied him. "No Jack, the *land* saved your life. *Wabasso* saved your life."

Jack considered Kubby, who now had that *time-for-a-high-five* gleam in his eye. The caretaker smiled and nodded as though he was welcoming Jack into some sort of select brotherhood. Jack nearly made the argument that, by the same token, it was also Wabasso that had tried to *kill* him. Instead, he let it go and Kubby finished dressing his knee.

"Try to keep it straight," Kubby said, lowering it to the floor gingerly. "And, I should probably change the bandage every day for a while." He sat up, hands on his thighs. "Now, let's check out that foot."

He lifted Jack's other foot up and carefully rolled off the bloody sock. Jack breathed a sigh of relief when he saw that he didn't lose any nails. He did, however, sport a long scrape down the side of his big toe. Kubby tended to the wound, and then addressed Jacks tattered hands. Those injuries took a little longer to clean. Kubby had to tweeze several needles and other debris out of the cuts, and through the process, applied a lot of stinging alcohol.

When Kubby had finished, Jack's hands resembled those of the mummified and he felt a profound fatigue settle in. He slumped into the office chair and rested his eyes as Kubby went to store the first aid kit.

"There's one more bit of treatment I have to give you," Kubby announced upon his return.

Jack's eyes darted up at him. He dreaded the prospect of any more poking and prodding at the hands of the caretaker.

"It's time to prescribe the painkiller." Kubby grinned and held up a Ziploc freezer bag. Jack eyed the bundle of green herbs inside it. He recalled the smoke wafting from this very room when he arrived in the office to check in.

"I can't smoke that." Jack chuckled.

"Oh, sure you can. In fact, you *should*." Kubby dropped onto his cot. "This primo blend has all kinds of medicinal goodness. It's just what you need to get over a cliffhanger-type -accident." He retrieved a rolled joint from the top of the bag and wet it in his mouth. He produced a Bic lighter from his pocket, but before he lit-up, he said, "Whoa, something's missing." He reached for the shelf beside his cot and pressed play on the stereo. Drums beat from the small speakers and Kubby nodded in rhythm as he sparked the lighter. He sucked hard and a cherry blazed. Jack caught himself starring as Kubby exhaled slowly, contentment dawning on his face. Lazy guitars began to whine.

"You like Credence, Jackie?" Kubby asked.

Jack perked up. "I *love* CCR."

"Me, too." Kubby took another long, easy haul.

"How old are you, Kubby?" Jack said, his eyes narrowing as he assessed the caretaker.

Kubby gave a squinty smile and smoke billowed from his nostrils. "Old enough to know better," he said. Then he reached over to offer Jack the joint. "Here…"

Jack dismissed it with a wave of his bandaged hand. "I haven't smoked in, what, twenty some years?"

"Wife don't like it?"

"No, it's not like that…well, yeah. I guess you could say that, but…"

"Here," Kubby said, not retracting his offer.

Jack eyed the wafting, white smoke. It danced seductively on the air.

"My arm is getting tired." The caretaker's elbow began to droop and he supported it with his free hand.

Jack relented and took the joint with his thumb and forefinger, but only held it and watched it sidelong while it smoldered.

Kubby said, "Tonight, at lights out, when you hit the hay, you're gonna see that cliff again. You're gonna feel like you're going over. You're gonna hang there, and you won't sleep a wink." He raised his brow and nodded at the joint.

Unless I smoke this? Jack thought. "I guess I might be a little on edge right now. What the hell." Jack inhaled the pungent smoke and it scraped its way down his windpipe. He tried to hold it in, but it fought like a badger for release. He erupted in a long string of coughing. Phlegm spattered into his bandaged hand. When he finally caught his breath, his eyes teared and he could hardly feel his throat.

"What do you think?" Kubby said.

"That's pretty fuckin' good," Jack said.

They laughed.

Back and forth the joint travelled, dropping ashes on the towel on the floor as it went. When it was little more than a nub, Kubby pinched it out between his fingers and dropped the remainder in the Ziploc.

Jack settled back in his chair and grinned all the way through *Fortunate Son*. He wasn't sure if he would be transported back to the cliff when he went to bed, but he was pretty sure he wouldn't be feeling his injuries. Already, his torn knee was a distant memory and even his hip tempered to a mere dull ache. "You know what's funny, Kubby?"

The caretaker lay back on his cot, staring at the rafters. "What, man?"

"After I got all banged up out there, I walked all the way back through the woods with no shoes on." Jack rubbed his mouth to battle the giddy laughter building deep down.

"Yeah, well, a man's gotta do what a man's gotta do, man."

Kubby raised his head and nodded his approval.

"But, I walked right past my cabin." Jack couldn't hold his laughter at bay a moment longer. He snorted as it burst out of him.

"All the way here to see this guy." Kubby pointed his thumbs at himself, proudly.

Jack caught his breath long enough to say, "Yes, but, I could have at least stopped in there to get a pair of shoes."

"Oh yeah." Kubby's face shriveled up in an exaggerated grin and his shoulders started heaving. "That *is* funny. Yeah, you're gonna end up like me." Kubby raised his leg to show Jack his filthy foot, nearly blackened by years of barefoot strolls and skipped baths. If they were outside, his feet would be barely visible against the soil. Kubby would appear to grow from the ground like a tree. For Jack, the thought was as sobering as a slap across the face. He looked down at his own bare foot and after slogging through the woods, it was well on its way to resembling Kubby's.

Jack sat up straight in his chair. "I should head back to my cabin."

"You want to smoke one for the road?" Kubby said, already sitting up and reaching for his Ziploc.

"No, but thanks for all your help, Kubby."

"My pleasure, man." Kubby raised his hand. Jack indulged him in a tentative high five. He figured he owed him that much. "Oh, and let me get you something for your feet," Kubby said, getting up. He searched his laundry heap and some seconds later, came up with a pair of tanned leather moccasins. "Here, for your journey back."

"Thanks, Kubby. I'll return them tomorrow."

The caretaker plopped himself back on his cot. "No rush."

Jack stood up and the room turned on its axis. He held the wall to steady himself while he fumbled the Native footwear onto his feet. "I think I could sleep for a week."

"Well, I got a roast in the oven over in the mess," Kubby declared. "If you're not feeling up to dinner tonight, I can save you a plate. Yeah, I'll leave it in the fridge. You can help yourself."

I wish I really could help myself, Jack thought. He considered the task that lay before him. There was work to do, waiting back at his cabin. It was the sole reason he had taken the long road to Wabasso Lake. He tested his battered knee as he took his first steps to the exit and wondered if it would serve reminder to the consequences of straying off the path in the future. *Lesson learned.*

A slender crescent moon hung above the lake. Wabasso's skin sparkled magically under it. It illuminated the beach, the pair of canoes, and the rocks lining the disused fire pit. The appearance of the night sky gave Jack a mild surprise. There had been plenty of daylight left when he limped into the office. Evidently, he spent far longer with Kubby than he thought. He thanked the caretaker's primo blend for the missing time.

The evening breeze carried the faintest chill. Jack found it refreshing. It served to wake him as he walked along the path past the mess hall. After a few moments in the night air, he was able to shake off the fatigue that had come over him in the office and he no longer felt the need to lie down.

He eyed the open windows of the mess, aglow in soft orange. Lively conversation and stray laughter drifted from inside. The other guests likely gathered in anticipation of Kubby's roast. The thought of joining them in his current condition didn't hold much appeal for Jack. He picked up his pace to avoid being seen as he walked by.

Jack fully expected his injuries to flare as he hurried down the path, but Kubby's painkiller was more effective than he could have imagined. His bruised hip, torn knee, even his battered foot did very little complaining. When Jack was safely past the mess, he slowed to a stroll, and finding the crisp evening air so agreeable, he decided to continue down the trail for a while.

He pictured the part where it veered close to the lake and thought it would be a nice place to sit and enjoy the view. To his right, he passed the series of side trails leading to the guest cabins. Thankfully, he didn't meet anyone along the way. Explaining his bandaged hands and pant leg ripped up to his thigh would likely prove too taxing at the moment.

He came to the final side trail heading to his own cabin and briefly considered stopping in for a change of pants and footwear, but the moccasins proved to be quite comfortable. He decided against it. Besides, he wouldn't be long. Despite being relatively pain free for the moment, Jack knew that bed rest would be the best remedy for his wounds.

The trail twisted sharply to the left. It led Jack further into the woods and away from the other guests. In his isolation, unpleasant thoughts loomed large in his mind once more. They seemed to lie in wait for him in the dark, seldom travelled places. Now those incessant phantoms closed in, swirling about him. Back in his cabin, his laptop waited for his return. The *block* waited.

Is that why I can't go back? Is that why I'm on this trail again in the dark of night? He wished he could walk to his car, get in and drive back to the city without stopping. He wished he could arrive at home to find his boys sleeping soundly in their old bedrooms. Neither outcome was possible.

I'm being punished, he thought. *I have to stay here. I have to stay with these…people. They know I'm a fraud. They know I'm a failure. This is a personal hell. And somehow I deserve it.* Jack recalled what Kate told him about Wabasso giving people what they need most. He chuckled silently. *Maybe she's right. Maybe I need this. Maybe I need to suffer.*

Jack stopped and, for the first time in many minutes, took in his surroundings. There was no sign of the lake. Trees grew close on all sides. The high tangle of branches and leaves supported by hundreds of imposing black columns filtered the moonlight. A silent, lifeless place, Jack couldn't hear so much as the stirring of insects among the trees. It was as dark as he imagined the ocean floor. Jack thought if he did see animals, they would likely bear phosphorescent spots and stripes, glowing eyes. He looked at the trail ahead. It climbed and snaked around the wide trunk of a dead tree. He knew this place. On the other side of that leafless tree opened a clearing where bald rock led to a bluff. Jack sucked in a breath and his throat quivered.

How did I manage to get here? he wondered. *It's not a simple case of taking a wrong turn. I had to cover a lot of ground to get here. Did my subconscious bring me here so I could face my fears?* He wasn't even certain that he feared the place. Sure he had that dreadful moment when he had to hang on for dear life, but did that constitute a fear of the place in particular? He didn't think so.

Did I come for something else, then? Perhaps what I thought I saw across the lake? Jack had to admit, it was a bizarre sighting—a building where he hadn't expected any building to be. There it was and then there it wasn't. And, Kubby's reaction to the sighting had been surprising. The caretaker did his best to ward off any thought of Jack venturing over there.

Jack considered continuing to the clearing. Surely in the dark, it would be harder to make out any structure half hidden by trees to begin with. Although, if there happened to be a building over there, perhaps someone inside had lit a lamp. It would make it easier to spot.

Jack eyed the trail behind him, where it descended into darkness amid the towering trunks. Ahead, the path twisted around the weather beaten tree. *Kubby probably doesn't want anyone crossing the lake because he grows his primo blend over there,* Jack concluded. *Who could blame him for wanting to keep his secret crop a secret?*

Jack continued his ascent. He reached the dead tree and stumbled when his moccasin hooked one of its bulging roots. Jack put his hands up to brace his collision with the tree and its coarse bark bit into them. He expected bolts of fresh pain to strike up his arms from his wounded hands. No such pain came. Jack chalked it up to Kubby doing a good job of bandaging them. He found a more secure foothold and resumed his climb around the tree.

He stepped out of the woods and the wan light of the crescent moon washed over him. The pale glow helped him pick careful steps toward the stony bluff. Once there, he peered anxiously across Wabasso's silvery surface. Jack released a long sigh while he scanned the distant tree line for his mystery structure.

There was nothing—no building, no straight roofline, no widows lit by lamplight. He was glad, he decided. Had there actually been a building standing over there, it meant, among other things, that Kubby had lied to him. Jack was a little relieved that wasn't the case.

Keeping a safe remove from the edge, Jack dropped his gaze to the south shore and the collection of glowing windows that comprised the retreat. The mess hall was easy to pick out. The other guests were likely inside, by now enjoying the roast. Jack's stomach grumbled when he pictured thick slices of medium rare beef piled alongside a heap of mashed potatoes smothered in gravy.

With so few guests at Wabasso, his absence at dinner was no doubt noticed. He decided he didn't want to appear rude or give the impression that he didn't value the company of others. At least he didn't want Kate to get that idea. For that reason, and a now constantly rumbling belly, he elected to hurry back to the mess. If he made good time on the trail, and quickly changed clothes in his cabin, he could still arrive at dinner at a decent time. He could blame his all-consuming work for his tardiness.

Jack approached the dead tree to find the mouth of the trail and halted in his tracks. He heard a troubling noise. It was a distinct grunting sound, perhaps a vicious animal. The snapping of twigs followed.

Jack backed away from the tree, into the clearing again. His heartbeat revved, his breathing shallow. Then he heard a word of English, then another. He loosed a sigh. It wasn't the growling of an animal that he heard, but the sound of a gravelly voice speaking. It had to belong to one of the other guests.

Perhaps a few of them had gone for a walk after their supper and found their way here. Jack waited for them to appear from the trail behind the old tree. He grinned and anticipated telling them about the start they had given him, but when they emerged from woods, his grin faded. The one in the lead was young, probably twelve years of age. The man who followed was much older—likely in his seventies. Jack backed up another step. These two were not guests. He recognized them.

The youngster wore a navy plaid shirt tucked into short pants and brown leather shoes. The elder had on neatly pressed woolen trousers braced by suspenders. His white band collar shirt stood stark against the night. It was appropriate wear for folks from their time.

They didn't notice Jack standing in the clearing as they stopped under the dead tree. They simply went on with their conversation. Jack saw the black eye the lad sported and he felt sick to his stomach. It was exactly the way he imagined it.

The old man laid a wide farmer's mitt on the boy's head. It had swelled knuckles that had been broken and rebroken in countless wars waged with other hard men. "Son," the man said.

The boy looked up at him, his lower lip showing the slightest of tremors.

"You're old enough to know—" the man started. Jack felt icy winds blow through his very core. He knew what would be said next, word for word, "—the true measure of a man don't come in inches and feet or pounds and ounces." The old man stared at the boy. "It don't even come in battles won and lost. It comes…"

Jack waited, afraid to move a muscle.

"It comes…"

The old man went silent. He stood perfectly still like a movie projection suddenly paused. The boy, too, waited for his grandfather to deliver that bit of crucial life changing advice. He searched the old man and swallowed hard. He raised a finger and pointed at Jack.

"Ask him," the boy said.

Jack thought his bowels might let loose. He took another step backward without the slightest thought of the bluff or its hundred foot drop.

Grandfather and grandson slowly turned his way. "How 'bout it, Hoss?" the elder asked. "You must know. What makes a man a man?"

Jack shook his head, unable to find his tongue.

"After all, you're the high riding, big money scribblin' asshole that decides all things, ain't ya? You stand there, lookin' like a drifter in your torn dungarees and your redskin slippers, and you tell me, what truly makes a man a man?"

"I don't think he knows, Grandpa," the boy said, matter-of -factly.

"I don't think he knows, neither." The old man straightened and set his jaw, as he seemed to come to some conclusion. "I don't think this city boy knows low from middlin'." He gave his grandson a stiff nod. "You best fetch the rope."

The old man moved fast and he was on Jack in a heartbeat. One big hand clamped on his arm, the other on the back of his neck. Jack fought to break free of the hold. He tried to pry open the old man's grip with his free hand. It was no use. The man possessed a strength that belied his age. Jack felt like a child, struggling in futility to get loose. "Get your fucking hands off me," he yelled.

"Got it, Grandpa," the boy shouted.

Jack looked over the man's shoulder at the boy. What he saw spurred his fight to a wild frenzy. The boy held several coils of rope. One of its ends was tied in a noose. He tossed that end up and over one of the limbs of the dead tree.

The old hangin' tree. The words boomed in Jack's mind like cannon fire. His voice erupted in a desperate howl. He frantically slammed his elbows into the man. The blows had no effect.

The old man set his jaw again and whirled Jack around toward the tree.

Jack was powerless to do anything but go where he was flung. He fell in a heap on the bald rock and before he could regain his footing and attempt flight, the clamps were on him again. He squirmed and writhed against the old man's grip and when the boy fit the noose around his neck, the battle in Jack reached hysterical levels. He lashed out at the boy, kicked madly at the man. His attacks seemed less than an inconvenience to each of them. They brushed his flailing arms and legs aside with ease.

The boy handed his grandfather the other end of the rope.

The old man gave Jack a cold and heavy stare. "Anything you want to say?" he asked.

Jack saw his chance for escape. He tugged on the rope to pull it off his neck.

The old man took up the slack and the noose tightened.

Jack changed strategies. He decided to make a plea for mercy, but his voice cinched off as the rope hoisted him off the ground. He searched the stony faces of Grandpa and Grandson and knew then that they were incapable of mercy. He dug his fingers under the noose to unlock his windpipe. Every arm length of rope taken up by the old man lifted Jack higher until he swung a good four feet from the ground. The coarse fibers of the rope bit into Jack's neck. He felt his trachea closing off again. His fingers couldn't hold his body weight a moment longer. They pinched into his throat. His legs kicked in a desperate search for something to stand on.

I'm going to die. Dear God, I'm going to die.

Jack gnashed his teeth to the point they might shatter.

"How long will he last, Grandpa?" the boy said, looking up at Jack without the slightest hint of compassion.

The old man held the rope and all of Jack's weight in one hand with ease. He spit on the ground, never taking his cold eyes off Jack. "That is entirely up to him."

Jack gasped for air. It didn't come. Darkness crept in from the sides of his vision. It enveloped the boy and his grandfather and finally everything clouded over black.

With his final scraps of oxygen, Jack screamed.

He jerked forward and groped feebly at the rope.

It was gone.

The boy and the old man were gone.

Jack's brain processed his surroundings at a snail's pace. It was dark. He was in his cabin, sitting bolt-upright in his cot. And he still screamed.

When he realised this, he slapped his bandaged hands over his mouth. The whole retreat had likely heard him, but the lingering dread from his nightmare superseded any shame he felt. It had felt so real. A sheen of sweat coated his skin, hair clung to his brow. His throat ached—bruised and rubbed raw by the noose—or could he have done it to himself? Could he have choked himself in his sleep?

Jack kicked his legs over the edge of the cot and his wounded knee delivered a yelp of pain. Outside the window a hook of a moon suspended over the lake. The sight of the placid waters under the clear night sky did little to quiet Jack's reeling thoughts. But, there was one thought he could settle on: *I'm never going to smoke anything Kubby gives me again.*

Chapter Five

Jack spent an hour sprawled on his cot, trying to get back to sleep and failing miserably. Every time he closed his eyes he saw the old man, his grandson and their wicked noose. Eventually, the terror that the dream infused in him began to abate. In its place pangs of hunger crept in. Soon, all he could picture was the roast beef waiting for him in the mess hall refrigerator.

When his stomach growled, he gave up any notion of getting more rest. He got up, careful not to jar his tender knee, and retrieved his phone from the desk. It was dead. He had forgotten to charge it. He would need to start the laptop to get the hour. The idea of opening it sent a wave of nausea through him. He decided against it. It was still dark out, making it either really late or really early. He supposed it didn't much matter which.

He switched on the cabin's lone light and pulled the waistband of his boxers down to marvel at the welt on his hip. The forget-me-not from his hiking mishap was about the size of a softball, purple in the centre with outer rings of blue. It would likely turn all the colours of the rainbow before it cleared up. He dressed in a fresh pair of jeans and a plain white tee shirt and squeezed his bandaged foot into a pair of Adidas.

A knock at the door froze Jack.

The image of the old man appeared in his mind, grim

faced as his gnarled knuckles pounded on the door.

Jack didn't move a muscle, didn't draw a breath. *Those maniacal country folk—they found me.*

Another knock issued.

Somehow they crossed the line between fiction and reality. Now they're here, outside my door. Jack drew a slow calming breath.

Okay, that's ridiculous.

I'm tired and hungry, and I need to get a grip.

Even after telling himself just that, apprehension filled his voice. "Who is it?"

"It's Kate," came the voice from the other side.

The tension bled out of Jack's muscles. "Kate? Is everything all right?"

He went to the door and opened it. She stood there, the hood of her red sweatshirt pulled up, her arms folded against the night chill.

"I'm sorry. I know it's late, but I saw your light on." Her eyes expressed a mingling of sympathy and concern. "Can I come in?"

"Of course," he said, stepping back. "Is everything okay?"

She entered and pulled off her hood. "I could ask you the same thing. I heard the, umm, some noise coming from here earlier."

"Oh...that." Jack's cheeks flushed. "I suppose I woke you up. I'm sorry."

"I'll bet you woke everybody up." She lowered herself onto the wooden chair.

Jack huffed a nervous chuckle and sat on the cot. "How embarrassing."

"Do you want to talk about it?"

"It was just a dream."

"I was hoping you don't scream like that when you're awake." Kate gave a smile that quickly faded when she got a good look at him. "What happened to your hands?"

"I fell and managed to cut myself." Jack folded his arms and tucked his bandaged hands in his armpits in a weak attempt to deflect focus from his wounds. "Kubby went overboard with the wrappings. They make it seem worse than it is."

"Jesus, Jack, you've had a rough start here."

His gaze drifted across the wood floor as he considered this. "Yeah, I guess things are starting to pile up."

Kate leaned forward in her chair. "Do you want to talk about it? Your dream, I mean? Sometimes talking about it helps you to get over it."

Jack's eyes met with Kate's and he felt diminished, like he was becoming transparent and Kate would soon be able to see all his secrets on full display. She would see his attraction for her. She would see his broken home. She would see the B word.

The last thing he wanted was another woman seeing weakness in him. He felt pathetic, small. "I don't know…" He cleared his throat. "I was dreaming about…" He stopped and decided on another starting point. "I have been working on this passage, this exchange between…well, I'm having some trouble with it. I just want to pull it off perfectly because it sets up a lot of what happens next in the book."

Jack cursed himself. If he had so much difficulty even describing his problem, how did he ever expect to overcome it?

Kate pursed her full lips and nodded.

"I guess it's been on my mind pretty much constantly. Anyway the dream was…terrible, a nightmare. You must think I'm out of my mind—a grown man having a nightmare."

"Why? It has happened to me," she said flatly.

Jack attempted to laugh it off. The noise he made sounded desperate, even to him. "I'm sure it happens to everyone at some point in their life."

"No, I'm not talking about having a nightmare. I mean, I had a dream about something I was writing."

Jack raised an eyebrow. "One of your novels?"

"The ending of one, actually. It was a western drama set in 1880's Oklahoma and I was trying to decide on how to close out a relationship between two characters. There is always this urge to close on a kiss, but I didn't think a kiss was warranted in this case. I didn't know what to do. I even thought about killing one of them off." Kate shook her head as though the experience still bothered her. "I must have fretted over that ending for days."

"Been there." *Am there.*

"Then I had the dream. It was simple enough. I dreamt I got up in the morning, left my cabin—you know, Number Two down there. I was on my way to breakfast. It was getting light out, a few minutes before dawn, so it was still kind of dark. Anyway, I started toward the mess and then I heard this noise behind me. It was so peculiar, but I thought I heard hooves on the path. So I turned around and came down this way to check it out, and I saw him."

"Saw who?" Jack gaped.

"My Texas ranger."

"I'm sorry…*who?*"

"One of my characters." Kate dropped her gaze and shook her head in solemn reflection.

Jack swallowed, his mouth dry.

"It took me a minute to realise exactly *who* I was looking at. It scared me to death. My first instinct was to turn and run. But, I just held still and tried not to make a sound, you know? He was riding away so he had his back to me. He was just the way I described him in the story: tall in the saddle of his bay-brown, wearing a long grey overcoat and matching Stetson. He just kept on his merry way and soon he went around the bend and was gone."

"And that gave you the ending you wanted?"

Kate grinned and turned her eyes up to the ceiling as she recited her ending for Jack. "Annie watched the ranger ride off, his Morgan at a steady trot. He didn't hurry the mare as he rode out of Annie's life forever, nor did he look back. The end."

Jack slowly nodded. *Perhaps it's not an exciting ending, but it is honest. Maybe that's what's missing from my approach—more honesty.*

Jack started to imagine what sort of advice would pass from a grandfather to his grandson on the subject of being a good man. It was so difficult to see past his own ideals—more accurately the yawning, empty pit where such ideals would dwell in a real man.

"There it is again—that face." Kate tilted her head and squinted somewhat as she studied him. "You get this look about you, like you're carrying heavy luggage or something."

Jack spared a glimpse at his laptop and sighed.

Kate leaned forward to snag his attention. "Whatever it is, just remember, this is the best place for you to be."

"Kate, I..." *I have writer's block.* "I have..." *Just tell her.* "I have two boys." Jack stood up and reached for the wall over Kate. He took down the picture of his sons at the beach and showed it to Kate. "This is Brian and that's Thomas. I'm having a hard time without them."

"They're handsome, like their dad." As soon as Kate said it, her mouth clamped shut. She wore the expression of a person who had said too much.

Jack admired the photograph a moment longer before returning it to the wall. "Do you want to see if we can get some breakfast?" he asked.

Kate seemed thankful for the diversion. She went straight to the door. "I'm way ahead of you."

The cursor blinked at Jack.

It had taken him several minutes to work up the courage to even start the laptop. It took several more before he felt able to face the screen. When he did, he saw those ragged sentences and his eye shot immediately to their end and that urgently blinking black sliver on the white page. It was roughly the size of a paper cut. It cut and cut and cut, bringing with it a slow and painful death. Soon it was all Jack saw on the page. He became aware of his heartbeat again. It grew louder. It rushed in his ears. It pounded in rhythm with the blinking cursor.

Jack rubbed his eyes and searched for a measure of serenity. It had been there when he ate a very early breakfast with Kate. It was there when he walked her back to her cabin in the first rays of dawn. He even felt a relative sense of calm as he sipped from his water bottle, waiting for the laptop to boot. Then it was methodically chipped away with every blink of the cursor. He reached into memory for one of the tips for overcoming writer's block his writing group had discussed. There were ten. He couldn't remember a single one.

He clutched the edges of the table and winced as though bracing for some sort of violent impact. His mind flailed for a lifeline. He tried to remember Kate's advice. *What did she say?* She had tried to tell him to relax, that he was meant to be here, but he kept going back to her dream. *She dreamed her ending. Did I dream mine, too?*

Jack saw the old man and his grandson standing under the skeletal limbs of the long-dead tree. The boy held the coil of rope.

Jack struggled to breathe. He pushed his chair back from the table and when he did, he could almost feel the spiny strands of the noose as it closed around his neck. He threw his hands out and shut the laptop.

Several moments passed before the atmosphere in the small cabin cleared. Jack's heartbeat calmed and soon the cabin became very still and very quiet. Jack treasured the peace in the aftermath of his latest failure until it was broken by the sound of footfalls on the steps outside. *Had Kate returned? Did she somehow sense my distress again? Just how much is she able to gather with those bright green eyes?*

The footsteps stopped outside the door, but no knocking followed. Jack eyed the simple wooden door. The porch boards creaked. He started to stand, but it occurred to him that perhaps he should keep quiet. He waited. Still no knock. There was another, longer creak, followed by a scuffing sound like pages being rubbed together. Then a piece of paper appeared under the door.

Jack got up and retrieved it from the floor.

It read, *Call your agent. - Kubby.*

Jack opened the door and found the caretaker a few yards down the path. Kubby stopped and turned. "Sorry to bother you, man, but your guy called the office a couple of times already this morning. He says it's real important you call him back. I tried telling him that I'll give you the message at lunch—"

"That's okay, Kubby," Jack said.

Kubby didn't make eye contact. He appeared genuinely uncomfortable having interrupted a writer's workday. "I didn't want to bug you, but the guy was getting kind of ugly about it."

"Yeah, Ted can be a nasty piece of business, when he doesn't get his way." Jack tucked the note in his pocket and looked back inside the cabin at the closed laptop. "Hey, do you want to come in for a while? We could hang out."

"No, I really shouldn't," Kubby said, still averting his eyes from Jack as though he was standing on the porch in his underwear.

"It's okay. I was taking a break anyway."

"I really can't."

Jack got the impression that it was indeed a strict rule for staff not to interact with guests when they were supposedly working. Despite the invitation, it was a rule Kubby would not break. "Okay, I'll catch up with you later then."

Kubby seemed relieved at having been let off the hook. "Okay, man. Later," he said and continued on his way.

Jack lingered in the doorway, watching the caretaker go until a stroke of red against the otherwise evergreen canvas lured his is gaze.

The cardinal had returned. It resumed its perch on the short maple tree in front of the cabin. Jack could see that it had snared a grasshopper. Tiny twitching legs protruded from either side of its beak. It turned its head and framed Jack with a peppercorn eye. If he didn't know better, he could have sworn the bird was judging him.

"What are you lookin' at?" he said.

The cardinal didn't budge.

Jack pulled the note from his pocket and told the bird, "I'm going to call him. I just don't want to."

When Jack reached the communal phone outside the mess hall, he found it in use. He considered returning to his cabin, but putting off this phone call would only serve to infuriate Ted further. Jack, too, would appreciate getting it over with. He wasn't sure what he would tell Ted exactly, but he knew whatever it was, it would be one hundred percent bullshit. He'd heap it high and deep and Teddy would eat it up. What choice did he have?

Jack didn't know the man on the phone. Tall with wavy blonde hair and sideburns, he was very Ivy League, standing there in his salmon-coloured golf shirt and tan khakis. His conversation appeared to be an animated one. Although not trying to eavesdrop, Jack learned that the man neared the end of a first draft.

Jack backed up a few feet to afford the man more privacy, but it didn't make any difference. The phone booth, if it could be called that, was three sided and had no door. The man, while talking excitedly into the receiver, saw Jack standing behind him some ten feet back, but didn't seem to mind. He continued his conversation with whom Jack figured was his agent or editor. There was a lot of smiling, a lot of laughter. It seemed there would be a lot of success. Jack turned away and kicked at the dirt.

He began to feel very exposed standing there, outside the mess, and he prayed for the man to free up the phone before somebody happened by. He didn't think he could tolerate another person asking about his bandages or, worse yet, why he screamed himself awake last night. Jack had decided he was going back to hide in his cabin, when the man on the phone raised his voice.

"Excellent, I'll see you in New York," he said. "Put the bubbly on ice!" After a pause, he responded with an emphatic,

"Yesssss!" and hung up.

Jack straightened and prepared to introduce himself and perhaps explain his bandaged hands one more time. The man turned from the booth, pumped his fist triumphantly, looked Jack in the eye and said, "Yesssss!" again. He proceeded to walk past Jack in the direction of the cabins without saying another word.

Jack didn't take offense. Had they tried to converse they would likely discover that they weren't even speaking the same language. Their situations were so different, so utterly opposite that they might as well have been members of different species. Perhaps the blonde man knew that.

Jack picked up the phone, dialed and prepared himself for a conversation with what he imagined was one of the pushier agents in the game. He didn't have much time to prep—Teddy answered on the first ring.

"Hullo."

That Ted himself answered and not his secretary came as a surprise to Jack. *He must be good and worked up.* "Hey there Ted, it's Jack. I just got your message," he said, doing his best to sound cheery.

"Good God, Jackie, I thought I would have heard from you by now. I didn't know if you made it there safe or not. For all I knew, you got lost or eaten by hillbillies or something. The hills have eyes up that way, you know?" A bit of dry laughter scraped out of Ted's throat. Jack waited for it to abate. Ted loved to laugh at his own jokes.

Jack drew a breath to speak, but before he could get a word out, Ted rambled on again. "Or you could have hit a moose with your car. You know how many people hit moose up in that country? Me neither, but it must be a lot. It's all I hear about from there."

"How are you, Ted?" Jack said quickly when he saw a chance to jump in. Jack never knew if his agent routinely had trouble hearing him or if he simply ignored him. In any regard, the result was much the same—Jack listened while a single sided conversation unfolded on the other end of the line.

"So how do you like the lake?" Ted went on. His voice became faint for the briefest of moments and Jack pictured him pulling away from the receiver as he reached for paperwork. "Is it as peaceful as everyone says? What do they know, anyway? Bunch of schmucks."

"The lake is very nice," Jack blurted.

"How's the work coming along? I'll bet the old word mill is pumping out some good stuff."

On the other end, Jack heard the rub of several pages being turned. He found the noise most unsettling. "Well, I'm working away."

"Super, super, that's great. Everything will be great." There came a pause. It seemed Ted didn't get the answer he really wanted.

Jack cradled the receiver under his chin and adjusted the wrappings on his hands. They were getting dirty and he looked forward to Kubby changing them. "I was told your call was urgent."

"Yeah, ah, listen Jack, I don't mean to pile stuff on your plate right now, but the shit is starting to hit the fan around here."

Ted took a rare breath. "Jack, the publisher called this morning. And I know what you're thinking. What the hell do they want now, right? Well, they're starting to use some pretty tough talk, Jackie. I told them, hey, relax, Jack's working on it. He's at Wabasso fucking Lake, birthplace of the bestseller. It's gonna be all right. Just settle down and you'll get your book. But, you know them, right? What can I say? They're yakking about their holiday book list and going on and on."

Jack rubbed the bridge of his nose between his fingers. "It's just more of the same though, right Ted?"

"Ah, no, Jackie. It's different this time. God...I'm sorry as hell about this, but they...they're talking about cutting your contract."

The news knocked the wind out of Jack. He had been preoccupied by mental blocks and nightmares featuring crazed country folk, but this wasn't some abstract theory or dream.

This was real. As real as the mess hall before him. As real as the phone in his hand.

"It gets worse," Ted continued. His voice was grave. It didn't seem to fit the Ted Marsh Jack knew. Jack's stomach soured. "There's a stipulation in your contract. It's meant to protect the publisher in the event a writer doesn't deliver on a book. Basically, it says they can claw back some of the money they advanced you."

"How much?" Jack ran his hand over his face and braced himself for Ted's idea of *worse*.

"Well, Jackie, you signed a three book deal. You delivered one book to press. It is their legal right to take back two thirds of the money."

Jack thought he might wretch.

"I couldn't be more sorry about this, Jackie. I know the trouble you're having with the ex. Hell, I've been there myself a few times." Ted's voice hitched. As usual, with mention of divorce, he had started to snigger, but thought the better of it. This was no time for jokes. "Now Jack, I've done my level best to keep the wolves off your doorstep, but there's only so much I can do."

"You said I had some time, before I came here. I thought the publisher was giving me a few weeks to finish the manuscript."

"You still have them. You do. But, they want to see chapters now. They want to see what you've got already. They, God Almighty, I hate having to tell you this. They're talking about taking what you have and getting one of their staff writers to finish for you."

"No way. No *fucking* way, Ted!" Jack wasn't quite sure why that upset him so. He didn't have nearly enough material completed for someone else to finish. All he really had was one incomplete paragraph, but the thought of some stranger taking his words, real or not, infuriated him. It was *his* old man, *his* boy, *his* hangin' tree, nobody else's.

"I know. I know. I flipped my lid when I heard that, too. But, Jackie, this is going off the rails in a hurry."

Jack made sure he was alone. He lowered his voice nevertheless. "I'm screwed then."

"Just hang on now, Jackie." Ted said in a consoling tone—another that did not sound at home coming from the agent.

Jack prepared for another blow.

"I asked them, if you showed what you had and it was good, and I mean, like, *The Long Night*-good, would they give you more time? Now Jackie, they didn't shit all over the idea. They said they would consider it. And seriously, that is the best shot you're going to get here. If they like what you show them, there is a chance we can pull this thing out of the fire. So you've got to parcel together what you got, give it a spit shine and send it to me pronto. Can you do that for me?"

Jack paused as he contemplated telling yet another lie. He decided to tell it. "All right. I'll do it."

"Good. We're all about buying time now. And Jackie, you're a good writer. When they see your work they will like it. There is a reason they signed you, after all."

"All right, Ted. I'll send you what I have."

"Make sure you do, Jackie." Ted slid into a voice better suited to his personality—a threatening one. "It could be the only way to keep this shit storm out of a courtroom."

Jack didn't find the caretaker at his usual post in the office. He went behind the counter. At the door to Kubby's quarters, he softly rapped. "Anybody home?"

The door creaked open under the weight of his knuckles, enough so Jack could see the empty room. Two more doors stood closed at the back of the front desk. Behind the first, Jack found a nineteen eighties era washer and dryer. Alongside them were tall storage racks containing cases of toilet paper, paper towels and a variety of cleaning supplies and implements.

Jack opened the other door. It led to a set of metal stairs that descended to a narrow corridor. A steady drone came from below, so faint that Jack didn't so much hear it as he could feel it in his bones. He paused, weighing his options. In all likelihood, Kubby could be found in the mess hall preparing the midday meal. If he wasn't there, he soon would be. There was no need for Jack to search every nook and cranny for the caretaker. Besides that, this stairwell was probably off limits to guests. He could almost hear Kubby explaining that the ownership didn't want him down there or that the staircase wasn't insured or some foolish thing. Even so, he started down the stairs. After the conversation Jack had with Ted, there was precious little left to worry him.

The sound of his footfalls on the stairs bounced off the stark walls. At the bottom, Jack proceeded down the corridor. The dank smell of mildew became overpowering. The very air felt wet against his skin. Jack realised then that the corridor didn't run under the office cabin, rather it led away from the building, toward the lake. Its walls, floor and ceiling were composed entirely of poured concrete. Two long fluorescent fixtures mounted on the ceiling lit the passage that ended after some thirty feet at a wide metal door. As Jack neared the door, the drone intensified, resonating in his chest.

Jack palmed the doorknob. Warm to the touch, it vibrated subtly as though alive with some inner energy. He pulled the door open.

Inside, Kubby looked up from a clipboard. His doughty expression of surprise soon faded to his customary grin. "Hey, man. Good to see ya!" He had to yell in order to compete with the drone, now formidable with the door open.

The mechanical hum issued from a generator as big as a sedan, situated to the right side of the large concrete room. Kubby had evidently been taking readings from the unit's many gauges. He joined Jack in the doorway.

"Sorry to interrupt," Jack said. As he got a better view of the room, and added, "Wow, this is impressive." He eyed a large black cable running from the generator to a tall electrical panel on the far wall. Two dozen smaller cables webbed from the top of the panel. They wound together across the ceiling and continued out the side wall. A boxy, wall-mounted fan unit exhausted fumes. All of the gear sported clean, bright paintjobs. The generator was yellow, the fuel tanks supplying it, orange, electrical panel, grey, fire extinguisher and hose reel, red. It was neat and orderly and organized and not at all like the man who maintained it.

The place reminded Jack of a spy novel he'd read as a kid. It featured a rustic campground that a terrorist organization used as cover for an underground, state of the art weapons manufacturing facility. This bunker seemed a little less perilous.

Kubby said, "Yeah, this is the mechanical room. It's what makes Wabasso tick. Pretty cool, eh?"

"I'll say. What does that do?" Jack pointed to a series of blue, refrigerator sized tanks lining the left side of the room. A thick pipe entered from the far wall and appeared to feed them.

"That's the water system," Kubby said. "Water goes through each of these holding tanks and gets filtered. That's the pump over there and that compressor keeps this last tank filled with air to pressurize the water so it runs nicely for our taps."

"Where does the water come from?"

"The lake."

"We're drinking from Wabasso Lake?"

Kubby beamed as he nodded. "I know. Cool, right?"

Jack felt a high five moment in the making. He tried to head it off. "Well, I'm sorry for chasing you down like this, but I really wanted to ask you something."

"Ask away, my friend."

"Do you have any more of that weed?"

Jack leaned back in Kubby's orange leather chair and eyed the fog of bluish smoke that obscured the ceiling. "Holy shit, am I ever high."

Kubby changed the disc in his stereo and reclined on his cot. Soon the Allman Brother's *Midnight Rider* began to play.

Kubby held up the noticeably depleted Ziploc bag and considered it.

"I'll give you some money," Jack said, watching Kubby take inventory.

The caretaker scoffed at the notion. "You're my guest, man. What's mine is yours."

"But, I feel bad, smoking all your stuff."

Kubby scratched his head. "You *should* feel mellow by now. Maybe we should light another."

Jack started to laugh, but the humor of the moment quickly died off and he went back to staring at the smoky ceiling.

"You seem a little bummed," Kubby said after a brief silence. "I might have something more upbeat. You like the Rolling Stones?"

"My wife left me." Jack surprised himself when he said it. He could think of many reasons to be *bummed*, but he didn't think that his divorce would be on the tip of his tongue. He just opened his mouth and there it was. He raised his head to gauge Kubby's response.

"What?" The caretaker said, wincing as though the news pained him. "That was stupid. You're a really nice guy."

"Oh, thanks." Jack softly chuckled while questioning the wisdom of Kubby's insights. "Anyway, she didn't really see it that way. She said I changed. I'm not the guy she married anymore."

Kubby squinted. "That's ridiculous. Who else could you be?"

Jack sucked in a steadying breath. "After I sold my first book, I quit my day job, you know, so I could concentrate on writing full time. She didn't like that so much. So, she just packed up and left and took the kids with her."

"Man, that's harsh."

"Yeah, she just took 'em away and told me I had to give her money to take care of them. They need all this stuff for school and soccer and astronomy club and I gotta fork all this dough over."

Kubby shook his head. "Astronomy?"

"All because she said I *changed*."

"You became a writer. Is that it?"

Jack sat up in his chair. "Well, I guess that depends on who you ask. Don't ask my publisher. They'll probably tell you I'm not."

"You are, though. This is a *writer's* retreat," Kubby said, turning up his palms. "That's why you're here."

"Ah, I don't know anymore. I don't even know if I want that." Jack sat with elbows on knees and laced his fingers together. "Five years, Kubby."

"Five?"

"Five years. That's how long it took me to write my first book. Five fucking years. Now I'm supposed to bang one out every year?" Jack shrugged. "Why did they think I could do that?"

"Who?"

"The publisher...their contract." Jack rubbed his hands over his face and groaned. "You see, I'm obligated to give them a book every year...never mind. It doesn't matter."

"What about the one you're finishing now?"

"It won't be done in time. I...I only have one page done."

"One page? That's not really all that much." Kubby scrunched up his face as though he was delivering bad news.

"Oh, did I say *page*? I meant paragraph." Jack went quiet. He read the sympathy in the caretaker's face and erupted in laughter, sinking back in the chair.

Kubby laughed, too, although he seemed unsure what was so funny.

"I'm screwed," Jack said after the moment passed. "Hey, why don't we light another joint?"

Kubby got up from his bed. "I think I have something a little more suitable for just such an occasion," he said, as he knelt down and reached under his cot. "You probably can't tell by looking at me, but I enjoy a cocktail every now and again." Kubby produced a tall bottle of *Canadian Club* whiskey. "I hope you don't think any less of me."

"I couldn't possibly."

Jack didn't mean to hurl an insult at his host. Luckily, Kubby didn't notice. He reinstalled himself on the cot and opened the bottle. He took a healthy swig that made his face prune up and handed the bottle to Jack. "Don't get down on yourself, man. It is not an easy thing, to write. If it was, everyone would do it 'cause it's like, the best job ever. You get to make books and read books and talk about books and people ask you stuff about books. What in the world could be better than that?"

"You make a good point, but I just feel like I'm in over my head." Jack took a swig that tasted to him like a blend of cough syrup and battery acid. He stuck out his tongue and expected to breathe fire.

Kubby took the bottle back and cleared his throat. "We are all apprentices in a craft where no one becomes a master."

"Who said that?"

"Hemmingway." He drank and sent the whiskey back Jack's way.

"Far be it for me to argue with him," Jack said before hoisting the bottle. More pleasant than the first, this mouthful raced down his throat and stoked a furnace in his belly. Satisfying heat spread throughout his body.

Kubby eyed the works on his bookshelf and in a sentimental tone, said, "We all go through slumps in this game, man. I should know. I found out the hard way, myself."

Jack balked. "You did?"

"Oh yeah, that's why I'm at Wabasso."

"You're losing me." Jack tipped the bottle again.

Kubby turned his hands up. "I thought you knew. I came here to work on a novel, same as you."

Jack thought he might spray whiskey across the room and had to battle to get it down. "Really? What happened?"

"Oh, I never finished. And, I never left."

"You're kidding me. How long ago was that?"

"Let's see." The caretaker made an absurd frown as he tried to fathom the year. "It was right after college, I don't know, twenty years ago."

"Holy shit. You don't look that old."

Kubby smiled sheepishly. "Oh, thanks, man. That's nice. You look good for your age, too."

Jack didn't think Kubby actually knew his age, but he was preoccupied with the dozens of questions flashing through his head. "So you just stayed…like, moved into the office cabin?"

"Yeah, I really liked the place and this job opened up. The ownership just let me stay on. And that was really cool because I got to stay and be a part of the writing experience. Even if I can't do it myself, it's still cool to be around those who can." Kubby accepted the bottle from Jack. He inspected the label. "In some small way I feel like I'm part of the process. Plus, I get to read all the time. And, sometimes, if I catch one of the writers in the right mood, they'll talk to me about their work. Also very cool."

"What happened to your manuscript?"

Kubby swallowed hard. "Oh, I still have it. I'm thinking about busting it out one of these days to work on it some more. I do that every couple of years. It's like, as I get older or grow up, or whatever, I'm able to add more to it. I figure by the time I'm sixty, it should be pretty well done."

They traded the whiskey bottle back and forth. A slur entered Kubby's voice as he talked at length about his never ending project. "This one time, I was reading through it and I realised, hey, nobody uses a *Walkman* anymore. I changed it to *Discman* to keep with the times, right? Next thing I know, fast forward a few years, and I have to change *Discman* to MP3 player. Now it's like *iPod* or *iPhone* or some shit like that. Someday it will be an implant behind the ear that people get their tunes from and I'll have to change it again." Kubby shook his head solemnly. "I sure hope I finish the story before that happens."

Jack had stopped listening. He considered his own manuscript. The air in the cabin began to taste sour, the walls too close. He stood. "Kubby, I gotta get going," he said, teetering on numb legs.

"We haven't changed your bandages yet."

Jack waved the idea off. "They'll be okay until morning. I really have to hit the road."

"Okay, well, thanks for dropping in." With some marked effort, Kubby got up from the cot. "We have to do this again, man."

"Yeah, thanks Kubby." Jack turned toward the door. The floor seemed to pitch and yaw under him. He had to grab the doorjamb for support.

"Hey, wait," Kubby said. "Parting gifts." He handed Jack the remaining half bottle of whiskey. "You might need this more than I do."

Chapter Six

Jack trudged through the sand that skirted Wabasso, stumbling a step or two to the side for every step he took forward. The contents of the bottle sloshed in his grip as he tripped along. The lake was still—a sheet of purple glass under a violet sky. For the second time in as many days, he managed to wait out sunset in Kubby's room.

The sky darkened to the east and more stars steadily emerged. In minutes, the retreat would be in darkness. Jack drank from the bottle and marveled at how quickly he became accustomed to the taste of whiskey. Either that, or it torched his palette, leaving it barren.

He slowly made his way up the beach, passing the overturned canoes and the stone ring of the fire pit. From there he could see the mess hall. Its windows were dark. The dinner hour had passed him by once more. The thought prompted a snarling grumble from Jack's empty pit of a stomach. "Oh yeah…it's chow time."

Jack staggered into the mess and lit the place. He let himself into Kubby's kitchen and went through the fridge. "Come to papa," he said when he found the glass container of leftover roast beef. He pulled it out along with a container of mashed potatoes and set them on the counter. In no time he arranged a heaping plate. He also arranged quite a mess of spilled food on the counter and floor. After successfully negotiating the controls of the microwave, he waited for his meal to heat. Cooking, he decided, was thirsty work. He hoisted the bottle for a slosh of whiskey. He ate at the counter, spilling more food about the place. By the end of his feast he had abandoned the use of utensils and he leaned against the counter, bottle in one hand, shank of beef in the other. Eating, he decided, was also thirsty work.

After his meal, Jack resumed his tipsy tour of the retreat, stopping briefly at the shower house to answer nature's call. He found the pathway leading to the guest cabins with a degree of difficulty that wasn't present in prior journeys. The walk somehow seemed longer tonight. Jack paused for another belt off the bottle. The path branched to the right, and through the trees and shrubbery he could see the cabin it led to. It was number two—Kate's cabin. The windows were lit, their curtains drawn.

Jack stood there several long moments. Since his phone conversation with Ted, all he wanted to do was get very high and then crawl under a rock and let the world pass him by. Now a part of him wanted absolution. Kate had told him that he was supposed to be at Wabasso. He wanted to know why she thought that. He wanted to know if she would still think that way if he told her about the writer's block that completely disabled him every time he so much as looked at his laptop. He drank while his inner debate continued.

A cool breeze tickled the hairs on the back of his neck. He decided to return to his cabin and he drank to that, too. *After all, Wabasso has rules about interrupting writers at work,* he thought. *She's probably working on some story where a lovelorn farm girl throws herself into the arms of the withdrawn yet gentle stable boy. I can't be responsible for stemming that kind of creative flow.*

Jack reached Cabin Six and climbed the steps, relying heavily on the rudimentary handrail. He went inside and dumped himself into the cot. Lying back, he faced the ceiling. His head felt thick, like marshmallows packed his sinuses. Back in his irresponsible youth, before marriage and children, he had on occasion, gotten himself considerably high. A time or two he had also gotten himself really drunk. Though never had he been both high and drunk at the same time. He didn't care much for it. At Kubby's, he felt like his head was lighter than air. Now the whiskey weighted it down significantly. He felt sluggish, useless.

"Better get used to it," Jack said out loud. "You got no job. You got no family. You got no reason to stay sober." Jack tipped the bottle again and realised it was empty. He groaned and let it drop on the floor.

The empty bottle slowly rolled to the corner of the cabin where Jack had left Kubby's moccasins. He loosed an exaggerated sigh and shook his head. He thought of the caretaker's incredible story. Kubby had come to Wabasso to write...and never left. *How the hell does that happen to a person?* Jack wondered. *How do you go from being a promising young writer to making sandwiches for guests and picking up after them? And he must have been talented, too. He couldn't have gotten into Wabasso, otherwise. Just how did he end up where he is today?*

A sobering thought occurred to Jack. He could see himself having to remain at Wabasso indefinitely—especially if he lost his contract. He'd have to sell his house. He already could barely afford his lofty alimony payments. In truth, he was only a step or two away from becoming another Walter Kubanowski. His stomach turned as those steps became clear in his mind.

Jack eyed the moccasins in the corner and the sight of them soured his stomach all the more. Those filthy shoes that filthy hippie couldn't be bothered to put on his filthy feet seemed to mock him. He got up with a mind to toss them out of the cabin.

The room spun when he stood and he had to lean on the table to steady himself. It took greater effort than expected to bend over, pick up the shoes and toss them into the closet. With the grungy things out of sight, Jack drew a few deep breaths to calm the tempest in his belly.

He was dumbstruck by how drastically his goals had

changed in such a short time. Once, he had anticipated the next contract he would sign—the one that would see him paid handsomely. That goal shifted to completing the contract he was under, to completing just one of the books he owed, then to completing at least a page of it. Now his goal was to avoid becoming the next homeless man to hideout at Wabasso Lake for the remainder of his days.

I don't even know if the ownership would let me stay, he thought grimly. *I may end up worse off than Kubby.* Jack shook that ugly thought out of his head. He didn't want to travel down that road. He was going to take the opposite road, one that would lead out of this dire situation.

And, that road begins right here, he thought, turning to the table and the laptop closed atop it. He stood over it and attempted to focus his impaired thoughts. *I can do this. All I have to do is forge ahead. Put something down. Don't stop no matter what. What were those tips again? Oh yeah, implement a schedule, and ah…set deadlines. I can do this.* Jack touched the latch of the computer and gathered in air like he was preparing to dive underwater. *Another tip…oh, right, think of writing as a job and not an art form, and…and try to examine the issues behind the block.*

He stopped. The air leaked out of him. He picked up the laptop and held it at arm's length.

Issues behind the block…

The words echoed through his mind. He saw the faces of his boys in the rear window of the silver minivan as they were taken away.

She didn't even look back.

Jack's tightened his grip on the laptop until his knuckles turned white and his arms shook. Closing his eyes, he lifted it overhead and, with all the strength he could muster, he threw it to the floor.

The sounds of wreckage filled the cabin: plastic cracking, wood snapping, components scattering.

A minute passed while Jack stood there, eyes shut, breathing deeply in an effort to douse his temper. During that time, he wished he would open his eyes to find the laptop still on the table, waiting eagerly to get to work. He wished he would find that he hadn't let his emotions run wild. Instead, when he raised the courage to look, he found the ruin between his feet. He rubbed his face to battle the coming tears and studied the laptop jutted from a split in the floor boards. He nudged the computer with his toe. It hardly moved. It was wedged into the boards as tight as an ax blade slammed into a tree trunk.

Jack dropped down to the cot and lay back again. He started to calculate how much worse he had made things. It proved immeasurable. Darkness crept in from the corners of his vision and it carried him into a deep sleep, but before it did, he saw a black fog rising from the floor. He recognized the entity, now freed from the laptop like a genie from its lamp. They were intimately familiar. It loomed over him as he drift-ed off.

From the personal journal of William Jessop:

12 June, 2012.

I spent most of the last week working on my Tanner Black series for the *Mill Street Literary Review*. Having contacted Black's agent for insight into Black's surprise retirement and coming up empty handed, I shifted my focus to his publisher. *Lightning Storm Press* is one of those hulking, faceless entities that seldom share discourse with lowly book reviewer-types like me, but when I made mention that I was an officer in Tanner Black's fan club (minor embellishment), I was told to expect a phone call from a senior editor regarding the matter. A Mr. Hustwick telephoned a few days later and stated that he would be happy to dish what he knew. "Anything for TTBF," he said.

"Right," I answered. I could not hide the apprehension in my tone.

"The Tanner Black Following…" he said, helping me along. "Perhaps you fellows don't use the acronym anymore."

"Er, no, we just call it *the following*," I said, without missing a beat (major embellishment).

We got down to business. Hustwick explained that he was a youthful twenty years of age when Black came onto the scene. He worked as a proofreader on Black's second novel and had risen to copy editor by Black's fourth. "Tanner was a permanent fixture at the publishing house to me," Hustwick recalled. "I came to see him as a sort of school chum, especially in those early days. Every year he came back a little older, a little wiser, and so did I, I suppose. We were contemporaries in the same business. We learned our craft together. Other writers came and went, but I could always count on Tanner's return every year.

"In fact, I was rather shocked when I received word of his retirement. The possibility had never entered my mind. He's far too young, I reasoned. Then it struck me. He's not at all young anymore, and neither am I. His notice left me feeling

96

the full weight of my years, let me tell you."

I asked what the notice exactly contained and waited while Hustwick seemed to debate how much he should share with a devotee he hadn't previously met. I listened to his breath, as I held mine.

"Without getting into specifics, Tanner indicated that he had a family matter to attend to. We at Lightning Storm Press respected his decision and left the door wide open to his return should he resume his career. Of course, it is all rather moot now that he has passed."

I agreed somberly, though I could think of nothing but this family matter and how it was responsible for derailing Black's career. I didn't press Hustwick for more information. He was already steering the conversation toward how Lightning Storm would honor Black's legacy. He said he was proud to inform Tanner's fan club that the publisher intends to re-release his entire series in the coming year and that an anthology is in the works that will include stories by popular writers of today intended to tie-up the series' loose threads.

I instantly understood why Hustwick had been so willing to reach out to me. The realization left me speechless, although I should not have been surprised that a hulking, faceless corporation was so eager to cash in on the dead. That the dead in this case was my favorite writer, however, hurt a little.

Hustwick proved helpful whether he knew it or not. He pointed me toward Black's remaining relatives; a list that turned out to be rather short. Mrs. Black passed away some ten years ago. She and Tanner did not have children. He did however have one niece. Kathy (I'll omit her surname to honor her request) is the daughter of Black's sister, Deborah (predeceased), and after some digging, I found Kathy living on the west coast. I contacted her via email.

She maintained that her relationship with Black, despite inheriting the bulk of his substantial estate, was not familiar. She said that he sent greeting cards on the major holidays and wrote the odd letter, but she could in no way delve into his character or surmise reasons he may have quit the business that was so good to him. She did, however, tell me that one of his letters had indicated that he'd grown accustomed to finishing his novels at a private writer's retreat and that he planned to return there to complete his latest project. It was to be a companion piece to his series in which the origin of his unstoppable, knife wielding killer was to be the focus.

This project, sadly, never made it to print. (As a fan, I'm dying right now.) It occurred to me that perhaps something at this writer's retreat caused Black's work to suffer. I decided to focus my efforts there. When I asked if she recalled any details about this retreat Black may have shared, Kathy could only tell me its name.

Wabasso Lake.

Chapter Seven

Sunlight poured through the window and spilled across Jack's face. He twitched a couple of times before covering his eyes with his bandaged hand. As wakefulness slowly took hold, various bodily pains reported in. He lay in the exact face-up position he had been in when he fell asleep. He stretched his arms and legs and shifted to his side to shield his eyes from the blinding light. The ache between his ears made its presence known. Inside his head a vice squeezed ever tighter. He licked the paste in his mouth and was reminded of the empty whiskey bottle rolling across the cabin floor the night before. He cringed. It was going to be a long day. Then he recalled what he did to his laptop, and despite his headache, he sprung upward in the bed. "No, no, *no*," he said aloud.

The top of the writing table was empty.

It was true. He didn't dream that he had destroyed the computer, he had actually done it.

He dropped his feet over the side of the cot and looked down at the wreckage. The computer stood on edge, half poking out of the floor.

The vise tightened.

Reaching down for the laptop intensified his headache. He had to wiggle the thing back and forth like a loose tooth to work it free of the floor. He sat upright and waited for the pain in his head to subside to a dull thud before inspecting the laptop. The casing was scratched up, but it didn't rattle when he turned it over. He entertained the idea that it may yet work—that is until he opened the lid and saw the cracks webbing through the screen. A few of the keys fell away as well. He closed the lid again and dropped it on the cot beside him.

He rubbed the sides of his head in an effort to soothe the ache. It did little good. He wondered if Kubby had *Advil* or *Tylenol* in that first aid kit of his. Even if he did, Jack reasoned, he would more than likely push his own brand of painkiller on him—the one he kept in the *Ziploc* baggie. That was the last thing he needed. What he needed now was some water to rinse his mouth, and of course, to fix the floor before somebody saw it.

He got down on one knee to inspect the splintered edges of the floorboards. They were hopelessly damaged and, short of calling in a carpenter, would remain so. He ran his finger down the edge of a broken board and eyed the darkened cavity beneath it. What he saw there seized his full attention and pushed any plans for repairs to the back of his mind.

An object lay inside the cavity. The thing, whatever it was, was about the size of a shoebox, whitish in colour. Jack scratched his stubbly chin and considered the possible peril in sticking his hand down in the hole to retrieve it. There could have been some critter or other burrowed in down there, something with many sharp, little teeth. He didn't especially like the idea of going to Kubby with another wound for him to dress.

Jack stooped lower and craned his head for a closer look. He still couldn't tell what the thing was and attempted to slide his hand in the hole to touch it. His bandages snagged on either side of the busted floorboards. He sat up on his haunches, debated for a moment, and then grabbed hold of one of the boards and pulled. It came up easier than expected. The next board came loose much the same way and in a few seconds he gazed down at the object positioned neatly between two floor joists.

It was a box wrapped in plain paper and tied with a length of black string. The paper had been white, but yellowed over time. Exactly how much time had passed, Jack couldn't fathom. He rested his hands on his knees and studied it for a moment. Had his boys been there, they would have screamed, "*Treasure!*" and plunged their hands into the floor to snatch it up. Jack felt considerably less excited. Curiosity was his sole motivation, but not only of what was inside the box, but for who had taken the trouble to put it there. The floorboards had been nailed down, after all. This wasn't the sort of hidey-hole in which people stowed their savings in the old days before banks and investments became the norm. This was a one-time installation—put the box in the floor, nail it shut and forget about it.

But why?

Jack covered his mouth and continued to stare at the thing.

It doesn't make any sense. This is a guest cabin, not a private residence. Whoever put this thing here obviously couldn't be sure they would ever be able to access it again. Maybe they didn't care if they ever saw it again. Or maybe…they wanted to make sure they never did.

That idea had Jack considering leaving the thing where it lay and nailing the floorboards over it once more.

My life is complicated enough, thanks. I can't be opening strange packages, hidden away by strange people. Of course, it could be money. God knows, I could use some of that right now.

That was reason enough. He reached down, hooked a finger under the string and picked it up and was immediately disappointed. The likely box bowed in the centre and its ends sagged as he lifted it out of the hole. As soon as he brought it up, the daylight revealed that it wasn't a box, but a stack of pages. There would be no money—no alimony for the ex, no astronomy club fees for Brian and Thomas.

Jack placed the stack on the writing table and sat down in the chair. The top page was blank and covered in a fine film of dust. He thumbed the bottom corner of the pages and saw double spaced lines of text flip by on each one. The text was in an old font that reminded Jack of the electric typewriter he learned to type on as a child.

"Holy shit," he said aloud when he realised what he'd found.

A bunch of typewritten pages hidden away at a writer's retreat...

"This is a manuscript."

Jack pulled his chair up closer to the table, his excitement building. He wondered if it was very old. Perhaps it was a first draft of some previously published work. Knowing the exclusivity of Wabasso Lake, it may have been the work of some renowned writer.

Maybe it is money, after all.

Jack worked the string off the baled pages. He took off the top page and set it to the left of the stack. Two words graced the next page. Jack read them aloud.

"Together, Dead."

There was no name, no date, word count, nothing other than...

"Together, Dead?"

Jack turned the page over, saw that the back was completely blank. On the top of the next page, in the stack, writing began without so much as the announcement of chapter one. There was no header or footer, no name anywhere, just the lone number one in the bottom right hand corner of the page. Jack set the title page face down to the left. He laid page one on top of it. Page two was the same—jammed with double spaced lines. Jack ran his thumb down the pile of paper to what he guessed was the half-way point of the manuscript and peeled it up. Page 157 faced him. It didn't offer a name, either. Nor did page 189, as he discovered when he flipped ahead. Page 203 was much the same.

Jack restored the pile so page one lay on top and he sat back in his chair to consider this new mystery.

It was so odd that the writer's name was nowhere to be found. Jack never wrote a single page that didn't bear the standard Jack Bishop header. He put his name on everything. Even the single paragraph of his latest sputtering effort was graced with his moniker. Whoever wrote this clearly didn't think the same way. Perhaps they didn't fear misplacing their material, or theft of it, the way most writers did. Even if that were the case, Jack figured a writer's sense of ego would prompt them to claim each and every page as their own. In fact, he believed most authors were born with an above average measure of ego. They needed it if they expected the public to read what amounted to be hundreds of thousands of words worth of their thoughts.

With that in mind, Jack debated on reading some of the manuscript. If this were his work that had been squirreled away from prying eyes, how would he feel about some curious stranger reading it? On the other hand, reading it may be the only hope for discovering its true owner. If he read some, and could explain its contents in detail, it might help to discover the identity of its author. Jack could admit, at least to himself, that he wasn't very well read outside of his genre, but Kubby would probably have a pretty good idea who wrote it.

Jack pulled up to the desk and scanned the first page. He could tell early on that it was a work of fiction. It opened with a man waking up at home. Jack thumbed ahead a several pages and read a few more lines. There, he got the impression that the character was perusing the contents of a derelict barn. Further ahead again, the narrative caught Jack's eye and he began to read more closely.

He ran the whetstone over the blade methodically, the way his father had shown him many years ago.

They had been preparing the rabbits they snared that day so his mother could make a stew. Jonathan had worked the knife through the rabbit flesh while his father watched on closely, advising along the way. He complimented his boy for his skilled work with the blade. Jonathan smiled.

His father did not. Instead, he said, "I don't suppose cutting up rabbits is always going to satisfy you, is it?" Jonathan did not understand. "You just make sure you tell me before you go after something…bigger." He held Jonathan with his stare. "Son, you make sure you tell me."

Jonathan had agreed, though to what, he was not exactly sure. He had been too occupied by the blade slicing through the musculature of the creature. He loved the sound it made when it cut through the cartilage in the joints. If he was quiet enough, he could hear the wet slurp of the meat when the blade severed it. He loved that sound above all. The sooner he had agreed with his father, the sooner he would pipe-down and let the knife do the talking.

The whetstone made a dry, pitiful scraping noise as it honed the blade. Jonathan grimaced as he continued to sharpen and wished he could lubricate the process with some warm blood. The blade wanted it. He knew the blade wanted it.

"What is this?" Jack said, sitting back. He rested his chin in his hand and stared off in the distance. Is this a horror story? He recalled the bookcase in the front of the office. It was home to many literary works completed at the retreat. None of them, however, was a horror novel.

I shouldn't get ahead of myself. I don't even know what this is, yet, Jack thought as he skipped further through the pages again. Though, the next section he read left little room for doubt.

...thrust the pry bar into the whirring spokes of the wheel and the bicycle locked up solid. The paperboy flew over the handlebars and onto the hard packed earth. He let out a screech as he skidded to a stop. He saw the blood spreading in his upturned palms and looked up at Jonathan. His face, a medley of pain and disbelief. "Why? Why did you do that?" he cried.

Jonathan did not answer. He did not even blink, as he closed in on the boy. In a few strides, he would be on him. He took the knife from his back pocket and held it up.

The boy's eyes went lidless and he screamed, polluting the air around them with the stink of fear. In desperation, the boy kicked at the ground, trying to run before he is even on his feet. He fell. He fought to scurry away like a beast on all fours and got nowhere. Finally, he saw that the newspaper sack, still slung over his shoulder, was hooked around the bicycle's handlebars. He reached the strap to untangle it just as Jonathan stood over him.

Jonathan's knife came arcing downward. The boy screamed again only this time it came out just a whisper. The blade severed his vocal cords.

Jonathan knelt down to watch the blood gurgle from the torn throat. He peered into the boy's eyes. They were dilated to their limits. His skin blanched. His expression perpetually begged a question.

Why? Slowly, the blood ceased to pump from the wound and turned to seep. Jonathan watched intently as the life drained from the boy. Still neither of them had blinked.

Jack set the page down and got up slowly from the table. His headache worsened and now his stomach threatened a bout of the dry heaves. The flutter in his stomach, Jack knew, was less likely a hangover symptom and more the sort brought on by excitement. He went to the door, opened it and looked outside. For what, he wasn't sure. Perhaps a bit of air would soothe his stomach. Maybe he wanted to make sure he wouldn't be interrupted if he dared indulge his curiosity and read more of the manuscript.

Still…

Reading another's work uninvited was akin to breaking into their home and rifling through their underwear drawer. It just wasn't done. In fact, if Jack suffered such an intrusion, he would be beside himself with rage.

Still…

Twerp twerp!

He wasn't alone, after all. The cardinal watched him from its preferred perch.

"Well, what would you do, smart ass?"

Tiny black eyes remained fixed on him.

"Would you respect the author's privacy? I don't see how. You don't respect mine."

He looked inside to the pages atop the table. His gaze lit upon the broken laptop on the cot, then drifted back to the manuscript. The cardinal screeched. Jack ducked reflexively as the bird leapt off its branch. It cut across the front of the cabin and over the trees.

The absurdity of his reaction left Jack feeling a bit foolish. He tracked the bird's vector as it curved toward the water. Then Wabasso stole his focus. It winked at him from behind the weave of tree limbs. *Whoever wrote that story stood right here,* he thought. *He stood here and admired the lake just like I am now. He smelled the water and the wildflowers. He probably stashed his story for a good reason. I should respect that.*

Still, if I did happen to read a little, no one would be the wiser.

Jack eyed the manuscript, waiting on the table. He looked outside again, this time for prying *human* eyes and then closed the door.

Together, Dead

I

Jonathan Dunn woke to ear-ringing silence. He had the dream again; the one where he got up from bed to find his mother cooking breakfast and his father reading the <u>Weekend Extra</u> and listening to the farm report on <u>KBX93</u>. He had hurried downstairs to find them in the kitchen, their lives going on like nothing bad had ever happened. The accident that claimed them, their funeral; surely those awful events were the dream.

Sitting up in bed, reality washed over Jonathan in a cold tide. They were gone. One moment, in the tomblike quiet of the old farmhouse, assured him that he was alone.

Jonathan swung his bare feet over the side of the bed and sat upright. A shiver ran through him despite all the sunlight filtering through his window. The walls were grey, the floors were grey. All the colour inside the house had been stolen away like the life it once held.

He dressed in his red and black plaid shirt and pulled up the suspenders of his grimy work pants. He found his muddy boots beside his door and another pang of sorrow surprised him. His mother never would have let him wear those boots past the mudroom, let alone up to bed. If she were alive to see the tracks he had likely made through the kitchen and up the stairs, he would be in for it. He would have been woken by her hollering. He would give anything to be woken by her hollering again.

Jonathan ambled downstairs and into the kitchen, boots in hand. The folded cardboard boxes his sister got at the market leaned against the wall.

<u>Is she coming by today?</u> he pondered.

He never did keep track of the passing days very well. On the farm, it never seemed to matter. One day was the same as the next, especially since they stopped planting the fields a few years back, in '89. Without a harvest, what was the sense in keeping time, anyway?

He stood at the kitchen sink and ran a glass of cloudy water from the old tap. While he sipped it, he looked out the window at the barn. The door was open again. Had he forgotten to close it? Maybe. He was pretty sure he remembered to close the house door and lock it the way Jill had shown him. "That's the important one," she had said last time she was here.

"Mom and Dad always locked the doors at night." Jill had said while she put food in the fridge. "You can remember to do that, right Jon? Jonathan? I'm talking to you. Pay attention."

"What?"

"The doors… I…" She breathed heavily. "Jon, you just have to be able to do this on your own for a little while."

"Lock the doors?"

"Yes, yes, lock the doors. And keep the windows closed. And turn off the taps when you're not using them."

"For a while?"

"Yes, just for a few days. I have some things to do at home, but I'll be back soon." She seemed angry, the way Dad used to get. "And, Jon, promise me you won't use the stove."

"Promise."

"There's bread and all kinds of potato salad and there's fruit in the pantry. Just, please, don't try to cook any-thing."

Jill's words echoed in his ears as he took the briefest gander at the stove. It was that open barn door that snared his curiosity this morning. He took a handful of oatmeal cookies from the tin in the pantry and went to the mudroom. The back door was open, also. Jonathan disregarded that detail and walked through it, eating his breakfast as he crossed the yard to the barn.

In other news, the search for eleven-year -old Jessie Carlson is still on. The boy was last seen setting out on his bicycle to deliver newspapers along Route 124. Police are asking individuals with any information to come forward—

Jill squelched the radio. She steered the car around a curve on the country road while cradling the phone between her chin and shoulder. "No, I don't know how long it will take me," she said, annoyance gathering in her voice like storm clouds. "I only know it would go faster if I had some help."

Jill Moore, formerly Jill Dunn, reached into her purse on the passenger seat and retrieved a pack of cigarettes.

"Sorry, I'm not going with you," replied a male voice. "But, someone has to watch the boys this weekend, remember?"

"I know. I know. I just dread the idea of trying to pack up the whole farm in a couple of days."

In the rearview mirror, she regarded the folded moving boxes piled in the back seat. She caught a glimpse of herself, as well. Her reflection proved rather disquieting. Her fair complexion paled to near-grey. The familiar roses in her cheeks had withered and died. She brushed a shock of red hair from her eyes and semi-consciously brushed again as though she could wipe away the spray of freckles on her brow, as well. A nervous tick she had not experienced much since childhood.

"What about your brother? Isn't he going to help?"

"Very funny, Luke," said Jill, pulling a cigarette free of the others with her teeth. "You are well aware of his disability."

"Actually, no, I'm not, and you're not, either. No one is."

"Luke, now is not the time."

"When will be the time? We can never talk about this."

Jill sighed. Of course he wanted to talk about this now. He was safely on the other end of a phone line, not within slapping distance. "Look, I know how you feel about Jonathan. That's why I didn't even ask you if I could bring him home to stay with us."

"I thought, for once, you were thinking about the safety of your sons," said Luke in a tart voice.

"He's <u>not</u> dangerous."

"You don't know that. He has never been checked out by a professional. Your parents kept him hidden away on that farm his whole life."

Jill plucked the cigarette from her mouth. "They were from a different generation. That's what people did with family who were—"

"Crazy?"

"Luke, I swear." In the rearview mirror, Jill searched her face for resemblance to her parents, to Jonathan. Thankfully, she saw precious little .

"Well, that's what he is, and I don't like the idea of my wife spending the weekend alone up there with him."

"Come on, Luke. You know I can handle him. He listens to me the same way he listened to Mom and Dad."

"He used to, anyway. Jill, their… passing, it changed him. It was written all over his face at the funeral."

Jill recalled her brother, sitting in the front pew, one of their father's suits ballooned on his slender form. "He was <u>sad</u> at the funeral. He just can't show it like everyone else."

"I know sad when I see it, and that wasn't it."

"All right, I'm prepared to be wowed.

What was it?"

Luke paused to gather his wind. "To me, it looked like something serious broke inside him. Like his last support beam snapped and he was about to come crashing down any minute."

Jill pinched the cigarette between her lips. She did not agree with her husband's assessment, but something in his message resonated. She would have been lying if she said she was not concerned their parent's death had taken a serious toll Jonathan, and the idea of heaping more bad news on him had her worried he would not be able to bear it. Telling him they were selling the only home he had ever known may prove too much. The thought of it scared her, but she did not let on. "Okay, Sigmund Freud. Thanks for the analysis."

"Yeah, that's what I get. I have serious concerns for your safety, and that's what I get."

"Don't be a baby. I understand…mostly. Jon <u>does</u> need help. That's why I arranged for the special care home in the city. In a few days, Jon will be living there. The movers will come and empty the farmhouse and we can put it up for sale. Once it's sold, we can close the book on this ugly chapter and get on with our lives." She marveled at how easy she could make it all sound.

"It can't happen soon enough for me."

"Luke, I appreciate your concern. I really do, but you don't have anything to worry about. Take the kids to a movie, get some pizza. Do some guy stuff this weekend, and I'll be home before you know it." She dug the <u>Bic</u> from her purse and lit her cigarette.

"Was that a lighter I just heard?" Luke's voice rose an octave. "Are you smoking again?"

"The turn-off is coming up. Gotta go. I'll call tonight. Bye."

"Jill?"

She hung up the phone on the dashboard, took a long haul off her cigarette and vented smoke slowly through her nostrils. Immediate relaxation resulted. More than a guilty pleasure, smoking was her crutch whenever her nerves were rattled, and Luke knew it. Right now, he was probably contemplating how uneasy she really was about this weekend.

Jonathan stepped through the open barn door and was welcomed by a draft of moldy, damp air and the smell of long-gone livestock. The barn's interior somehow remained dark, in sharp contrast to the sunny summer morning outside. It seemed to hold shadow like a miser horded cash.

There was no electricity here. The Dunn's could never afford to get it wired, but that inconvenience did not hinder Jonathan. He knew the inside of the barn like the inside of his bedroom. Eight paces and a right turn got him to the tool bench where he could find an array of screwdrivers, wrenches and files. Another three paces got him to the wall hooks where the yard tools hung. He knew the rusty old sickle waited there, beside it, the posthole diggers, and beside them, the ax.

Jonathan had no interest in any of those. Moreover, he no longer cared that he found the barn door wide open when he woke this morning. The only thing he could think of whenever he entered the old building was what he would find thirty paces toward its centre. That was where his footsteps on the plank floor started to sound hollow; where he would find the hatchway down to his special room, his secret room.

He was heading in that direction when it struck him how bold he had become. Before the death of his parents, he would never have dreamt of visiting his room in the light of day. They would surely have caught him. That would have been trouble. Now they were gone and with that loss came a vast freedom. All he had in the world was his room, and the trophies inside it.

His eyes adjusted to the darkness by the time he counted twenty paces and he could see his destination; a patch of floor cleared of straw and debris. He could see the outline of the hatch, and he could see that it was also open.

A cold draft blew between his bones as the consequences dawned on him. Someone had been in his place, his secret place. Someone had seen his trophies. Maybe someone had touched them, or worse yet, stole them.

He hurried to the hatchway and plunged a leg into the thicker, harsher darkness below. He knew his foot would land on the top rung of the rough ladder he had built years ago. His other foot followed with-

out the slightest hesitation and he proceeded blindly downward. He had done this
countless times, always in the cover of
night when his parents were asleep, always without a guiding light.

From the bottom rung, Jonathan reached
upward and found the pull-string exactly
where he expected it to be. He gave it a
sharp tug and the hatch closed overhead,
sealing him in. For a moment, he relished
the smell of the earthy air and the perfect silence of his special place. He almost forgot the panic that nearly overcame him when he had found the entry
opened to the world. Any worry over the
theft of his prized possessions oozed out
of him as he stood there on the dirt
floor, his back to the ladder. He could
feel that nothing was missing or even out
of place. He was that attuned to the
space.

He reached to his right and grasped the
handle of the twelve volt flashlight he
kept near the foot of the ladder. At
first, he squinted against the glare, and
then slowly he peeked at the circle of
light as it played over the chiseled
earthen walls and the six-by-six beams
that buttressed the room against collapse.

The shelves Jonathan had built from
scraps of his father's fence lumber,
lined either side of the ten foot by four
foot room. They were fully stocked, all
his trophies, present and accounted for.

Jonathan went directly to his favorite
one and snatched it from the shelf. It
was a scrap of a flower print dress. He
held it to his face and breathed in the

116

faded scent. Apple blossom. That was what she smelled like, that lady at the market. That was why he followed her home.

He brushed off the surface of the shelf, folded the rag and carefully returned it to its place. Next to it, he shone the light on a set of car keys, truck keys, actually, and as he fingered one of them, remembered the man he had come upon, broken-down on the roadside. Jonathan had said he would help, and he watched the man tinker away under the hood; that big, heavy hood. He closed his eyes and saw it come crashing down again. His breath fluttered as he exhaled.

Jonathan's light spilled over the shelving illuminating the salesman's pocket watch, the lock of Sally Thompson's golden hair, the drifter's backpack and the shriveled, severed hand that once belonged to one of his father's hiredmen.

He aimed the light at the far overhead beam. It was adorned with the skulls of a few dozen barn cats in varying degrees of decomposition. Controlling the farm's feral cat population may not be very sporting, but it was something to do in the many boring days that lingered between run-ins with bigger prey. His dad had never seemed to mind.

At the centre of the beam hung the skull of his very first victim. Faye. Jonathan never left his special place before paying tribute to his first lady. Losing Faye did upset his dad. The reliable, old dairy cow did not go easily. It amazed Jonathan how many times he had to swing the ax. Faye had kept bawling. She

117

had woken his parents before he finally did her in. When his father came upon Jonathan in the field, covered in blood from head to toe and standing proudly over Faye's hacked up carcass, he exploded in a rage. He laid a licking on the boy, the likes of which neither had ever seen. The next day, Jonathan's father got the tractor and dragged Faye to the compost pile and buried her. That night, Jonathan dug her up and took his trophy.

That was before Jonathan built his trophy room. He had hidden the skull in his bedroom closet and lovingly ogled it every day while its flesh slowly sloughed off and its smell grew worse and worse.

When his father investigated the rotten odor and found the trophy in Jonathan's room, he gave him a beating that topped the first one.

Even now, when Jonathan viewed the cow skull, it welled up feelings of pride, but mostly pain; a titillating mixture he had never been able to evoke with any other trophy, try as he may.

Jonathan killed the light and set it in its place before climbing out through the hatchway.

The air in the barn was noticeably fresher, and breathing it always gave Jonathan a twinge of grief. It served as reminder that he had returned to the real world above.

He stood in the dark, watching the hatchway in the floor and ruminated over what he should do about it mysteriously opening. If someone did find his trophy room, they were good enough to leave things be. It was obvious, they only wanted to look, and who could blame them? Jonathan grinned as he considered his fine collection and he hoped that, if he did have a guest, they were impressed with what they saw.

The crackling sound of car tires on the dirt driveway stole Jonathan from his thoughts. Outside the barn doors Jonathan saw his sister's yellow Honda coming to a stop beside the house. His open-door dilemma had to wait.

The real world called.

Chapter Eight

Jack propped his elbows on the table and laced his fingers together. He sat for several moments, thinking about what he'd read. Ultimately, an ugly emotion crowded its way into his thoughts. He had more and more difficulty pushing it away. Shuffling through the pages, he reread a couple of sections, gave them some consideration.

This could be tightened up a little here, he thought, *and this part requires a little more depth. I mean, if this were my work, I would perhaps expand on this Jill character's dilemma. In fact, if it were mine, I would probably…*

Jack pushed his chair back from the table as he felt the full impact of an especially devilish idea.

If it were mine…

No, absolutely not. I can't do that.

He stood up to distance himself from the pages and began to pace, taking care not to step in the gaping hole in the floor.

This is somebody's manuscript. They put hours and hours of work into it. It belongs to somebody, and Kubby will probably know who.

He stopped at the centre of the floor and looked down at the hole where the manuscript had hidden.

Kubby might *know who.*

It doesn't matter if he does or if he doesn't. I can't use this. I can't even think of using it. That is stealing, plain and simple.

Jack couldn't imagine an offence more taboo among writers than stealing another's manuscript. Writer's block, well, people could at least understand that. The idea of a writer battling a block almost seemed heroic when compared to cheating to get around it. Stealing—plagiarizing—*that* was a cardinal sin. *That* was unforgivable.

"That settles it," Jack said. He went about gathering up the pages, tucking them in his laptop bag. He stowed the bag in the closet and set out in search of Kubby. He would discover the manuscript's rightful owner and get it back to them straight away. All he needed was the help of a man with a drug addled memory.

As he stepped outside, Jack glimpsed one of the other guests walking past his cabin along the main path. The man, brown haired and dressed in a red long-sleeved shirt, took determined strides. Jack didn't recognize him, but started to wave hello. The man didn't notice him, or perhaps more accurately, pretended not to. He merely continued his steady pace and when Jack reached the path, he was already out of sight.

Jack thought that was a little strange. The man would have had to break into a jog to get around the bend in time to vanish. Then he considered some of the other guests at Wabasso and he decided that *strange* was only the tip of the iceberg when it came to these folks. The rude behavior didn't bother Jack much, though he foresaw an awkward encounter with the man when their paths inevitably crossed again. A few yards down the trail, Jack's thoughts shifted away from his run-in with the man—or lack thereof—and back to the manuscript. Moreover, he considered how he would approach Kubby about it.

Jack arrived at the mess hall. As soon as he entered, he made a bee line to the kitchen counter. On the other side, Kubby watched over a large omelet sizzling on the gas grill. He slid a spatula under one side of it and bent slightly at the knees, an expression of intense concentration covered his face. Jack offered a greeting, but Kubby gestured to silence him. The task at hand fully consumed the caretaker. He bit his bottom lip, then carefully raised the spatula and flipped the omelet. Only after succeeding in his maneuver did he shift his focus to Jack.

"Sorry 'bout that Jack, but I don't want to make a mess out of this."

"Yeah, sure. Listen, Kubby, there's something I have to ask you." Jack paused, scratching his chin while he hunted for the perfect way to pose his delicate question.

"If you're going to ask him for that omelet, you can forget it." A voice called behind him. Jack turned to the nearest table and found Kate smiling up at him.

"Oh, hey Kate. Didn't see you there." A nervous smile crossed Jack's lips.

"What did you want to ask me?" Kubby said, now shifting his attention to cleaning up his work station.

Jack, unable to look away from his fetching colleague, said, "Umm…it can wait." What he really thought was that his question was best asked in privacy.

"Cool. Come see me after breakfast," Kubby said as he wiped his hands on his pants. "We should really change those bandages, anyway."

"Yes," Jack said. "Good idea." *Great idea. We can talk then.*

"Join me, Jack," Kate said and nodded at the vacant seat across from her.

Jack started toward her table. That's when it occurred to him that he hadn't changed clothes in a day or showered in two. He prayed she wouldn't be able to detect his likely odor—a pungent combination of sweat and *Canadian Club*—across the table. He sat down slowly on the bench so as not to raise a draft. "Good morning," he offered.

"Not hungry this morning?" she asked, balking a little.

Jack scanned the kitchen counter where a few cereal boxes stood next to a glass pitcher of milk. Further down was a basket of assorted muffins and bagels. There were two more pitchers at the end—one containing orange juice, the other, some pulpy red fluid he guessed was V8. The flutter in his stomach had not abated and the mere sight of food actually excited it.

"No, I'm not. When I'm concentrating on work, I guess my appetite suffers a little. I can't even think of eating right now."

"So work on your draft is going well?"

"Yes," Jack said. He tried to think of something to say that wasn't a total lie. "I guess you could say that I've reached a pivotal point in my story. I'll have a big decision to make very soon." Sharing that sliver of truth raised a cold sweat on his neck. He wondered if Kate could see the sheen forming.

How would she react, he thought, *if she knew what decision I had to make? What if she knew I was entertaining the idea of stealing someone else's story and passing it off as my own?*

"That's wonderful," she said.

In her emerald eyes, Jack saw the purest honesty. She was happy for him, happy that his work was coming along, that he'd overcome whatever obstacle had been blocking his progress. Jack couldn't have felt worse.

Kubby arrived at the tableside and set a plate down in front of Kate. It held a side of toast and the steaming omelet that he no doubt took pains to fold perfectly with the spatula. "A cheese and asparagus omelet for the lady," he said. "And can I get you anything, sir? Coffee?"

"Maybe just some water," Jack said, hoping a little hydration would quell his hangover. Kubby nodded and promised to return.

"Oh my God. This smells so good," Kate said, closing her eyes and tilting her head back. "How could you not want one of these? When I'm working, my appetite kicks into high gear. I swear I gain like ten pounds every time I finish a novel."

Jack tried not to look at her plate as she dug in. "Umm, Kate, I was wondering…"

"Uh-huh?" she said, glancing up at him with her mouth full.

"This might sound a little odd, but remember the other day? You told me something about the retreat, about Wabasso."

"What? Like where to find the showers?" The wisecrack seemed to surprise even her. Trying to suppress her laughter, she said, "Kidding. I'm kidding. Sorry."

Jack breathed a nervous chuckle. "No, you said something about this place and how it can *give* you things...things you might need."

The corners of Kate's lips curled up in a devious grin. "Did you receive a gift already, Jack?" When she said *gift*, she raised an eyebrow.

"Maybe..." Uncertainty filled Jack's tone. He considered his next words very carefully. Fortunately for him, Kubby supplied a welcomed distraction. The caretaker returned and set a tumbler of water down on the table.

"There you go, my friend. Compliments of the house." Kubby stood beside the table, with the expectation one might see in a waiter who just delivered a bottle of fine wine. Jack clued in that he was supposed to taste the water and give his approval. He raised the cold glass and sipped. The mouthful remained cool even as it raced down his throat.

Jack gave an eager nod for Kubby's benefit. "Very good. Excellent." In the following seconds, Jack decided his description was no exaggeration. As soon as he swallowed, the liquid had a calming effect on his stomach. He drank again, this time, deeply. When he set the glass down, the nervous flutter in his core had gone.

Kubby raised his hand: step one of the high-five process.

This time Jack happily indulged. The passing of his nausea was indeed cause for celebration. He lifted his hand and the caretaker clapped it loudly.

"That was a good one," Kubby said. He made his way back to the kitchen, whistling some tune as he went.

Kate took another bite of her omelet and smiled as she chewed. "I think you're a good fit here, Jack."

"Umm...thanks." Jack felt a satisfied grin spreading on his

face and he couldn't shake it off. He wanted to get back on topic now that he and Kate were alone again. He leaned in to the table. "About those gifts you mentioned. I just want to be clear. What sort of gifts are we talking here? I mean, how obvious is it when you get one?"

Her brow furrowed now. "I'm not sure I follow."

"There he is!" A voice boomed from the mess hall entrance.

Jack looked over his shoulder to find Warren walking in, his rotund friend, Ralph, trailing.

"There's our resident H.P. Lovecraft," Warren continued. They approached the table and Warren patted Jack on the back. "Tell me, Jack, how are you settling in?"

Jack turned to face forward. "Just fine, thanks," he said flatly.

"Are you finding our little lakeside retreat peaceful enough for pursuing your work?" Warren asked, feigning concern.

"Yes, I'm very comfortable here."

"That's queer. Because, I could have sworn I awoke to your screams yesterday." He elbowed his sidekick and they shared in giddy laughter.

Jack gnashed his teeth and continued to stare straight ahead. He laced his fingers around his water glass and gripped it tightly.

"I told him that you were swept up in your story," Ralph said, holding his belly as though his laughter might actually split his sides. "I said that's just how a horror writer can tell they have something special—when reading their own prose is so very frightful that they simply can't help but scream in terror."

"Why, Ralph," Kate said as she reached across the table to take hold of Jack's hand. "Those were screams of pleasure. Can't you tell the difference?"

Kubby erupted in laughter. Warren and Ralph glared in his direction. Warren's scorn was enough to silence the caretaker.

Jack felt heat rising in his cheeks and prayed it wouldn't

show.

Ralph muttered something under his breath.

Warren gave the pair a wry smirk before seeking out other sport. "Mr. Kubanowski," he bellowed. "Why do I not smell ham?"

"Oh, dang! I forgot," Kubby blurted then busied himself at the grill.

Warren and Ralph bid them a good morning and seated themselves at the next table.

Kate gave Jack's hand a subtle squeeze before taking hers back. "Don't let them get to you," she whispered, and started to work on her breakfast again. "So, what were we talking about before they interrupted?"

Jack glanced over his shoulder. He found they were still the focus of Warren and Ralph's attentions, though they tried to appear otherwise occupied. "Maybe we can talk about that some other time."

Kate studied him for a moment and offered a fleeting smile. "Sure."

Jack's appetite returned with a vengeance. While watching Kate enjoy her omelet, he decided to ask Kubby for some eggs of his own. He ate three scrambled eggs with whole wheat toast and a side of Warren's ham. After that, he asked for a rasher of bacon and more toast. Of course, he washed it all down, not with juice or coffee, but with the finest, most refreshing water he had ever known. Wabasso Water.

Having long finished her breakfast, Kate waited with Jack while he devoured his. The pair made small talk, touching on every topic from their hometowns to liberal politics. When Jack finally had enough, he thanked her for the company and Kate departed for her cabin to resume her work.

Jack felt a twinge of envy after she left. He envisioned Kate simply sitting in front of her laptop and typing. Writing was likely that easy for her. Jack had never been able to simply begin the creative process at will. Conversely, he couldn't turn

it off when he saw fit, either—say when he was called for dinner or when he was supposed to take the boys to the park.
When he caught a good wave, he had to ride it out. Sometimes it lasted for days.

The caretaker finished the breakfast service, and after he
cleaned up, Jack followed him back to his quarters. Jack sat on
the cot, Kubby on his old desk chair, and they went about
changing Jack's bandages. Kubby leaned in close and inspected the cuts in Jack's hands. They had scabbed over nicely and
he gave a grunt of approval. "I don't think you're gonna need
these wrapped again," he said as he fished through the first aid
kit. "I'll just clean them real good and stick some Band-Aids
on 'em."

Jack watched Kubby produce the little brown bottle of
rubbing alcohol from the kit and he winced. *Not this again.*
Though, when Kubby dabbed a generous quantity of the stuff
on his palms, it didn't sting that much.

"That's a pretty good sign, they're healing up," Kubby said.
"You're a fast healer. Do you meditate?"

"Meditate?"

"Yeah, like, mind over body, to speed up the healing process?"

Jack shook his head. "Nah."

"Well, you could've fooled me," Kubby said. He replaced
the bottle and took a few Band-Aids from the kit and began
fixing them to the larger cuts. Jack didn't think they would
stay in place for long, but he didn't protest. The caretaker
stuck the last of them on. "Now, let's check on that knee."

Jack gently removed his tennis shoe and lifted his foot up.
Like before, Kubby rested it on the chair between his legs. He
rolled up Jack's pant leg and went about undressing the
wound. Jack watched as the layers of bandage grew redder and
redder as Kubby stripped them away. The knee was still plenty
tender, but other worries nagged at him now, like how to
broach the subject of the mystery manuscript.

*Should I just come out and tell him about it? That would elimi-
nate any chance of me claiming the thing as my own and getting*

myself in a heap of trouble when its rightful owner comes forward. That would be the prudent course.

Jack waged an internal debate, changing his mind every few seconds. A dozen scenarios flickered through his head. He imagined how easy it would be to put his name on *Together, Dead*. He pictured Warren and Ralph getting the news that he had finished his work ahead of schedule and that his book would hit store shelves by the holidays. The smiles were wiped clean-off their smug faces.

He imagined the phone call from Ted Marsh. He'd call to report how pleased the publisher was with his submission. He'd call him *Jackie-Baby* again and tell him how much he admired him for coming through under such extreme pressure. The best part would be the reprieve from the demands of his contract. *I'd have a year to finish my manuscript. Isn't that what Ted said? 'We're all about buying time now.'* The very thought of it had excitement flaring in his core again.

Jack settled that emotion with a sobering thought. *I'm still talking about plagiarism. It's just so wrong—more than that—it is a crime. For all I know,* Together, Dead *went to press years ago. Is it really worth the risk? How much am I willing to put on the line just to find a short cut around this…block?*

The B word rattling around in his head hurt more than the split in his knee. To this day, his troublesome block remained firmly in place. There was no advice, no amount of concentration, no secret technique that could help him push through it. *I've suffered it for so damned long…maybe I was meant to find that manuscript. Maybe, in some way, I earned it.*

Jack's mind wandered back to the day the block rose up his path. If it wasn't fully erected on that day, certainly its foundation was laid in place.

Kubby cleared away the rest of the wrap and the bloody gauze from his knee and grimaced at the gash beneath. "Dude, this doesn't look too good," he said, pulling back from smelling range.

No…this doesn't look good at all, Jack thought, but it wasn't the wound that was foremost on his mind.

"I better give it a good cleaning," Kubby said.

"Okay." Jack's voice was monotone.

Jack barely registered Kubby picking out the alcohol bottle from the kit. He was back at the front door of his house, watching his boys being hauled away. Their faces in the rear windshield, growing smaller and smaller until they went around the corner and disappeared altogether. Their mother didn't hurry the minivan, nor did she look back as she drove out of his life forever.

"This is gonna hurt some." Kubby said, holding a saturated cotton swab poised over Jack's torn knee.

"Okay."

Kubby gingerly dabbed alcohol onto the red and swollen edges of the tear. Jack felt his leg burst into flames, tasted acid in his mouth. He balled his fists and squeezed his eyes shut as they filled with water. For a moment, he thought he might scream out, but a calm and collected inner voice spoke up instead. It said, *take it...you* have *earned it.*

The burning sensation ebbed. Jack repeated the words to himself. Tension bled from his muscles and he opened his eyes. Kubby continued to blot the cotton swab along the edge of the gash. It still stung, but just a little. Soon, Kubby applied a gauze pad treated with *Polysporin* to the wound. He began wrapping a fresh length of bandage around the knee and said something about buying more of the stuff on his next trip to town. With the dressing complete, Kubby rolled the pant leg down and carefully set Jack's foot on the floor. Jack felt significantly better, though he knew it had little to do with the treatment.

He closed his eyes and saw his block before him—that miserable, black wall of stones and mud and guilt. To his left, he saw a path leading to the edge of the wall. It was a way around and he knew if he took it, he would find daylight on the other side.

Jack gathered a breath and took the first step.

"Say, Kubby, I wanted to ask you..." He hesitated, searching for the right words. "Umm, can you remember a guest ever claiming to have lost something in one of the cabins?"

Kubby stopped repacking the first aid kit and put some thought into an answer. "Hmm...lost something?"

"Yeah, like maybe somebody left Wabasso, but they left something behind by mistake. Did you ever hear anything like that?"

"I don't think so."

"Nobody ever said they forgot anything...say in Cabin Six?"

"Nope. Did you find a wallet or something?"

"No."

"Oh," Kubby lowered his voice as though broaching a sensitive subject. "Did you lose your wallet?"

"My wallet's fine." Jack rubbed hard on his brow. "I was just wondering if anyone ever forgot something...important—something they'd need, something they'd really miss."

"Nothing comes to mind." Kubby's face suddenly lit up. "Oh yeah!"

"You remember something?"

"Yes."

Jack's breath hitched in his throat. He saw his opportunity unravel in an instant.

"There is a Lost and Found box under the counter in the office."

Jack sighed. Kubby's inability to follow the simple conversation sapped his energy reserves.

"I'm pretty sure that you'd only find a *Dodger's* hat and a *Frisbee* in there, but you can check it out." Kubby closed the lid of the kit and paused, an expression of confusion coming over him. "Come to think of it, that Frisbee might be mine. Hey, do you feel like throwing it around for a while?"

"Umm, I should probably go easy on my hands right now."

"Oh, right. Good call. I'm game if you change your mind."

Jack's thoughts drifted back to his secret manuscript.

Kubby can't offer much help in discovering the author's identity—at least not without me divulging more information and then I'd be declaring outright that I found the work. Maybe I should ask someone else. Kate might be able to give some insight. She's been coming to Wabasso for years. If anyone has heard of a long-lost manuscript at the retreat, surely she has. Then again, maybe asking Kate is too risky. She's too keen. She won't settle for I found something in my room like Kubby did. She'll ask questions and it won't take her long to figure it out.

Maybe using the manuscript is too dangerous. I don't even know the likelihood of getting caught. Am I really so desperate that I'd take a chance like that?

Jack already knew the answer to that. He slouched.

Of course I am.

"Well, there you go, Jack-man." Kubby tossed the first aid kit onto the cot. He raised his hand for a celebratory high five. "You're on the road to recovery."

Wabasso appeared very different when Jack stepped out of the office. Gusts of south bound wind stirred her grey surface to a chop. Branches and shrubs snapped on the sharp breeze and sand flew up from the beach. Jack shielded his eyes as he passed by. He walked as fast as his hobbled knee would allow, past the mess hall and the communal shower house, to the path leading to the guest cabins. The wind ripped through the pocket in the trees, hurling spray from the water and the first droplets of what promised to be a prolonged rain storm. Jack wondered why the weather wasn't the centre of conversation in the mess hall. Then he remembered this was North Country, moose country, and here, weather was said to change as fast as a man can change his mind.

Jack glanced to the right each time the path broke off to one of the cabins. He found their windows awash with lamplight; their inhabitants hard at work. Soon he would be as well. He smiled in spite of the headlong wind.

When he reached Cabin Six, his sodden tee shirt clung to his skin. He threw the door open and it sent the empty whiskey bottle skittering across the floor. He secured the door, turned on the light and went directly to the closet to retrieve his laptop bag. He opened its flap and eyed the lineup of pens in their respective built-in slots. He had fine tipped black markers, highlighters of green and pink and yellow, blue ink ballpoints, but his focus went to the end of the line where he kept his red *Bic* felt-tipped.

Big Red, he thought of it, affectionately. The very pen he used to mark up his first draft of *The Long Night*. Back then, he used to print out each chapter upon completion. It was a prideful thing, to print pages of work—especially for a full time employee of the power commission with scarcely enough free time to indulge in such a hobby. He saw each chapter as a trophy. It was his secret art, and if it could be said that those pages were the canvas, then surely Big Red was the brush.

He didn't simply slash red ink through his words and scratch notes across the page, he often used a ruler when drawing a line through a word he intended to cut. He used his best free hand box lettering to make his notes. His pages would continue to be trophies.

Jack pulled Big Red from the slot and took off its cap. He set it on the writing table, at the ready. He reached into the bag and clutched the stack of papers within and pulled them free. He set them on the table beside his editing pen. Instead of sitting down, he backed up.

These pages were the answer to all of his problems, yet he hesitated. He took a few deep breaths and shook his hands out to limber up. Once he had stretched, he continued to stand away from the table.

What's the problem? he wondered. *You already decided, right? What's the holdup?*

Maybe the act of sitting down to work on someone else's manuscript gave him pause. Maybe it was the sight of Big Red waiting to make its mark. Either way, Jack had trouble proceeding. He realised that this was the point of no return. Once he started to read again, once he began editing these pages, he would be a thief. He would forever be a thief.

What if I get caught?

What if it doesn't even make it across Ted Marsh's desk?

True. Ted had read enough of Jack's work to be able to detect the shift in style. Then there was the genre. While it was horror, it seemed to be *slasher* fiction. Jack never really read those, let alone entertained the idea of writing one. All he knew about them was that promiscuous women die first, liquor and drug use is certain to get a character killed and the virgin survives an attack by the killer, who seems to be killed himself, but who lives to kill another day.

The sparse rules weren't much to go on. He didn't think it was enough to sell the manuscript as his own, but he had one thing going for him. Neither Ted nor the publisher knew what to expect from his submission. Jack hadn't given them the slightest idea of what he was working on for the simple reason that he didn't know. He hadn't gotten that far.

Jack could finally see benefit from his weakness. He released a breath and picked up Big Red from the table. He looked at it and imagined it carving a path through a monstrous black wall.

"I'll change it just enough," he said softly. "I'll make it *mine*."

Together, Dead

II

Jill could look at nothing but the big white farmhouse as she rolled up the driveway. It used to warm her heart to see the place. Years had passed since she last felt happy to be here. The place represented too much illness, too much death, and now, too much work. The house actually appeared larger than she remembered, and the thought of trying to pack its contents in mere days had her reaching for her cigarettes again.

She brought one to her lips while stopping the car, but when she saw Jonathan emerge from the barn, held off on lighting it. She had always tried to set a good example for her younger brother when they were growing up, and Jill's habits died hard. She tossed the cigarette into the dashboard ashtray and got out of the car, forcing a smile for the young man who represented all that was left of her family.

Her smile disappeared when she took full notice of his appearance. His clothes were filthy. His complexion was pale. His sunken cheeks were scruffy with several days of brown growth. He was growing out of the maintenance-free buzz cut their mother had always given him, and his demeanor, the vague expression of confusion he kept, seemed more profound than ever. Jill could have burst into tears as she watched him approach.

"Hi, Jill," said Jonathan, his voice void of any highs and lows that would suggest emotion.

"Jonathan… Jon, are you okay?" She could scarcely believe how sickly he looked after spending the week alone. Two weeks on his own would be the end of him.

"Yes," he replied in that flat tone and stopped, keeping a six foot buffer between them.

"Have you had anything to eat?" she begged, battling the urge to take him in her arms. The Dunn's had never been a particularly affectionate family. Love was something shared, but not expressed. Seeing Jonathan up close, his bloodshot eyes helped Jill to keep their conservative distance. A hug would likely do more harm than good. An unusual gesture like that might have served to upset him more than anything.

"Cookies," answered Jonathan, and Jill believed him. He seemed like a man who had been surviving on crumbs. But, why? She had left plenty of food in the house. She thought of asking him, but let the argument die before she made it. It was abundantly clear how much care her brother required.

Forgetting to lock a door or close a

window was one thing, but it seemed that he could not clean himself or even feed himself. Her parents had done more for him than she could have imagined.

She had been off the farm for over ten years now. When she left, Jonathan was not yet sixteen; still at the age when most boys needed a lot of help around the kitchen and laundry room. Back then, Jill had considered his many limitations almost normal.

Their mother had never complained about how much attention he needed. In recent years, Jill got the sense that her brother was more of a handful than her mother let on, but one look at him and Jill knew it was worse than she dared dream.

How can it be this bad? One thing is certain, she reckoned. If he refuses going to the care home, his argument won't have a leg to stand on.

"Let's go inside," said Jill. "I'll make you some breakfast. Are cheese and asparagus omelets still your favorite?"

Jonathan gave a nod of assent and walked past her toward the door.

"Afterwards, we have some work to do." Jill watched him enter the house.

At least, I'll have some work to do, she said to herself when he didn't respond.

"Want some more juice?" asked Jill, resting her hand on a plastic orange juice container.

"Yes, please," said Jonathan, head lowered over his plate at the kitchen table.

She poured while he mopped up bits of

egg with a piece of toast.

"Did you have enough to eat?" she asked.

"Yes," he said, robotically.

Jill took a break from packing up the kitchen, and set the large cardboard carton on the floor. "Okay, Jon. I have some things I have to talk to you about."

Still chewing, he set his empty stare upon her.

"I mean, you know why I'm here this weekend, right? You know what all the boxes are for?" When he kept mum, she went on. "I'm here to pack, Jon. Pack up the house? So we can sell it?"

He abruptly stopped chewing and swallowed hard.

Jill approached the table. She gripped the back of an empty chair and in her most apologetic tone, said, "Jon, you can't stay here on your own. It's too much for you."

Jonathan searched the surface of the table for clues to what was happening.

"And, I live too far away to come here to watch over you."

Something outside the window drew Jonathan's attention.

"Jon, please listen to me. This is really important. I arranged for a place for you to stay in the city. It's nice and clean and there will be other people there to spend time with. And there are people there to cook for you, too. They have a doctor to check up on you, and they do a lot of activities and stuff. When I was there, they were getting ready for movie night. That sounds nice, right?"

Jonathan continued to stare out the window.

Jill moved to block his view and wrestle his focus away. "I think it will be really good for you. I'm sure you will make some friends-"

"No." He looked up at her, unblinking.

"Now, Jon, you never know. There are a lot nice people there. You'll see."

"No. I'm staying."

"That's not an option, Jon. I'm sorry, but you really have to do this."

Jonathan locked his jaw and stared straight ahead, as though the discussion was over. "I'm staying here."

"You can't! You can't stay here." Jill pulled back from the table. She tilted her head back in frustration. "Who's going to take care of you? Who's going to cook and clean and do your shopping and make sure you wash yourself?" She brought a hand to her brow and sucked in a breath. "It's too bad Mom and Dad aren't here, believe me, I know, but they're gone and we have to make some difficult changes. We _are_ selling the farm."

Jonathan aimed his glassy stare out the window like he sought a second opinion from someone outside.

Jill picked up an empty cardboard box and shook it in front of him. "Now, take this to your room and pack your things. Jon, look at me!"

Jonathan got up so quickly, his chair skittered across the floor behind him. Jill flinched and then stood there fence-post-stiff as he crossed the floor in two strides. He took the box from her, tore it in two and tossed it aside. "I ain't never leavin' here," he said bluntly. Before he left the kitchen, he turned back.

"You'd need a team of draft horses to drag me outta here."

Jill knotted the ties of an over-stuffed garbage bag and propped it beside the other two she had filled. She had been working steadily since Jonathan stormed off, hoping the distraction would calm her down. So far it failed to do so. She inhaled slowly as she eyed the boxes packed with the contents of the kitchen cabinets.

The task before her seemed enormous, but her thoughts dwelled elsewhere; darting from her mother to her father, and more often than not, to her brother and the temper he had displayed. She could not remember him ever moving so quickly. He had sprung out of his chair like a viper striking from the tall grass. For an instant, his eyes changed. They narrowed. They hinted at some deep underlying malice.

They were her father's eyes.

Jill wiped her brow and found that her hand trembled, and her anxiety quickly turned to anger. She had lived too long with her oppressive father and his liquor-fuelled rages to suffer even one moment of Jonathan's insolence. She desired more than anything, to barge into his bedroom and dole out some of the wrath her own boys knew so well, but it was not as simple as that. It never was with Jonathan. He needed more help than anger, more pity than rage.

Jill walked down the hallway from the kitchen and past the parlor. The room was virtually untouched since her parents' death. Her father's slippers waited at the foot of his armchair. His newspaper was folded over the arm. Mother's needle-work sat ready on the chesterfield, her empty teacup on the end-table.

Seeing the items served a fresh dose of sorrow. Jonathan had been living in this environment alone, for a week. He had been living amid their parents' things the entire time. Every room, every cor-ner, of the house bore some reminder of them. The feeling was not lost on Jill as she had packed her mother's good china in the kitchen, and she could only imagine how strongly it affected Jonathan.

She climbed the stairs and walked past the master bedroom, the door to which was thankfully closed. She stopped at Jona-than's door and knocked on it gently. "Jon, are you okay?"

There was no answer.

"Jon, can I come in?"

She held her ear to the door and grasped the handle, waiting for a re-sponse. When none came, she turned the knob and eased the door open. The over-ripe smell of sweat and stale air wel-comed her.

"Jon?" She peeked inside to find him sitting on his bed, hands on his knees, staring out the window. He took no ac-count of her entry. His focus remained glued to something outside. "Jon, are you okay? I'm sorry about earlier. We have to talk about this, but we shouldn't let it upset us. Jon?"

Jill sat down on the bed beside him. Only then, did he seem to notice her. He slowly turned from the window and regarded her with distant eyes. All the rage those eyes had contained before had bled away and he resembled his usual semi-vacant self.

"Yes?" His voice was also devoid of anger or sorrow or any other emotion.

"We can talk about things later. For now, why don't we get you cleaned up? I'll run you a bath. Would you like that?"

"Yes."

"Do you have any clean clothes? Clean, you know, clothes? No? Okay, I'll do some laundry while you're in the bath." Jill waited for some reply from him. All she got was his blank stare. "Okay, I'll start that bath."

Jill tested the water in the half-filled bathtub with her hand. It was far too hot for her, but that was how Jonathan liked it. She retrieved a fresh towel from the linen closet for him and laid it on the toilet tank.

She turned and was startled to find Jonathan standing behind her. She gasped in her moment of surprise. He barely blinked.

"Jon, the water's ready. Umm… toss your dirty clothes outside in the hall." She edged around him, toward the door.

He dropped his trousers before she was even out of the room.

She hurried out.

A moment later, Jonathan tossed a ball

of dirty laundry out the open door. Jill scooped it up and headed for the cellar. She held the dingy clothes as far from herself as she could. They reeked of dried, old sweat. She had toilet trained two boys and had yet to experience this kind of stink in their laundry.

Jonathan slowly lowered himself into the tub. The water was just right, hot enough to break the threshold of pain. It stung the tender flesh of his genitals as he sunk to the bottom and the breath quivered out of him. His chest turned a pinkish hue. The half dozen scars that striped his body would glow red when he got out. They would be obvious, those scars his family believed he had collected over a childhood spent on a working farm, each one a mishap of either sewing or reaping. Did they ever dream he had gotten them in pursuit of his trophies?

He let his arms float. The heat seemed to migrate to his knuckles. They pulsed.

He made a fist with his right and released and clinched it again. He closed his eyes and thought about his trophy room and the severed right hand displayed there. The slightest smile passed his lips as he pictured the withered grey appendage in its place among his other keepsakes. He thought about the day he collected it and the memory brought him a full grin.

The hard look had gone out of the farmhand's eyes. Jonathan had noticed that about him right away. Since the day Mr. Dunn had hired the man to help with the potato harvest, he had this hard look about him. Jonathan had supposed it was the bearing of a man put to task. This man had decided he would not rest until his work was done. That look remained, even when he and Jonathan were ordered to turn the compost heap while the rest of the family conducted business in town.

The farmhand went about the mindless work like it was of utmost importance. The heap of festering decay became his main focus. To that point, he did not notice when Jonathan moved behind him and raised the shovel.

Then that hard look was gone.

Waking, tied to a chair, gagged at the mouth, the farmhand seemed like an entirely different man. He was small and weak. His grungy, thrift store attire no longer told the story of a man used to hard labor. It was the dress of a homeless man.

Absolute panic filled the farmhand's red rimmed eyes. When the first droplets of blood mingling with sweat ran from his matted hair and down his cheek, he started to thrash and he screamed a series of vowels into his gag.

Jonathan trusted in the nylon ropes that bound the farmhand's arms and legs, but he questioned if the old wooden chair would hold up to the abuse. It was one of his mother's kitchen chairs, sent to the barn long ago with a broken rail for his father to repair. The farmhand gave the thing all the fight it could bear. The arms of the chair started to bend.

Jonathan decided to finish his business quickly. His family would return soon, and when they did, the farmhand would be gone.

    That's how it goes with these shiftless men-for-hire, his father would likely say. Gone on a drinking binge as soon as you pay 'em, never to be seen again.

    Jonathan heard those exact words more than once and this time would have been no different.

    Jonathan took up the ax and the farmhand's eyes widened. His howling intensified.

    "I told you not to show me up in front of my father," said Jonathan. "Yeah, you work hard, mister, too damn hard for your own good."

    An expression of pleading swept across the farmhand's face. He shook his head, flecking drops of blood on the ground.

    Some hit Jonathan's legs. He did not care, just like he did not care that the farmhand offered the sincerest of apologies for his transgressions. It did not bother Jonathan at all that the man showed up on his family's farm and worked circles around him. Jonathan figured that most regular men need an excuse, or a reason, for killing. So he gave him one, hollow as it was.

    Jonathan, on the other hand, did not need anything, but to hear the sound of flesh tearing and bone snapping. He liked the sight of blood, but it did not compare to the sounds. The sweet sounds of death.

    He cradled the ax, felt its weight. He inspected its flinty grey head, tapering to a fine silvery edge. It was recently sharpened and the thought of its cleaving ability sent giddy waves throughout Jonathan's body. He loved all blades, but none so much as the ax. Like him, it had a one track mind. Once you start to swing it, there's no taking it back. Whatever was in the way was getting chopped, getting killed.

Jonathan stepped close to the struggling farmhand. He watched as the man fought against his binds. His flailing was feverous; one second, balling his hands into fists, the next, stretching his fingers open to their limits then clutching the arms of the chair.

Jonathan held the ax head over the man's bony, exposed wrist. Its shiny bite hovered above the bare joint. At once, the farmhand ceased his thrashing and eyed the ax head. Jonathan figured the man was as much in awe of the moment as he. Surely, the man was savouring it, too.

The peaceful moment was over in a blink. Jonathan raised the ax in both hands for an overhead swing. The man burst into a fit of bodily jerks and muffled shrieks that trumped the ones that came before.

The ax came down.

For a split second, the barn went silent.

After two ticks of a clock, the farmhand exploded with squeals akin to those of swine at the slaughter.

Jonathan hardly registered the man's agony. He delighted in what he heard, when he lowered the blade, splitting skin, cracking bone. Even the sound of the chair arm splintering as the ax busted through it was exhilarating.

Jonathan held still, trying to catch his breath. He dropped the ax in the dirt beside the man's amputated hand. He knelt to pick it up and a line of blood shot past him at eye level. Jonathan stood with the hand, caressing it, bending and pointing its digits this way and that. What mere seconds ago belonged to the farmhand was all his, now and forever.

The writhing farmhand had pulled his stump free of its ties and held it to his chest in a feeble attempt to stem the blood flow. He screamed until his face was tomato red. Blood vessels swelled in his neck to the point of bursting. All the while the gush of blood continued.

Jonathan had watched intently, waiting for the life to drain out of him so he could move him to the compost heap and bury him in. His screams had already began to fade. Jonathan had held the severed hand closer to his face and spread its fingers as though he was a palm reader. A ribbon of blood had tailed from its ragged end as he had inspected its lines and compared them to his own.

Jonathan lifted his hands from the hot bath water and inspected the lines crisscrossing his palms. He considered the possibility they had gotten longer since that day in the barn. He could have sworn they did. He felt the overwhelming urge to see his trophy again.

The basement stairs squeaked and thumped as Jill carefully picked her way down. At the foot of the stairs, she switched on two bright fluorescent fixtures overhead. They illuminated her father's workbench, a large, white deep freezer and a neat pile of firewood in the corner. In the opposite corner, she found the washer and dryer. Beside them, a wash basin and a short section of counter top.

She tossed the dirty clothes in the washer, added detergent and started a cycle. She found clothes in the dryer. Some of them were Jonathan's, some were their parents'. She pulled them out and began folding them on the counter. It did not enter her thinking just what she would do with her parents' clothing. There was no need to hang them in their closet or stow them in their drawers. Yet, in her distraction, she simply folded them and stacked them, nonetheless.

Her gaze drifted across the counter and to the laundry sink and inside it. She stopped folding and stepped closer to the sink. She dropped the sweater she was holding on the floor. In the bottom of the sink was a long kitchen knife with a serrated blade and a black wooden handle amid a puddle of dark red fluid.

Blood.

Chapter Nine

Jack flinched when the knock came at his door. He set Big Red down on the writing table, cursing his jumpiness. He stood and gathered up the marked pages of the manuscript and stuffed them into his laptop bag. Like a drug house denizen with the law beating on the door, he hid his stash in the closet.

"Just a second," he yelled, quickly assessing the room. The hole in the floor stood out. He took his pillow from the cot and covered the damage with it. His breath was still short when he opened the door to find Kate, bouncing on her toes and smiling.

"Hey Kate," he said, trying to tame his hair by hand. "What's happening?" He looked over her shoulder and noticed for the first time that the sun had set. He'd been so wrapped in his work that he had missed the evening meal—again.

"Jack, I'm here to collect you," she said.

"For dinner? Yeah, I kind of got on a roll and lost track of time."

"Umm, sorry, but you missed that," she said dismissively. "I'm here 'cause we're having a send-off for one of the other guests."

"Oh, really? I kind of have a lot of stuff to do..." Jack

trailed off as he looked back to his writing table, Big Red waiting.

"Come, now. All work and no play makes Jack a dull boy." He gave an insincere chuckle.

"Besides, it will be fun. We're having a bonfire on the beach. Kubby is bringing stuff to make S'mores."

"Umm, yeah, that sounds like fun, but..." He turned his gaze to the table again and this time, it fell on the pillow that hid the hole in the floor.

"Jack, I'm not leaving here without you." She folded her arms across her chest.

Despite her slight frame, Kate suddenly appeared the immovable object. Jack was familiar with this kind of strong willed resolution. He used to see it in his former wife when they locked horns over household duties or something to do with the kids. He decided to save them both a little time by foregoing a standoff. "Okay. I guess I can take some time away from the grind. And I mean *some* time. I can't spend all night at this thing."

Kate gave him half a smile. "Bring a sweater."

They set out on the path bound for the beach. Jack heard scraps of music on the night air. He could also detect the faint smell of wood smoke on the cool breeze. He grinned at Kate by his side.

She had been watching him.

"What?" he said, defensively.

"Nothing." she said, finding humor in his unease. "It's just that...you look good right now."

"Oh, just now? Thanks, I guess."

Kate faced forward. "You know what I mean. You usually have this serious scowl on your face, like you're sitting at the high stakes table or something, but it's gone now, for the moment, anyway."

"I'll take that as a compliment then."

"I wouldn't go that far," she said.

Silence crept in and Jack became acutely aware of the sound of their footsteps on the path. It was a comfortable sort of silence—the kind that true friends seldom notice and lovers come to cherish. Jack broke it, nonetheless.

"So who's leaving the retreat? Please tell me it's Warren."

Giggling, Kate said, "You don't think you'd be so lucky? Frasier Strom is leaving. I'm not sure if you know him."

"Tall guy? Moustache?"

"That's him. He just finished his draft this week."

"Hmm, I wonder what that feels like." Jack recalled his brief encounter with the man, how he pumped his fist in triumph as he concluded his phone call.

Kate confidently negotiated a slight bend in the darkened path as though she had strolled it a thousand times before. "It's a time honored tradition at Wabasso for all the guests to gather to give the departing writer a fare-thee-well."

"And, S'mores are a part of this tradition?" Jack chided. Less sure footed, he caught his toe in the dirt and nearly stumbled.

"They are when I'm involved, buster."

"I haven't had one of those since I took the boys camping. When was that? Two years ago? No, three?" The tree coverage diminished and permitted more moonlight to show the way. Kate's hair appeared black in the diluted light, her skin, all the more fair.

"Kubby went to town today. He said he was going to stop by the liquor store to get something for those of us with more adult tastes."

That reminded Jack that he had to discretely approach Kubby to ask him if he could find him a replacement laptop on one of his supply runs to town. *I'll tell him mine has a virus or that the battery is fried or something like that. With any luck, the second hand store will have something I can use. It doesn't have to be much, just capable of word processing. Big Red is doing the job just fine for now, but I can't very well send a stack of red lined pages for Ted Marsh to show the publisher. And to make changes to the manuscript in broad strokes, I'll need a PC.*

"Jack, are you still there? Hello?" Kate studied him, her brow raised.

"Sorry. What did you say?"

Perhaps a little cross that Jack had lapsed to daydreaming, she continued, "I said you won't have to speak at Frasier's send off tonight since you don't know him. At these things, everyone has to say something nice about the departing writer, even if they don't really mean it. It's a pain. You'll see what I mean when we send Warren home."

"Something tells me I'll be shoving off before him," Jack said, failing to mask the satisfaction in his tone.

"Really? Your story is coming along?"

"Yeah, it actually *is*. The finish line is in sight."

"So, that explains the look." She searched him again. "It's relief."

Jack grinned. "I guess."

Kate gave him a pat on the back. "That's great. I was starting to wonder if you were having some real trouble with your work."

Jack's pleasant demeanor faltered. In his mind, the black wall rose up before him. Kate's mere allusion to his writing *trouble* seemed to give it new life. It blotted out all light ahead of him. He had found a way to cheat it, but it would remain. It would be there waiting for him the next time he tried to create. The idea squeezed the air out of him.

"Well, I'll be sorry to see you go. It's nice having some fresh blood around here." She gave him a playful nudge with her elbow.

Jack saw sparks in the distance, leaping into the night sky. He and Kate had reached the mouth of the pathway where the vegetation lining it gave way to the coarse sands of the beach. Closer to the water's edge, five figures formed a semicircle around the stone ring of the fire pit. The glare of the impressive bonfire spared only their darkened silhouettes, but Jack could easily pick out long-haired Kubby and rotund Ralph Deakins from the group. As Jack and Kate walked across the beach, their shadows spread across the side of the mess hall, its walls, like all the trees surrounding it, glowed orange in the fire light.

Jack pushed all thoughts of his writer's block, and the negativity it evoked it, aside. He forced an amicable smile, as he braced himself for socializing. He would stay for an hour or so—long enough to appease Kate, short enough to keep his sanity. He hoped it would count for something.

Kubby detected their arrival before the others. He turned from the four foot high flames to watch their approach. "Hey, the gang's all here."

Warren spoke up next, his tone laden with derision. "Oh, let those two have the bench. I'm sure they'll want to curl up together by the fire."

Ralph snorted.

"My man Jack can sit wherever he wants," Kubby said. "How 'bout a brew Jackie-boy?"

"Yeah, sure," Jack said as he and Kate closed the remaining distance to the gathering.

The bonfire threw golden light over their features. Warren and Ralph stood together to the right. Jack ignored them. It was becoming easier to do every day.

"Here." Kubby handed Jack a bottle. "You'll like that. It's from the Clover Hill Brewing Company—possibly, the best micro-brewery in the area. Hey, you remember Pierre, right? He can't get enough of the stuff."

"Umm, we haven't really met, yet," Jack said. "Hey, Pierre. How are you?"

Pierre sat in a lawn chair, using a long stick to stir the fire. He had an almost sullen look about him. He gave Jack a silent nod and returned his focus to the fire. It released a swarm of fireflies each time he poked it. The cool greeting was more of a reaction than Jack got when he first saw Pierre in the mess hall, working through his lunch break. He wondered if Pierre was warming up to him.

Jack drank from the bottle. He wasn't much of a beer fan, but he could see why people liked the brand. Kubby had a Coleman cooler filled with more bottles bobbing in the ice like buoys on the ocean. Beside the cooler, the portable stereo from Kubby's room played. *The Rolling Stones* held the spotlight.

"Do you guys know each other?" Kubby said, gesturing to the man standing beside him. Like the first time Jack encountered the man, he was neatly dressed. He wore a mint coloured golf shirt tucked into pleated khakis and brown leather loafers. Jack admired his shoes. They reminded him of the alligator skins he had lost while hiking.

"No, haven't had the pleasure. Not officially, anyway." Jack offered the man his hand. "Hi....Jack Bishop."

"You were the fellow waiting to use the phone the other day." He wrung Jack's hand. "Frasier Strom. Sorry I didn't stop to say hello then, but I was a tad excited."

"Think nothing of it." Jack took his hand back and worked the effects of the fierce handshake out of it.

Kubby looked past them to where Kate settled in, fireside. "Can I get you a beer, Madam? We have red wine, too."

"You know what I want, Kubanowski," Kate scolded playfully.

"Oh yeah. I almost forgot. I've got the stuff right here." He retrieved a shopping bag from behind the cooler and took it to Kate. He handed her a bag of marshmallows, a couple of chocolate bars and a sleeve of what Jack guessed were honey wafers. That's what he had used the last time he made S'mores.

"So, congratulations are in order," Jack said to Frasier.

The writer bounced subtly on his toes. The smile that appeared on his face was far less subtle. His teeth were Colgate-white, his blonde moustache, perfectly trimmed. He parted his golden hair flawlessly to the side. Jack wondered how he managed to keep so well groomed at Wabasso. Jack had trouble dressing in clean shirts.

"Yes, thank you."

"Do you have a release date yet?" Jack asked. He felt it was a bit of a silly question, though he reached for something to talk about and it was marginally better than, *so, where do you get your ideas?*

"Nothing concrete, but I suppose it will be out sometime next year."

"What should we expect this time around?" Jack said, feeling a little guilt for implying he'd actually read Frasier's work before.

"More of the same. I tend to stick with what works best for me. So it will be more anxious, young men who become bitter, old men." He looked at Jack sidelong. "I understand you write thrillers."

"I do."

"That's fantastic." Frasier beamed all his pearly whites. "It must be fun. With all the excitement those sorts of stories bring, I'll bet you don't get even the slightest undertow of melancholy when you're writing."

Jack thought the comment was slightly odd. He considered it while he took a swig of beer. "Not that I can say. But, there are...other feelings. Dark ones. Sometimes. But, I guess it's part of the process. You just hope it's worth it in the end."

Frasier stepped closer to Jack, shrinking the already pinched space between them. "Ah, completing a manuscript, it's truly the greatest of feelings isn't it?"

"Maybe so." Jack thought that holding his baby boys for the first time wasn't too shabby either, but he kept the thought to himself.

"I'm sure I don't have to tell you that." As Frasier spoke, he rested his hand on Jack's shoulder and gave it a rub.

The gesture, Jack felt was a friendly one, but also too friendly for the occasion. "Oh sure, sure," Jack said as though he'd been down that road a hundred times or more.

Frasier removed his hand, much to Jack's relief. Hoping to discover less awkward ground to converse upon, Jack asked, "So what's next for you?"

"Home." Frasier said the word like it was the punch line of a joke. "I leave early in the morning."

Jack noticed Warren and Ralph. Their faces took on a sinister aspect in the light of the fire. They watched him and shared close words as he conversed with Frasier. "You must be happy to be getting away from here and back to civilization," Jack offered.

"Oh, Mr. Bishop," Frasier said in a shame-on-you tone. "If it were up to me, I'd never leave Wabasso."

Jack started to smirk at what surely was a quip, but then he saw no joking in Frasier's eyes.

"Hey Jack, show me how *you* make one of these," Kate called as she tore into the bag of marshmallows.

Thankful for a way out of this exchange, Jack excused himself and went to sit beside Kate on the long wooden bench by the fire. She skewered a marshmallow on a sharpened stick and handed it to Jack. "Don't say I never do anything nice for you," she whispered. The mischief in her smile told Jack she wasn't talking about preparing a marshmallow for him.

He glanced over at Frasier who had struck up a conversation with Kubby. "That was starting to get a little weird," he said under his breath.

"I have no doubt about that," Kate said. "As a rule I try to stay away from certain people around here." Jack gave her a knowing grin and positioned his marshmallow near the flames. Kate brought hers alongside it. She turned her stick as her S'more filling started to brown. Pierre watched it intently. When Kate noticed, she offered to make him one.

"No thanks, dear," Pierre replied. "I'm afraid I was born without a sweet tooth."

"I'd like one," Warren said.

Kate tossed him the bag.

He scowled.

"Oh shit," she said. "Smoke..." The gentle breeze had shifted inland and sent fire exhaust in her direction. Kate squinted and turned her head as it rolled over them.

Jack said, "I hate pink bunny rabbits."

"I'm sorry?" Kate gasped.

"I hate pink bunny rabbits," Jack said again. "It's like a mantra. You repeat it and the smoke goes away. I don't know how it works. It just does."

"Fine, fine. I hate pink bunny rabbits, too. I really do."

As if on cue, the breeze changed course again, wafting the smoke with it. Jack took a breath of clean air. "See? Works every time."

Kate's jaw dropped. "Wow, it's like magic."

"I know. It's strange how often saying that silly phrase makes smoke go away. My boys taught me that one."

"I *loathe* pink bunny rabbits, as well," Pierre exclaimed.

Jack and Kate peered across the fire pit to find him rubbing at his eyes. In moments the smoke that hampered him started abating. He blinked hard a couple of times, looked at Jack. "Holy shit. It *is* magic."

The three of them erupted in laughter. The unusual sight of Pierre's giddy reaction had Jack laughing all the harder.

Warren called out, "Speech! Speech!"

Ralph joined in the refrain, begging the guest of honor to say a few words. Jack figured they were having too much fun for Warren's taste and he just had to pour water on their moment. Kubby turned down Mick Jagger and company.

Frasier smiled and waved as he was given the floor. He took a moment to gather his thoughts. "Well, I suppose we are here tonight to honor Wabasso Lake's oldest tradition. We are sending a writer home. I have always enjoyed these evenings—even the ones we held in the mess hall when the weather didn't agree. For me, it is always bittersweet to be the one who is departing. Bitter, because I have to say goodbye to such excellent colleagues, and sweet, because I may succeed in getting another book on Wabasso's bestsellers shelf."

Kate released a barely audible groan.

"It's the best feeling, isn't it, finishing a manuscript? It's a high that has no equal. And we deserve it, do we not? We go through hell to get here. To quote Maya Angelou, 'There is no greater agony than bearing an untold story inside you'. I believe that's true. We put so much of ourselves into our work. Like fragile first-time lovers, we obsess, we pine. We forego sleep, meals, companionship. We suffer…"

"*Yes,*" said Warren.

He appeared to hang on Frasier's every word. Jack found a new level of dislike for him. He doubted that Warren had any idea what it was truly like to suffer for his work. *Does Frasier*

Strom know, for that matter? Jack wondered. *How does he have the nerve to sermonize about suffering? Did he sacrifice his family? Did he choose a love of words over his loved ones only to be abandoned by words in the end?* A black anger boiled in his stomach. Jack could explain what it really was to suffer only that would involve exposing a nerve too raw for the open air. At the end of his stick flames engulfed his marshmallow. He scraped it off on one the stones lining the pit.

As Frasier continued his speech, Jack glanced up at Pierre. He stirred the embers, blankly. It became clear to Jack. Pierre had tuned out. He had the bearing of a man who wasn't there by choice. He didn't like socializing with these people. He might have hated these people.

"...yes, we do suffer. So, when we finally reach this moment of accomplishment, of fulfillment, we should enjoy it. Savour it, because it doesn't last. Alas, we submit our work and the joyful part is over. Some editor, somewhere, starts picking our achievements apart, bit by bit. They cut and slash and hack and rearrange. In some cases, it will hardly feel like our work when they're finished. But, that is okay. And everyone here knows why...because we have a new project waiting in the wings, a new obsession, a new lover. It's waiting to take over our lives, to disrupt our sleep, quell our appetites, derail our social lives and return us once more to Wabasso Lake."

"Here, here," Ralph shouted. He and Warren clapped emphatically.

The others joined in with less enthusiastic applause.

"I love it when you come here to work, man," Kubby said as he stood beside Frasier and slapped a hand on his back. "I'm really gonna miss you."

Jack figured this must have been the part of the tradition Kate warned him about, when everybody gushes over the departing writer. He marshaled his patience.

"But, I'm gonna miss your practical jokes most of all," Kubby continued. "Remember when you replaced my copy of *Catcher in the Rye* with the French edition? I saw it there on my shelf and I was like, hey, I know I read this like a hundred times, but I can't read French, can I?"

"I had you wondering," Frasier said, wagging his finger.

"Or that time you dumped out my body wash and filled the bottle with hot sauce."

"Yes. I had to wait for a week before you discovered that. It was excruciating, waiting for you to take a shower."

Kubby didn't seem to notice that he was the brunt of yet another joke. "Well, you kept me on my toes. I can't wait 'til you find your way back here."

"Thanks, Kubby. I'm not sure when that will be, but something tells me you'll still be here."

"Of course, I will!" Kubby reached his arms around Frasier's waist and hoisted the writer off the ground in a bear hug. "I ain't never leaving this place," Kubby roared as he manhandled Frasier. "You'd need a team of draft horses to drag me outta here!"

The words burrowed deep inside Jack's grey matter. All other thoughts instantly dissipated. Nothing else existed in that moment except for those words, the man who said them and the manuscript where Jack first read them. *Draft horses... drag me...outta here.* Jack's body locked-up, unblinking, unbreathing, as he watched Kubby and Frasier jostle playfully. With great difficulty, he swallowed and mustered his voice. "What did he say?"

Kate chewed on her S'more a couple of times. "Nothing smart, anyway."

"No. What did he say about draft horses?"

"I don't know, Jack." Kate's eyes narrowed. "What does it matter?"

Pierre watched him with mild curiosity.

Jack got up and rushed toward the caretaker, kicking sand about wildly. He grabbed Kubby by the arm, knocking the beer bottle from his hand. "Easy Jack," Kubby blurted.

"Jack, what's wrong?" Kate said, but her voice seemed to be coming from some far off place.

Kubby became Jack's sole focus now.

"What did you just say?" Jack demanded.

Kubby seemed to be seeking some meaning from Jack's question for a few stretching moments. He finally said, "Oh, that was just an expression...you know...wild horses couldn't drag me away."

Jack shook his head and pulled Kubby closer. "That's not what you said. You didn't say wild horses. You said *draft* horses."

"Oh, well, I meant the same thing."

"But, I've never heard anyone say draft horses before. Where did you get that?"

Kubby's face slackened to a dumbfounded demeanor. He shrugged. "I don't know. I guess I picked it up somewhere."

Jack's lips peeled back to show his clenched teeth. "What do you mean, you picked it up somewhere? You must know where you heard it, for fuck sake!"

Kubby's expression shifted then from confusion to one of concern. "Are you feeling okay, Jack?"

Jack looked around him. Kate had stood up and now gaped at him, wide eyed. The others did, too, aside from Pierre who remained fixated on the flames, and Warren who sniggered into his hand. The full result of his outburst sank in. He quickly released Kubby's arm.

"I - I'm sorry. I..." Stunned by his own aggression, he stumbled backward a couple steps. He fished for something appropriate to say. Once again, the right words abandoned him. He turned and headed toward the guest cabins.

"Jack?" Kate called. "Where are you going? What happened?"

"Let him go," Warren said. "He doesn't belong here anyway."

That cruel sentiment didn't hurt Jack in the slightest. Other statements, ones involving draft horses, had left him numb. He could think of nothing but the man who had used the odd expression—not Kubby, but the other man—the one who dressed in red plaid.

* * * *

Jack threw open his cabin door and went directly to the closet. He retrieved his laptop bag and in one fluid motion, ripped the bundle of pages from it and flung it to the corner. He sat at the writing table, banging his injured knee as he did. The wound pulsed fresh agony through his body, but Jack barely registered it. The pages he'd slapped on the tabletop preoccupied him. He cut the pile in half like a deck of cards then pared down the remaining handful a few pages at a time. Then he found what he was seeking—a red scrawl in the margin of one of the pages reading, *replace with WILD*. An arrow accompanied the edit note and Jack read the words it pointed to.

Jonathan got up so quickly, his chair skittered across the floor behind him. Jill flinched and then stood there fence-post-stiff as he crossed the floor in two strides. He took the box from her, tore it in two and tossed it aside. "I ain't never leavin' here," he said bluntly. Before he left the kitchen, he turned back.

"You'd need a team of draft horses to drag me outta here."

Jack reread the final sentence and read it again. His stomach churned. There was no mistake—Kubby had said those exact words. He didn't change so much as a syllable. Jack sat back in the chair and rubbed his face with both hands. His mind circled the events on the beach searching for an answer that made sense. He counted the words in Jonathan Dunn's quote. There were seventeen. Kubby spoke all seventeen of those words in the same order as they were written in the manuscript. Coincidence had to be ruled out first.

Jack toyed with the possibility that he had incorrectly recalled what Kubby had said .He didn't think that was likely. If it had come out differently somehow, he wouldn't have been so struck by it. He wouldn't have had such a sure feeling of déjà vu. His thoughts continued to turn and eventually they took him to a darker place. Those dismal thoughts told him that Kubby was only able to quote from the manuscript because he knew precisely what was *in* the manuscript. If that were the case, Kubby must have known he would have gotten a reaction from Jack.

"He's playing with me."

Jack propped his elbows on the table and rested his head in his hands. His brow was cold.

Could it be that he planted the manuscript here, knowing I'd find it? Could this be some kind of joke? Is it some cruel-hearted initiation into the Wabasso Lake fraternity. Christ, they could all be in on it.

He pictured them now, sitting around the bonfire, laughing at his expense. He got up and walked a lap of the floor. His gaze drifted over the barren shelf, to the closet and down to his duffle of clothing. He stopped. His focus fell on the pair of moccasins near the corner of the room. Kubby had loaned them to Jack when he showed up at his door, barefoot and bleeding. He had dressed Jack's wounds.

"No," Jack said aloud. "He wouldn't. He doesn't have it in him."

Walter Kubanowski may be absent-minded and stoned much of the time, but he also gives without a thought for himself. He doesn't possess the kind of evil intuition required to play such a nasty trick. The look on his face when I grabbed him said it all. He was honestly concerned for me. Most people would have shoved me on my ass.

Jack's thoughts shifted to Kate. It pained him to picture her taking part in some ruse designed to humiliate him. It also didn't feel right at all. Like Kubby, he had only known her for what amounted to days, but she had been so kind to him, and she openly disliked Warren. That spoke volumes.

"Coincidence," he breathed. "Maybe it's just coincidence."

The idea didn't sit right. He stopped pacing, locking his

eyes on the manuscript. He had to admit, he didn't know what exactly happened on the beach. He needed more information and there was only one place he could get it.

He went to the table and sat down. He restacked the pages and thumbed to where he'd left off. He laid the unread pages in front of him and set the rest to the left, facedown. Given recent developments, he was less sure than ever about claiming *Together, Dead* as his own work. Regardless, he picked up Big Red and took off its cap. Perhaps, he wanted to complete his edit. Perhaps, he needed whatever sense of security gripping Big Red granted him.

Together, Dead

III

Thanks for coming so fast, Mom," said Luke, opening the front door wide.

"What's going on?" she huffed. Her jacket hung haphazardly from her shoulders, revealing the pink kitty-cat sweater beneath. The absurd garment stood in sharp contrast to the dread in her eyes. Rattled, she nearly tripped on the toy fire engine on the floor of the entry as she stepped inside. "You said on the phone it was some kind of emergency." Her octagonal glassed slid down her nose, and when she adjusted them her eyes appeared to bulge all the more.

"Yes, it is," said Luke with apprehension. "I have to go and help Jill at the farm. She's packing this weekend."

His mother sighed, shedding a good deal of the tension in her shoulders. "Oh, Luke. How is <u>that</u> an emergency? Haven't you known for days she was going up there?"

"Well, yeah…" Luke gave the back of his neck an anxious rub.

She dropped her hands to her sides.

"Why didn't you plan ahead? I don't understand this. I'm missing Bridge club."

"I just thought she could handle that stuff and I would stay here with the kids."

"Doesn't she have a whole house to pack up?" She shrugged off her jacket and hung it on a free wall hook by the door then stared at her son, hands on hips. It was the accusatory stance Martha Moore had come to perfect over the years. "Both of her parents passed away and you let her go up there by herself to box all of their worldly possessions? What kind of a husband are you?"

"Come on, Mom. The kids…" Luke ran his hands through his hair and bunched the dirty-blonde mane behind his head. "Maybe I made a mistake." He loudly exhaled.

Martha's register dropped into shame-on-you range. "I thought we raised you better than that."

"Okay, okay, I know I should have gone with her."

"So why the sudden change of heart? Did she call and lay down the law?" Martha grinned at the idea of her son on the hot seat.

"No, I haven't heard from her. It's something else." Luke bent and picked up the toy fire truck by his mother's feet and carried it into the kitchen. He placed it on the island beside a pile of dirty dishes.

"What is it, Luke?" she asked, following at his heels.

"I'm not sure, Mom. We sort of argued last time we spoke. It might be that…"

"Are you guys…" Martha made sure her

grandsons were not near enough to over-hear her words, and whispered, "…having troubles?"

He began clearing some of the dirty dishes from the island and took them to the already half-filled sink. "Troubles, no. We don't really have time to get in trouble."

Martha smirked. "Well, what did you argue about?"

Luke wondered how much his mother really wanted to help or if she simply enjoyed watching him in turmoil. Grudgingly, he said, "Jonathan."

"Her brother? The retarded one?"

Luke rolled his eyes at his mother's bluntness, but on some level, found himself appreciating the cruel nature of her description. "Yeah, I guess I didn't like the idea of her spending the weekend alone with him."

Martha reflected on that for a few seconds then asked, "You don't think he is dangerous, do you?"

Luke paused his dish-clearing. Staring with the plate in his hand, he mulled over the question. "I don't know. He's… he's not well, you know? Her parents could always handle him, but, I don't know."

"You don't have to say it. I understand," she said, raising a stop-sign hand. "When I was your age, people like that weren't extended all the rights and freedoms they get today. Families took care of them, yes, but they weren't allowed to do as they like. Now, when you go to the grocery store, you don't know who you might run into. There are crazies everywhere. Every couple of weeks I read about a murder committed by somebody with—what do they call it—mental health issues, or whatever. It's scary."

"Yes, it is," said Luke. He looked out the window over the sink at his boys rough-housing in the backyard.

"So what does Jill plan to do with him, anyway?" Martha said with half a chuckle that again hinted at some sadistic enjoyment of their difficult situation.

"She wants to put him in a home. I suppose she can now that she was named his legal guardian when the Dunn's died." Luke reached for a towel on the counter and wiped his hands with it. "She's breaking the news to him this weekend."

"This weekend?" Martha moved beside him. "How did he take that news?"

"I have no idea. I haven't heard from her. She's probably still mad."

Martha latched onto his arm. Her eyes adopted a firmness he was not used to seeing in his mother. "What if she's not still mad?"

"Mom?"

She plucked the towel from Luke's grip. "Get your ass in your car and get up there, now. Or do I have to go in your place?"

Luke regarded his mother for a moment and then looked out at the boys again. "Okay, I'll just say goodbye to—"

"No. They'll be fine. You don't have time to waste. Go!"

Luke gaped as the urgency that gripped his mother infected him, too. It set his heart to thumping. He did not say another word, simply snatched his car keys from the island and headed for the door.

The sound of his car door closing brought his sons to the gate in the fence surrounding the backyard. Their grandmother emerged from the house and Luke watched them greet her as he started the engine. He heard their confusion as <u>Nanny</u> tried to brush-off the fact that their father had to leave in such a rush. He backed out of the driveway and Martha shouted, "Call as soon as you get there."

Luke nodded and sped off.

Jill gawked at the knife in the sink. It could not possibly be blood on it. <u>Surely, there is some reasonable explanation</u>, she told herself. Her heart sank when she realised how she would have to get that explanation.

Upstairs, her younger brother (she had not been able to call him her <u>little</u> brother since he was nine) was soaking in a warm bath. He was a grown man with a man's strength and a child's wit. She did not even consider that the blood was his; that he might have accidentally cut himself. The idea simply did not feel right. All she could think of now were worst case scenarios and a husband's warnings.

What would he say if he were here to witness the knife in its revolting puddle? The clucking of "I told you so," came to mind. Jill could almost hear Luke's voice on the stale cellar air. It was not admonishment that she heard, it was another warning. <u>Take it</u>. <u>Hide it</u>. <u>Don't' let Jonathan get his hands on it</u>.

Jill peered at the blade a moment longer then broke out of her trance. "This is ridiculous," she said aloud, shaking her head. "He's your brother. Just ask him."

She walked to the stairs and caught herself tip-toeing as though seeking to avoid detection. He's not dangerous, she thought as she straightened and started to climb. If he's really not dangerous, why do you have to say it? And why is your heart beating so hard, right now?

Jill crested the stairs on the second floor, still tentative. "Jon?" she called. "How's the bath? You need anything?"

She found the bathroom door open and cautiously peeked inside. The only trace of Jonathan was a tub full of brown water. The towel she had set for him remained untouched and a series of foot-sized puddles lead from the tub and out the bathroom door.

"Jon?" She called again. "Do you need some clean clothes?" Or a towel, for God sake?

She continued her search in Jonathan's bedroom. His absence did little to calm her agitation. It made it worse.

In the hallway, she passed her parents' bedroom door and stopped. She still felt like the room was off-limits to her like it had been throughout her youth. There were many unspoken rules in the Dunn household. This was not one of them. "Stay out of our room" had been uttered often, so much so that entering it now gave her pause.

Is it the same for Jonathan? she pondered. Or is it another rule lost on him like washing before dinner and making his bed?

Jill gathered a breath and turned the doorknob.

"Jonathan?" she whispered.

Jill first noticed the hint of Chantilly Lace on the air. It was her mother's favorite perfume. The scent refreshed Jill's grief, but she was instantly distracted by the out-of-place item in the room.

Propped against the four post bed was a red bicycle. She gawked at the odd sight for a moment while several questions formed in her mind, the foremost being, what the hell was it doing here?

Dismissing the no-entry rule of her childhood, Jill walked over to the bike for a closer look. A grungy, white sack hung from its handlebars. Its label was well-worn, but she could make out Kings County and knew instinctively the rest read Herald.

Something shifted on the edge of her consciousness. She should know this bicycle. She searched it from front to back and fixated on the rear wheel. Most of its spokes were broken as if something had been jammed into it while it was spinning. Certainly, that would have resulted in a horrific crash for the rider. Jill's stomach lurched as she considered it. Somehow she got the picture of how the bicycle came to be here.

She could not breathe. She felt the overwhelming urge to call her husband, to tell him he may have been right about Jonathan.

Jill rushed from the master bedroom, sacrificing stealth for haste. She pictured her car phone on the dash of her Honda as she bounced down the stairs. She would call Luke, ask his help. He'll know what to do. Surely he's rehearsed calling the authorities concerning Jonathan's behavior.

The plan stalled on the runway.

Outside, Jill could see the phone through the Honda's windshield. She also saw Jonathan emerging from the barn, wearing only soiled work pants and still wet from the bath. He dragged a shovel behind him as he strode toward her with purpose.

She thought of trying to disarm his volatile mood with a warm smile, and then decided that an aggressive stance may be her only chance to bring him to heel. She attempted to summon their father's voice.

"Jonathan," she grumbled. "You stop right there!"

The only trace of their father presence was in Jonathan's eyes. They were narrow slits of rage.

"No more talk," said Jonathan, still closing in. "I ain't never leaving this farm." His voice was a flat line, bereft of feeling. It belied his actions. He raised the shovel now in both hands. "You ain't, either."

The breath froze in Jill's chest. She could not even scream as Jonathan drew nearer, his untied workboots kicking up dirt. Her own feet started to kick, started wildly galloping for the safety of the Honda. She got there, got the car between them.

Jonathan continued toward her at the same deliberate pace, as though he was in possession of the car keys and he would not be troubled much if she were to get in and locks the doors.

Jill did just that.

She slammed the driver's side door behind her and hit the lock. Flinging herself across the passenger seat, she swatted the other door lock, as well. Jonathan stopped a few feet from the passenger side. Jill did not dare hope that he had broken-off pursuit. His eyes gave no reason to believe it. She snatched the phone receiver off the dash as he raised the shovel over his shoulder.

Her thumbs went to work on the phone, dialing her home number, but when the first shovel-blow struck the windshield, her focus was broken. The second blow landed, webbing cracks throughout the windshield and sprinkling her with tiny splinters of glass. She gathered her voice and screamed.

Her trembling hands dropped the receiver into the foot-well as another blow connected and showered her with chunks of glass. This time, the spade broke all the way through.

Jill instinctively pushed herself away from the dash and continued to push and kick until she found herself in the backseat. Her mind reeled as she tried to find a course of action, but all she could do was scream. In fact, she had not taken a breath that did not come out as a shriek.

Think Jill! For Christ sakes, think! she demanded. He's gonna be in here any second, now. What are you gonna do when he gets in? When he—

It took a second for her to realise that Jonathan had ceased his attack on the windshield. She saw the spade protruding through the glass, jerking back and forth.

It's stuck!

She climbed into the driver's seat, unlocked the door and bolted in the direction of the road. A few yards down the long dirt driveway, she hazarded a peek behind her. Jonathan did not pursue. He was so preoccupied with the jammed shovel that he did not seem to notice her escape.

The blood rushing in her ears was nearly as loud as her feet hitting the dirt. Then the sound of shattering glass outdid them both. When she glanced behind her this time, she ran a little faster. The deepest, darkest dread sent fuel to her legs.

Jonathan had freed his shovel, and he sprinted after her.

Something about the unusual sight of Jonathan running pushed her fear to hysterical levels. This might be the last thing she ever saw.

She heard something else and was shocked that it was her own voice. She screeched the same thing over and over again. "Luke, help me!"

Tears overflowed her eyes and she felt the strength ebbing from her legs. Her body betrayed her. It gave up. Jill turned to steal a glimpse of the madman she used to tow around this very farm in their Radio Flyer wagon. She hoped the sight of him in his murderous pursuit would urge her body to run harder, but

she could not focus on him. The shovel
filled her field vision. It came spinning toward her: spade, handle, spade,
handle, darkness.

Luke slowed down for a sharp turn in the
rural route. He knew the Dunn's driveway
opened nearby to the left, but he always
overshot it, even with Jill in the passenger seat to guide him. Despite the aid
of a midday sun, he still did not trust
himself to find it. The over-growing al-
der brush conspired to keep the place secret, like the Dunn's themselves had conspired to hide their slow-witted son from
the world.

Seemingly from nowhere, a break in the
ditch appeared. Luke turned the car abruptly and aimed it between the encroaching bushes. After the brief nails-on-
chalkboard scrape from branches on either
side, the car poked through on the driveway. Luke eased up the sloping dirt lane-
way and under the arched sign that once
proudly announced arrival to the farm:
DUNN DREAMIN' in rusty wrought iron letters.

For the Dunn's, it meant they had finally realised their dream when they
moved onto the two hundred acre spread.
For Luke, it held an entirely different
meaning. It said the dream was over.
Something had been dormant here, something dark and sinister. It was awake
now, and life would never be the same for
Luke and his family.

His heart was in his throat as he
neared the white clapboard house and ad-

jacent weathered barn. To Luke, the setting was ominous and drear, and yet the
first sight of his Jill would instantly
brighten it. If she emerged from the
house, waving to greet him. If she apologized for not calling. If she smiled and
thanked him for coming to help. Hell, if
she hurried outside to let him have it
for taking so long to get here, the knots
in Luke's stomach would immediately untangle. As he rolled to a stop beside the
farmhouse, his only company was the hard
pulsing in his chest. It pulsed all the
harder when he realised his wife's car
was not here.

Maybe they took a break from packing
and went for ice cream. The idea of the
Dunn siblings sharing a sundae at a sun-
bleached picnic table at the Second Scoop
among a throng of other families would
have normally struck Luke as laughable.
Some dreadful inner voice told him this
was no day for laughter.

He attempted to find reason for Jill's
absentee car. Maybe she parked it behind
the house, out of the searing sun. Maybe
Jon went for a drive. In Luke's suspi-
cious mind, neither of these ideas could
hold water. He considered the look his
mother gave him as he had left home. Her
expression burrowed into his mind like a
tic. The worry on her brow, the fear in
her eyes, he kept seeing it and it revved
his anxiety.

He called before he was even out of the
car. "Jill!"

The sound of his voice deadened against
the two story house.

"Hello, are you in there? Jill?"

The windows revealed nothing but a dim reflection of the yard as Luke approached the doorstep.

"Jill?" he begged again.

When he got no reply, changed his plan. "Jonathan? You here?" The mere mention of his brother-in-law's name tightened the knot in his belly. "I came to give you guys a hand," he said loudly as he reached for the doorknob. "I—" his next fabrication faded to silence. The door was locked.

Shielding his eyes from the beaming sunshine, Luke searched the yard for any sign of the siblings. All he saw was a carpet of weedy dirt leading to the barn. The barn door was ajar. It was only open a foot, but it was wide enough for a person to slide through.

Luke wondered if Jill was inside. Maybe she didn't hear me calling. Maybe she's so busy packing stuff up, she didn't notice the car pull in. Maybe… All his excuses sounded a weak. The only thought he had that seemed to fit right now was the one telling him that he should be very worried and very cautious, too.

He walked toward to the imposing structure. It seemed to grow exponentially taller as he drew nearer and the darkness behind the door deepened with every step he took.

"Jill?" he said when he got there.

"Guys?" came out, little more than a whisper.

He started to call for her again, but choked on her name as he peeled back the barn door to let the daylight play over the yellow bumper of her car.

Why in the world did she park in the barn?

He noticed that the hood was propped open and the _whys_ started to pile up. He made his way to the front of the car, sinking further into the strong grip of the shadow within. In fact, he could not make out any of the engine. He would need a flashlight for that and trying to find one in the darkened barn was a fool's errand.

He rested a hand on what he thought was the fan shroud. Still warm. The engine had been running not that long ago. He yearned for sunlight and he started for the doorway before he became consciously aware he was doing so.

Something on the dirt floor between his feet grabbed his attention. It was the faintest twinkle, a tiny reflection of the outside light. Luke bent down to get a better view.

The pewter letter J that hung from the chain with the rest his wife's keys lay there, scarcely visible. Luke knelt to pick them up. As he did, he heard the shuffle of feet in the dirt behind him. The footfalls sounded with purpose, in rapid succession. Luke barely had the time to plant a knee and begin to turn. He glimpsed only boots, coiled legs. Lightning flooded his vision and darkness followed.

Chapter Ten

J ack walked to the edge of the bluff and looked down. Below him, flames engulfed the retreat. Each burning building a blight on the perfect dark. He watched with indifference. The only thing that interested him was the lake. Blacker than the dark of night. A hole in existence. Moonlight, starlight, even the fire-glow could not escape its hungry pull. Somehow he knew that if he went over the bluff and fell into it he would fall for eternity. He would never reach the bottom.

Grunts came from the woods. Jack turned from the bluff and walked before the leafless tree—his old hangin' tree—to await his guests. Soon a young boy and his grandfather would appear from behind it, and Jack knew what they wanted. They did not care about first drafts or deadlines or whatever might please a publisher. Jack did not, either. In this place, those things had already passed him by. What they wanted was the answer to a question—an answer that Jack did not possess.

The figure emerged from the woods. Jack expected the old man to lead his grandson into the clearing, but as this person got closer, a sickening feeling swept through him. This was not an old man. This was a young man; tall and lean, taking long, determined strides. This was Jonathan Dunn.

Every impulse in Jack's brain told him to flee, but his body betrayed him. He went rigid as Jonathan stopped mere feet from him. He stood within arm's reach—striking distance—perhaps not within Jack's range, but definitely within Jonathan's. He laid his stony stare on Jack. His eyes were shadowy under a thick ridge of brow. His face, narrow, high cheekboned. Jack had already seen this face. He had imagined it with the help of *Together, Dead's* narrative, and now he can scarcely believe how accurate his imagination was, right down to Jonathan's closely cropped brown hair and his filthy work trousers. As Jack continued his silent assessment of his visitor, it occurred to him that he still could not move a muscle and he still had not afforded himself a breath.

Jonathan released a subtle sigh. He appeared almost malnourished, but Jack did not see that as a weakness, rather something else to fear about the murderous young man. Like a rogue timber wolf, Jack reckoned, he ate just enough to stay alive, so he could continue to stalk and continue to kill. The silence stretched between them and soon Jack could smell smoke from the fires below. It tickled some deep nerve ending in his body he no doubt shared with his oldest ancestors. It yelped about the danger associated with detecting smoke in a forest. But, its internal orders to run were overruled. Jack knew if he so much as flinched, this wolf would pounce.

"You ain't figured it out yet..." said Jonathan, finally. An Appalachian twang seasoned his words. The very sound of it struck at Jack's core as though something seized his groin and gave it a hard squeeze. He did not expect that accent for one moment. The manuscript made no mention of it and yet there it was, as much a part of him as his sharp jaw line or his bony knuckles. The accent anchored the young man to this world. It made him real. It made the smoke real and the fire real. And the lake below them, like some kind of gateway to the underworld, it was real too.

"Figured what out...Jonathan?" Jack sputtered.

"How you get the true measure of a man."

Jack tried to speak, but his tongue clung to the roof of his mouth. He answered by shaking his head.

"That's 'cause you're lookin' in the wrong place. You want that old man and his runt boy to tell you. Well, they can't. That's something every man has to decide on his own. You ain't no different. You gotta look to yourself for the answer."

Smoke began to thicken the air and a few sparks glided between them like streamers on the night.

"I made my mind up on that a long time ago," said Jonathan. "Now I know, the true measure of a man don't come in inches and feet or pounds and ounces. It don't even come in battles won and lost. It comes..."

Jack felt the sting of burgeoning tears. If he blinked, they would overflow. He could not take his eyes off Jonathan. He suddenly longed for the nameless grandfather and grandson. They possessed such vacant, empty gazes when they spoke. There was nothing to them and Jack could see that. He could see through them, all the way to the other side. Jonathan Dunn was different. In his eyes, Jack saw volumes and volumes of sinister intelligence. He also saw the reflection of the blaze and wondered if that fire might be coming from within the young man and not from without. He was supposed to be a simple farm boy, but Jack saw no evidence of that.

"...it comes in how he handles fear."

There was an ax in Jonathan's grip. The sight of it sent a shockwave the length of Jack's body, tensing every muscle. He could not comprehend where the ax came from. It just appeared like an extension of Jonathan's arm. Jack eyed the ax's freshly filed bite. The moonlight played over it.

Jonathan went on, "Does he handle fear or does he let it cripple him? Does fear make him stronger or does it get the better of him?" He held up the ax head and inspected its nasty edge. He turned it over, let it dangle at his side and set his stare on Jack again. "I decided a long time ago, I wasn't gonna be a man who lived in fear. I was gonna be a man *to* fear."

Jonathan started forward.

Jack's body suddenly quit its self-imposed paralysis. His muscles all loosened to the point he nearly voided his bowels. He threw himself back from the advancing killer.

Jonathan took the ax in two hands.

Jack retreated as far as the bluff would allow. He peered over the edge at the black void that was Wabasso Lake. To his left, the fire had consumed much of the retreat and now spread through the woods, its appetite insatiable. Jack crouched and turned to Jonathan.

The killer slowly stepped across the clearing. He did not make use of his long strides, rather he took his time. His expression was euphoric. When he blinked, his eyes stayed shut unusually long. It dawned on Jack that he was savouring this moment just like he did when he killed the hired hand.

Jack looked down again and rated the odds of survival should he jump. Across the lake, inland from the forbidden shore, something snagged his attention. A warm light poking through the screen of evergreen. It came from a window. Kubby had denied the building's existence, but there it was, in the exact place Jack had seen it. In that instant, Jack decided if he survived the drop, he would swim there. He would get inside the structure and brace the door against all comers.

Without hazarding another glimpse of Jonathan Dunn or his ax, Jack jumped. He cleared the rock face and the debris skirting the water's edge and he fell toward Wabasso Lake.

He did not stop falling.

Jack lurched upright in his bed and wrapped his arms around himself. Slick with sweat, the touch of the night air on his bare back made him shiver. He scanned the dark cabin for the presence that had been so real. Too real. Only when he was sure he had no uninvited guests, did breathe a sigh. His throat felt sore and he worried that he had screamed in his sleep again.

He heard a noise outside his cabin. His windpipe locked up. A scuffling was followed by a soft thud as someone started to climb his porch steps. He *had* screamed. Now one of his neighbours came to find out why. He looked at the dark pocket where the door stood and waited for his visitor to knock.

The doorknob turned.

A click came next and the door unlatched. A shaft of moonlight appeared, a widening split in the darkness, as the door crept open. Jack could only watch as the blue light grew. A sense of anticipation bloomed in his chest. He breathed deeply and felt a tickle in the bottom of his lungs. His pulse quickened as the unannounced guest came inside.

A silhouette appeared in the doorway. Shadow hid any facial features, but Jack saw the tinge of flame in her shoulder length hair.

He watched without blinking.

She did not speak. She reached for the tails of her night gown and pulled it off over her head.

Jack's lips parted as he watched the moonlight touch the side swell of her breast and the arch of her hip. She came toward him, tantalizingly toward him. He scarcely registered the glittering puddles her bare feet left as she crossed the moonlit floor.

She lowered herself to the cot and Jack detected the scent of the beach, of Lupines and Star Daisies and dew. "I—" he began.

She silenced him with a kiss. He slid an arm around her waist. Tiny rivers trickled down her skin and onto his. He pictured her naked body swimming Wabasso's black waters under midnight stars and the thought of it sent the blood pumping to his pelvis. He pulled her close and as one kiss broke off another connected. She clutched the bed sheet and tore it off.

In one fluid motion, she kicked a leg over him and pinned him down. Chill droplets from her hair sprinkled his chest. He wriggled to get out of the shorts that had become too snug.

She helped to release him and he shuddered as she took him in.

He prayed he wouldn't be too quick. She didn't make it easy. She moved as though she knew exactly what he liked. The way she shifted atop him, the way she planted one hand on the centre of his chest, the way she reached behind her and groped his scrotum with the other, every motion pushed him further to his limit.

He cupped either side of her face and lake water from her hair tracked down his arms. He ran his hands across her chest. Hard nipples pressed against his palms. He pinched them between his fingers. She gave a little moan and ground herself into him, taking him deeper. When he could no longer prevent the rush, he clamped his hands on her hips and his legs went stiff until he was spent.

She became still. Though it was too dark to see, he was certain her eyes fixed on him. She didn't make a sound, not even a breath, but she watched him. Jack ran a finger down her cheek and thought of all the ways things would be different between them from now on. She folded herself atop him. He felt her against his chest, cold and impossibly wet, as though water oozed from her very pores. He sought to warm her with his embrace, to dry her stubborn flesh. Before he had a chance to, she pushed herself off him. Padding to the door, she bent and scooped up her gown.

Jack whispered as she faced the lake and dressed. "Wait. Please."

She turned to him and pressed a finger to her lips: "*Ssshhh.*"

With that, she stepped outside and faded into the night.

Jack lay back in his cot, unable to suppress the flutter in his chest or the grin on his face

From the personal journal of William Jessop:

28 June, 2012.

As it happens, Wabasso Lake is a very well-guarded secret. Almost too well guarded, but not for this tenacious investigator. I did, however, have to beat the bushes for weeks before I got the first real sniff at the retreat or any of its associates. Finally, a literary agent I am friendly with (not Black's) delivered on a phone number. It put me in touch with a man who sat on Wabasso Lake's ownership committee. Adding to the mystique surrounding this story, I pegged this owner as reluctant to go on record. He didn't give me his full name. He called himself Mr. K and insisted I do the same. Maintaining secrecy was high on his list of priorities, but he did give me something no one else had until then.

He granted me an in-person meeting.

His office was located in the city. A ten minute bus ride and a two block hike put me at his doorstep. You might say it was in my own backyard, but the landmarks along the way were all that I found familiar that day. I entered the six story building housing Mr. K's office and made my way into the lobby.

Mr. K emerged from one the adjacent rooms to greet me. I have come to think of this—and I have thought about this encounter many times over the last few days—as quite strange. Usually, the wealthy employ very un-wealthy underlings to receive their guests. He came out of his office alone. In fact, it seemed we were the only two people in the significant set of offices.

He cut an impressive figure. Tall with his long, gelled hair gathered in a ponytail, he kept his thick beard neatly trimmed in straight edges. He wore a dark blue suit and matching tie. My eye ultimately drifted to his rather expensive looking loafers. They shined as though polished mere seconds before.

He shook my hand and welcomed me to join him in his office.

I took a seat in front of his lavish hardwood desk. His high back leather chair was far more luxurious than mine. It left me with the sense that I had approached the crown, though the rest of the room could have been described as barren. Aside from his desk and chairs, the only other furniture was one of those mini-bar carts.

He went directly to it and offered me a drink. I declined and he poured himself two fingers of dark liquor from the lone bottle on the cart. As he did, he said, "I am of Polish descent. My surname, I'm afraid, is a mouthful to some. I ask friends and colleagues, alike, to call me Mr. K. It prevents any awkwardness."

He sat and the leather chair murmured as it took his mass. "I understand you have questions about Wabasso Lake," he said, cutting to the chase.

"Yes, I do." His forthrightness caught me a little off guard.

He set his drink down on the empty desktop and tented his fingers. "I will tell you what I can, but you must understand, I am a member of an ownership committee and as such, I cannot divulge certain facts without the unanimous permission of the board."

"Of course." I held up my pen and notebook to indicate my desire to take notes.

He flashed the briefest smile. "Fire away, Mr. Jessop."

"What is Wabasso Lake, exactly?" I said, following his lead and getting right down to business.

Mr. K gave a faint smirk and took on the air of a man whose time was about to be wasted. He answered in slow, measured words. "It is a private retreat reserved for writers of a *certain* quality who wish to work in solitude. The accommodations are meager and may leave some guests wanting, though the beauty of the lake is beyond comparison."

"Who determines the quality of the writers?" I asked.

"The ownership committee, of course. We weigh the applications of all prospective guests and decide which authors we would extend invitation to."

I scribbled his responses on my notepad without taking an eye off him. "Was Tanner Black an applicant or an invitee?" I asked.

Mr. K pushed his chair back from the desk and crossed his legs. "Ah yes, Mr. Black. How unfortunate. He left us before his time." There was compassion in his tone, but it sounded a little forced.

"There are some who say that his work suffered while he attended Wabasso Lake."

"I have never heard of this," he said with a flick of his hand.

I leaned forward, eager to point out, "He was unable to finish his most recent project. That much is fact."

Mr. K took up the glass and swallowed his drink in one gulp. "*If* Mr. Black had difficulties working at our retreat, I am confident it had nothing to do with the venue. The vast majority of our guests have very productive visits."

"Difficulties were not the norm for him." I flipped through the pages of my notebook, making it seem as though I had plenty of evidence to corroborate my claims. "He had an impressive track record of delivering novels to market nearly every year for the past thirty years."

Mr. K took no notice of my ruse. He raised his empty glass in one hand and looked through it. "Mr. Jessop, to suffer decline is to be human. Age affects us all. Perhaps you lit upon the effect it had on Mr. Black."

I paused. I had a follow up question in the chamber, but I was unable to pull the trigger. My mouth started to water. I swallowed and felt the contents of my stomach do a barrel roll. Of all the times for nausea to strike, during an important interview had to be the worst. It had never happened to me before. I took a deep breath, but it did nothing to refresh me.

Mr. K took the opening to expand on his point. "At Wabasso, great pains are taken to ensure the needs of every writer are met and exceeded. We create the ideal work environment. There simply are no distractions. Only writers are permitted so every guest has a heightened appreciation for privacy." He set his feet on top of the desk and crossed his legs at the ankles. I noticed he didn't wear socks in those expensive loafers. He continued his shameless promotion of the retreat. I wanted so much to brace him, to put him on the hot seat, instead all I could think about was the freshness of the mayonnaise in the tuna salad I had for lunch. Finally, he said something that jogged my focus. "…the ownership committee is very particular in this regard."

"Who is on the ownership committee, exactly?" I managed to ask.

Mr. K set his glass down, perhaps a tad more heavily than intended. The ensuing knock reverberated in the sparse room. "I am not at liberty to name the committee members. Just know that we are great supporters of the literary arts," he said. He perked up as an idea occurred to him. "Mr. Jessop, why don't you satisfy your curiosity by visiting the lake? That is against our usual practice, but I'll make an exception in your case. I'm certain once you see it you will find that it is a perfectly fine place to work. I might add that you should be careful while driving there. There are quite a lot of moose in the area and the beasts do tend to roam the roadways." He winced as though taking note of my appearance for the first time in our conversation. "If I may say, Mr. Jessop, you don't appear to be feeling all that well."

The sweat beading on my brow gave credence to his observation.

His expression went blank.

"I-I apologize, but I'm afraid I'll have to cut our interview short." With that feeble statement, I got up to leave.

I hurried out through the lobby, and with some effort, made it to the trash barrel at the street corner before I vomited.

Chapter Eleven

S unlight flooded the cabin and Jack's eyes peeled open. He sat at the desk, his face atop it. Saliva puddled under his cheek. He raised his head and went to wipe at his mouth when he realised a few of the manuscript pages were stuck to his hand. He sat up and tried to smooth out the crumpled sheets. He arranged them back in proper order and stacked them with the others.

From the wall over his desk, Brian and Thomas looked down on him. In the picture, they grudgingly smiled, squinting in the sunlight. For the first time Jack noticed that the boys' expressions could be interpreted another way. Perhaps they weren't a couple of kids grinning in the sun. Perhaps they were wincing like they were hurting. Or perhaps there was pity in their expressions—pity for the man taking the picture. Jack took the photograph down and traced a finger over the boys' faces.

What am I doing here? Why am I in this strange place, getting caught up in story stealing and wild conspiracy theories? I should be home. I should be with my boys.

Jack unfolded the crease in the photograph to reveal the blonde women he kept tucked out of sight. He eyed the root cause of his financial woes and the ultimate reason for his desperate trip to Wabasso Lake. Unlike her sons, she didn't smile for the picture. Her mouth was a thin line, an expression she had perfected. Through happiness and sorrow, sickness and in health, that expression hadn't faltered often. Age formed lines around it. She grew with it. Or it grew with her. Jack wondered if she wore it as she drove the boys away from their home for the last time. Maybe she had smiled. He didn't know. She didn't bother to look back.

He folded her out sight. Once he had Brian and Thomas tacked on the wall again, he sat back and let his gaze fall to the manuscript. He remembered reading about Luke's arrival at the Dunn farm and discovering his wife's car in the barn. Jack figured he had fallen asleep after that. He turned through the pages to where he'd left off.

Nevertheless, Jack didn't find anything in his reading that would explain how Kubby was able to quote the manuscript so accurately. Maybe it was a misunderstanding. Maybe he was hearing things.

"What the hell is a draft horse, anyway?" he said aloud. As he put the strange occurrence behind him, he glanced down at the manuscript. There at the top of the page, written in Big Red's bright ink were the letters,

DUNDREMN

Jack stood up and stepped away from the table. He rubbed his face with both hands before returning to the unfamiliar handwriting. "Oh shit," he breathed as he examined the foreign word.

He had no idea what it meant. It wasn't English or any language he recognized, and it appeared that someone wrote it with their wrong hand or with their eyes closed or...

Like I wrote it when I was asleep.

"Shit." He dropped himself onto the cot. "*If* I wrote that... *If*..." He buried his face in his hands and groaned as an idea took hold. If he indeed wrote that word, without any recollection or even understanding of its significance, it meant the situation had sunk to a new level. It meant this story had dug its way into his psyche like a tick into a dog's hide. It already had him seeing things and hearing things, and now it played on his subconscious. He pictured a bloated white worm, working itself deep into his grey tissue, tunneling as he slept, dropping insane ideas as it went.

Something hit the window. Jack yelped as the pane violently rattled. He sprang to his feet to assess the damage. Another object struck the glass as Jack arrived at the window and he shielded his face. Crouching, he attempted to catch a glimpse of the assailant.

His mind immediately conjured images of the Warren and Ralph. He wondered if they had given up on the subtleties of practical jokes and resorted to simply pelting his cabin with rocks as a means to irk him. He would not have been surprised to see them on his path, cradling armfuls of stones, yukking-it-up, as they readied another volley.

When Jack stole a look outside, he didn't find a pair of immature authors, though what he did see surprised him all the more. He caught the cardinal's approach. The little red bird fanned its wings wide and slammed feet-first into the window. Its tiny black talons scratched at the glass. Its wings batted away. As fast as it came, it withdrew, finding a perch on a nearby pine and screeching a warning.

Dumbstruck, Jack's mouth fell open.

Another screech issued. Another swoop attack followed.

Jack jerked back from the window as the bird slapped and scraped at the glass. So violent was its attack, he fully expected the bird would kill itself if it continued. He considered opening the window for it. If the blasted thing wanted in the cabin so badly, he didn't see the harm. As the bird voiced another threat from the pine tree, Jack got the picture. He reached for the wall switch and turned on the light.

The cardinal fell silent.

Several peaceful seconds passed. Satisfied there would be no further attacks on his cabin, Jack sat down on the edge of the cot. From there he could see the bird, now darting about in search of other points of interest.

Jack was glad he could help to sort the situation out. He only wished all problems were so easy to solve. He eyed the manuscript on the table.

At the very least, he thought, *I should take a step back from the thing. It has me acting like damned fool.* He considered his behavior at Frasier's send-off and shook his head. *Fine, it's settled, I'll take a break from it. I have a lot of apologies to give and a lot of amends to make. Better get started.*

Jack bounced down the steps and hurried onto the path leading from his cabin. The pungent scents of Wabasso's greenery met him. A warm breeze fanned the rich aromas over him as he took the path. He was instantly refreshed. He supposed he owed the sensation to his decision to distance himself from *Together, Dead* for a while. He could already feel the tension bleeding from his muscles, and once he made his apologies for last night's regrettable behavior, he would feel even better. That, coupled with a few good meals and some solid sleep, would have him set to rights in no time.

After a brief pit-stop at the shower house, he would visit the mess hall. If he could apologize to the other guests as a group, he figured it would be marginally less awkward than begging their forgiveness individually. With any luck, he would catch Frasier before he left for New York. Frasier deserved the bulk of the apology. After all, it was his party that Jack ruined.

Jack had picked up steam, breaking into a jog, when he saw a figure walking ahead on the path. He started to yell a greeting, but his voice stuck to his throat. He immediately doubted he would get a response. He didn't the last time he greeted the man in the red shirt. The mere sight of him was enough to make Jack's knees lock and skid him to a stop. This time, he was close enough to see the man's shirt. It was not only red, but it was plaid.

A chill formed in his tail bone and marched to the nape of his neck. Initially, he was quite certain he hadn't woken in his cabin this morning. He had to be sleeping. This had to be a dream, because he could have sworn he saw Jonathan Dunn round the bend in the trail and disappear.

He found his voice then. "H-hey," sputtered out of him. "Wait. I want to talk to you."

Despite the inner warnings from his deepest bowels to keep his distance, he pursued. He passed the bend and the trail evened out before him. It was empty. Whoever wore that red plaid shirt—and Jack still held a hope it wasn't Jonathan Dunn—had managed to pull another disappearing act. The trail branched off to Jack's left. Cabin Five—Frasier's cabin—was down there, tucked secretly amid the trees. A low hanging branch swayed as though someone had just pushed it aside while running past. That was enough evidence for Jack, and seconds later, he pushed it aside as well.

Cabin Five came into view a few yards down the trail. Similar to Jack's cabin, only more given to the shadow of its taller, more oppressive neighbouring trees. No one appeared to be home. Jack could see nothing in the windows, but the sun dappled day reflecting back at him.

His mind still played catch-up with his body. He refused to accept that he had followed Jonathan Dunn. It could have been anyone. Hell, it could have been Frasier out for one final lakeside jog before returning home. That made sense. A two-bit character springing to life from the pages of a stolen manuscript simply did not. Jack knew this. He clung to it, and yet, his skin broke an icy sweat.

He leapt up the porch steps and knocked on the door. It sounded oddly hollow.

"Frasier, are you in there?" Jack called.

He prayed his neighbour would come to the door, towel around his neck, perspiration dotting his brow, fresh from a jog in his favorite plaid shirt. Perhaps a pair of headphones would explain why he hadn't heard Jack's greeting on the trail. He knocked again.

The door creaked open a few inches, as he rapped.

A spoiled fruit stench escaped the cabin. Jack recoiled and waved a hand in front of his nose. He called for Frasier through the opening and as he did, caught sight of the blood inside. His jaw went slack, his pulse quickened. He pushed the door open wide.

All the furniture had been pushed to one side of the cabin, the desk overturned. The shelving unit had been tossed atop the cot. It all seemed to be moved to make room for a solitary wooden chair in the centre of the floor. A lake of congealing blood around it. Jack covered his mouth and nearly doubled over as the trash can smell of rot assaulted him again. It left a sour film on his tongue.

Despite the flash of nausea, he stepped inside, careful not to set foot in the pool of gore. The buzzing of black flies overpowered him once he was out of the rustling summer breeze. Dozens of flies circled the chair, landing for split seconds at a time before lifting off again. Jack wondered how he didn't hear their dizzying drone from outside. He felt the bubbling promise of vomit rise from his core, but he forced himself to look more closely at the chair. Certainly, he would need to describe the ghastly scene to the authorities at some point.

Scraps of rope hung loosely from the chair. Some lay in the blood around its legs. More clung to one of the wooden arms. The other arm was broken apart. Jack bent to inspect the busted arm. It was splintered where it joined with the chair back, like it sustained a heavy blow.

Fresh panic flooded his chest. The image of Jonathan Dunn flashed through Jack's mind. He pictured him in this very cabin. He saw him swinging an ax downward, blade shearing flesh and bone and busting through the arm of the chair. Jack staggered backward, too weak to stand. He slammed into the wall behind him and slid to the floor.

Then he saw the rest of the blood. It had sprayed on the front wall and up across the ceiling. Jonathan's victim had flailed his severed appendage madly in his final moments. The poor bastard had fought to get away and only succeeded in painting the walls with his own lifeblood.

Who was the victim?

The question marked the return of Jack's rationale, followed by a succession of other thoughts. *Where is the body?*

I need to get help.

Kubby needs to see this.

He needs to call the police and evacuate the retreat.

The final thought had Jack kicking to get to his feet and hit the trail running.

Where is Kate?

"I just saw her at breakfast like ten minutes ago," Kubby said, his face awash in confusion. "What's going on, Jack?"

Jack bent over and sucked wind, having sprinted to the office as fast as his legs could carry him. He spoke in short bursts between breaths. "You're sure...she's okay?"

"Yeah. Are *you*?"

Jack fanned the air, gesturing for Kubby to come with him. "No...I need help...Cabin Five."

"Frasier's cabin?" Kubby walked out from behind the front desk.

"I think something...happened to him."

"I can't see how, Jack," Kubby said. "He left Wabasso this morning. I personally saw him off."

With his hands on his knees, Jack articulated the scene as best he could. "There's blood. Lots."

"*Blood?*" Kubby stopped in his tracks, his jaw unhinged.

"Yes, lots."

"What the hell is going on with you now, Bishop?" Bellowed a voice behind Jack. He turned in time to see Warren enter the office, Ralph at his heels. "We saw you running across the retreat like a mad man."

Jack stood straight, still chasing down his breath. "Something happened in Cabin Five."

"What were you doing in there?" Ralph asked, placing hands on his broad hips.

Jack ignored him. "There's a lot of blood on the floor. There must have been an accident or something. I don't know, but somebody could be seriously hurt...or worse."

"Blood?" Warren said dismissively. "What do you know

about this Kubanowski?"

"Nothing," Kubby said. His face tensed with determination. "But, I'm gonna check it out."

Ralph gave a disapproving shake of his head. "Frasier probably got a paper cut or the like."

"I said it was *lots* of blood," Jack spat.

"Maybe we should have a gander at this, too," Warren said without much interest.

"Yes, fine," Jack said pushing between them and heading out the door. "Let's just go. Hurry!" He broke into a run toward the guest cabins. He looked back and found Kubby keeping pace behind him, his bare feet pounding the ground. Warren and Ralph ambled after them with little urgency.

"We'll have to call the police. How long does it take them to get here?" Jack said.

"I don't know, man. I never had to call them before." Kubby replied.

"Is there anything here if we need to arm ourselves...for protection?"

"*Weapons?* No way, hombre. I've never held a weapon in my life. I'm not gonna start now. I'm a pacifist."

"You might be changing that policy after you see this."

They passed the beach and a few seconds later, the mess hall. They hit the path leading to the cabins and Jack glanced down the trail that went to Cabin Two. Kubby noticed and said, "Seriously, Jack, I just saw her. But, we can stop in and check on her, if you need to. I'd say this qualifies as an emergency."

Jack considered Kate's late night visit. He decided it would be best if their next conversation was a private one. "I'll go to see her after," he said. "Did you see Pierre this morning?"

"Umm, no, I haven't seen him since last night."

"Did you actually see Frasier leave?" Jack huffed. His wind failed him again. His breaths no longer refreshed his burning lungs.

Kubby mulled this for a few seconds. "Well, I saw him

head toward his car with his bags. I didn't really see him get in and drive off."

They turned toward Cabin Five without slowing down. Jack wondered if Kubby's bare feet found all the little rocks and twigs his tennis shoes had. If they did, Kubby didn't show any sign of discomfort. He stomped the terrain every bit as hard as Jack did.

The cabin came into view and Jack abruptly stopped. Something was different. The cabin door was closed. Kubby nearly piled into Jack. He took a cue from Jack and went portrait-still. "What?" he whispered.

"I thought I left the door open," Jack said as softly as he could. Starving for air, he could hardly control his voice. "I'm pretty sure I left it open."

Kubby's brow furrowed.

"Somebody might be in there," Jack said.

The caretaker's eyes widened and he turned them toward the cabin.

Jack started forward. He paused and listened for any indication of a presence inside—a footstep on the wooden floor, the creak of old furniture, the squeak of the metal cot. Kubby seemed to be listening intently, too. He had tucked his hair behind his ears as if to afford himself an advantage. Their eyes met. Jack tilted his head toward the door. Kubby nodded.

They started up the steps.

Jack wished he was armed with something—even an ax of his own—and he wondered if Kubby had second thoughts about his pacifist's lifestyle. They climbed the stairs and one of the steps whined. Jack winced. If there was someone inside, by now, he knew *they* were outside.

They gathered at the front door, shoulder to shoulder. Kubby's expression told Jack that he had his back no matter what they found inside. Jack hoped Kubby read the same thing in his eyes. Unblinking, they nodded, faced forward and bent slightly at the knees in readiness for anything. Jack raised his hand to the doorknob. His fingers trembled. He wrapped them around the knob, turned it and threw the door open.

Jack stepped inside. His mouth fell open. He brought his hands to his face and groaned into them. "No, no, no."

The caretaker looked around the cabin and turned his bewilderment on Jack.

Jack opened his eyes and scanned the interior of the perfectly tidy cabin. The table stood under the left window, the chair pushed under it, the shelves set neatly adjacent. The cot rested against the other wall, made with military precision. And the floor—the sight of it made Jack groan again—was spotless. No blood pooled at its centre. Not a single drop. The walls and ceiling were the pristine white of freshly fallen snow.

"It wasn't like this," Jack said, getting to his feet. He went to the middle of the room and felt the floor where, only minutes ago, the bloody chair stood. "There was a huge puddle of blood." Jack went to the table and pulled out the chair. "And, this was broken." He peered at Kubby, pleadingly.

"It looks okay, now," Kubby said tentatively. "And, there's no blood in here. None that I can really see, anyway." He stepped inside and perused the space. His gaze met with Jack's and he must have seen the desperation in his eyes, because he added, "But, that's good. No blood is a good thing, right? That means nobody got hurt. There's no emergency. Crisis averted."

Jack turned away, his eyes bulging and red rimmed.

"Well, it would appear you've done it again, Bishop" Warren said, poking his head in the doorway. "I don't think we've ever had anyone at Wabasso do crazy half as well as you." He smiled in smug satisfaction.

"Okay, Warren, it's really no big deal," Kubby said. "Jack was just concerned about our safety is all. We should be glad he's watching out for us."

Warren laughed and shook his head. He and Ralph crowded into the cabin and began their own appraisal of its contents.

"I was in here not ten minutes ago, and all the furniture was over here," Jack said, waving his hand. "That chair was in the middle of the floor with blood all around it. I saw it! Now there could be someone very dangerous still here at Wabasso so we—"

Warren scoffed, "Oh Bishop, don't you get enough jollies writing your foolish drivel? Do you really need to invent, what did you call them, *real life terrors* to chase around, as well?" He loosed a chuckle.

Jack looked at Kubby and Ralph then back to Warren. He seemed to be enjoying this latest embarrassment far more than the others. Too much, actually—like he had some personal interest in this outcome. The revelation hit Jack like a shot in the chest. He gaped at Warren. "It was you..."

"I beg your pardon," Warren said, indignantly.

Jack pointed a finger inches from Warren's face. "You did this. You set this up—left the blood here for me to find and then you got rid of it before I could bring witnesses."

"That's absurd." Warren turned away from the accusations, making his way toward the door.

"You must have had help, but you did this!" Jack crossed the floor in two strides and grabbed Warren by the collar. "Where's your friend?" he roared as he worked a hand toward Warren's throat. "Where's your friend in the red shirt? It's Frasier, isn't it? He's still here."

"Let go of me!" Warren struck at Jack, but his every attempt break loose failed.

Kubby and Ralph seized Jack by either arm and pulled him back, only to have Jack drag Warren along, too.

"You're fucking with me!" Jack yelled. "You've been fucking with me since I got here!"

"Let go. Let go. I'm...cho...king," Warren pleaded, his voice a dry rasp.

"Admit it, Warren! Admit it, you bastard!"

"Please Jack," Kubby yelled. "Take it easy."

The sounds of struggle mingled together. Feet thundered on the floor, voices flared, Warren wheezed and gagged, but one voice cut through it all. "Jack!"

The men froze, and those who were able, turned toward the door where Kate Hargrove stood, red faced, her hands balled into fists. On sight of her, Jack released Warren who fell to his knees, coughing. The others let go of Jack. Ralph bent to assist his friend. Jack could almost feel heat in Kate's stare. He dropped his gaze shamefully to the floor. Kubby looked at them both and offered a shrug.

"Well? What do you have to say for yourself?" Kate gazed skyward as though she couldn't bring herself to look at Jack. "I mean, you lost your mind at the bonfire last night, and this morning, I find you trying to *kill* Warren? Are you some kind of loose cannon, or what?"

Jack sat on the steps to his cabin, while Kate paced in front of him. Something in the way she folded her arms and the straightness of her posture reminded him of the stern spinster of a teacher he had in fourth grade. The only thing missing was a yardstick to crack him over the knuckles with.

"I don't know. I'm sorry," was all Jack could manage.

"You were *crazy*. Your eyes rolled back in your head like a fucking shark. Jesus, two grown men couldn't drag you off him. What on earth is going on with you?"

Jack simply shook his head and stared at the ground, his feet, anything but her eyes. "I'm sorry, Kate."

"I know. You said that already. How about telling me what happened in that cabin?"

"Warren, he just got to me. He talks too much. You know that." Jack found he kept turning his palms up as he spoke. He folded his hands on his lap to stop the nervous tick. If Kate had even the most basic training in detecting dishonesty, he figured she would have known he was hiding something.

"Did it have anything to do with last night?"

"Maybe." *But, what part of last night are we talking about?* he thought. *The mishap on the beach or your late night visit?*

He took a deep breath in hopes of quelling the rebellion in his stomach. When he saw the blood in Cabin Five, all over the floor and up the walls, he felt the bile rise in his throat. Now he felt sicker still. The possibility that the gruesome scene he discovered was some sort of psychotic delusion meant he *was* sick. It was a notion he had trouble facing. Instead, he pushed the conversation elsewhere.

"I had a pretty disturbing dream last night," he said to the ground. "I guess it shook me up a little. And you know the other thing that might have my head spinning today." When he raised his head, Kate had stopped pacing and intently regarded him. He felt the corner of his mouth start to twitch. Regardless of how frightening the dream may have been, he knew it didn't lead him to assault Warren, but it was easier terrain to negotiate than what he really saw in Cabin Five. He gave her the choice: *shall we discuss the mania that comes with life at Wabasso or should we confess the feelings we have for each other?*

"Tell me about your dream," she said.

Jack tried to mask his disappointment. Clearly, she wasn't ready to face what had happened between them. He did his best to go along with the diversion. "I can't remember much about the dream, just that the retreat was burning. The fire consumed everything and spread into the woods, coming my way. And the lake…it wasn't there. It was like a deep hole in the Earth or something."

Kate's glare softened and she turned it toward the surrounding trees. "Umm, did *everything* burn in your dream, like, all of Wabasso?"

"Yes."

She scratched the back of her neck, still scanning the distance. "Was there anyone else in the dream with you? Did you see anyone you might have known?"

"As a matter of fact, I did." The severity in Kate's expression put Jack off guard. It became plain to him that she was not simply asking to avoid talk of other issues. She needed to know about his dream. He indulged. "It was really kind of strange, Kate. I met one of the characters from my manuscript."

"Did this character speak to you?"

"Yes. He did."

She stared at him. Now Jack wondered, if he was capable of discerning subtleties in body language, what he might have gleaned from Kate's. Tension seemed to have bunched the muscles in her shoulders. She stopped blinking altogether.

"What did he say?" Her voice was barely above a whisper.

He said that fear is the only way to get the true measure of a man, he thought. Saying that to Kate would only bring on more questions. If he answered those questions honestly, he might admit he had stolen another's story. He might say that the guilt of stealing said story led him to see things that weren't really there. Jack wasn't ready to face any of this.

Jack shrugged. "I...I can't remember what he said."

Kate's heavy stare lingered a moment longer before she cracked a tentative smile and nodded. "Just as well," she said. "It's probably not important. What is important is what's troubling you. And I know all about it, Jack. It's that *story*."

Jack's limbs went numb. He felt see-through, like Kate could learn all of his secrets in an instant. She could read what was in his head, in his heart. She knew a great deal already. For Jack, an uncomfortable amount. *What story does she mean?* He thought. *The story I came here to write or the one I stole?*

"What story?" he said, his voice desert-dry.

"The story you're writing, of course," she said. "You're totally obsessed with it."

His breath rattled out of his chest.

Kate sat beside him on the step and wrapped her arms around her knees. "You know, I've seen this before. I saw it in my ex-husband many times. He used to lock himself in his office and work on his drafts, day and night. He ignored everything else. Pretty soon, he *forgot* about everything else. He forgot how to act around people, how to be a friend, how to be a husband. All that mattered was his work. Today, that's all he has, and I feel sorry for him. It's a shame it comes to that sometimes. I mean, it happened to you, didn't it? That's why she left you, right?"

Jack envisioned the silver van carry his family away. He turned away from Kate so she wouldn't see his eyes glisten over.

Kate brought a hand to her mouth. "Shit. I'm sorry. I shouldn't have…I overstepped."

He waved her apology off. "It's okay. It's in the past," he said, but his head hung a little lower as he did.

She turned toward him and her hair tumbled over her shoulder. "I just want to help you. Jack, you're still new at this. You didn't know where to draw the line—where to build fences between your work and your life. That's a hard one for a writer to figure out. I mean, we can take our work with us wherever we go. It's not like we punch-out at five o'clock and leave it behind at an office. It's always there, wherever there's a laptop or a pen and paper. We can devote as much time as we want to planning our stories. I can't tell you how many times a girlfriend has been talking to me over coffee, and in my head, I'm somewhere else—deciding what will break my character's heart next time around. I know as well as anyone, it's hard to find a healthy balance. It really is."

She put her arm around him and gave his shoulder a squeeze. "I see you struggling, and I don't like it. You're a good man, Jack, but you're getting in way too deep. When was the last time you ate something?" She looked down at his wrinkled and stained shirt. "Or showered? Or put on clean clothes?"

Jack shook his head slowly. *How could I disagree?*

"Those are all warning signs. You have to recognize them before you go too far—before you do something worse than choke the life out of Warren Hellickson."

Jack laughed softly, and as he did, felt his whole body loosen a little.

"So, here's what I propose." Kate stood up and folded her arms across her chest again in her take-charge sort of way. "I will go to the mess and make you something to eat. While I'm doing that, you take a shower and change into something clean. After you eat, you're going to come with me for a paddle in the canoe and we're just going to chill out for a while."

"Chill out?" Jack's gaze dropped to the dirt. "I'm not sure I know how anymore."

"Just follow my lead." Kate held out her hand. "You're not working today. You're not reading or editing and *definitely* not writing. You're taking the day off, even if I have to force you at gunpoint."

"Since you put it that way." Jack took her hand.

She playfully groaned as she pulled him to his feet.

Jack gave her the most sincere smile he could come up with. It still felt fake.

Kate waited outside while Jack got his shaving kit and a change of clothes from his cabin, before starting toward the shower house together. It occurred to Jack that Kate may have been escorting him to make sure he didn't wander off to Warren's cabin to renew hostilities.

As they walked, Kate offered a smile. Jack wondered if he really could follow her good-intentioned advice. Could he take a day off from story stealing, from seeing things, from the steadily building dread deep in his bones? If so, Kate had given him the finest gift he could ask for. He could push all that stuff aside and for one day, forget about publishers and plagiarism and Jonathan Dunn. Though, even as he made a concerted effort to clear the murderous farm boy from his mind, he pictured the man in the red shirt again.

Who is he?

What if Warren really had nothing to do with what I saw in Cabin Five?

Jack exhaled as though he urgently had to relieve pressure in his chest before he reached the bursting point. Kate patted his back. He tried to smile, but his face felt frozen. *What if the manuscript is somehow becoming reality?*

Kate stopped. "Meet me in the mess in fifteen?" she said.

They had reached the shower house. Jack snapped out of his daze and registered his surroundings. "Sure."

"It's going to be okay, Jack." Kate gave his arm a reassuring squeeze.

Somehow, Jack didn't think so in the face of this latest revelation. The bloody chair in Cabin Five was straight out of a scene from *Together, Dead*. Then he considered the most troubling of all. *Did I actually see Jonathan Dunn on the trail—a living, breathing person who stepped from the pages of the manuscript—a character from a horror story made flesh?*

"You'll feel better after you eat something," Kate said, taking a step away. "Go ahead, get cleaned up."

"Kate," Jack said. "Do you remember the day I got here, you told me something about Wabasso—something I didn't really understand?"

She squinted as she tried to pin it down.

"You said something about Wabasso giving people what they need most."

"Oh, yes." Kate beamed as they touched on her favorite conversation topic.

"What did you mean by that, exactly?"

"Oh, just that Wabasso can...I don't know." She searched the surrounding trees and shrubbery for the right words. The warm breeze tickled the blossoms around them. Nearby a crow cackled. "It can...*inspire* you to do great things, if you listen closely to what it's saying."

Jack glanced back the way they had come. Down there, in his cabin, a bundle of pages gave him all the inspiration he could handle. He turned back to Kate. "What if you don't like what it has to say?"

Chapter Twelve

Jack pressed his forehead against the wall tiles and let the steaming water from the showerhead run down his back. He had intended to take a quick rinse to freshen up, though the heat working on his muscles convinced him to linger under the deluge. He had turned the hot water up twice, already. There was no hurry. He had the place to himself.

The large shower room housed eight stalls, finished in stark white subway tile, floor, walls and ceiling. A single drain in the centre of the sloped floor gurgled loudly as it swallowed the run off. Poor ventilation allowed Jack's hot shower to produce a palpable fog. In its midst he felt cut off from the outside world and was thankful for it. Kate likely had lunch ready for him by now, but that could wait. He needed a few minutes to lick his wounds. She meant well, but she hadn't spared his feelings outside his cabin. She was downright blunt. She was also downright wrong.

Well, mostly wrong. Working too hard on his manuscript wasn't to blame for his erratic behavior. He hadn't stormed out of Frasier's party so he could get back to his cabin to resume his work. He didn't shut himself in there, chasing after a deadline all hours of the day and night, forgoing meals. *But, there was one thing she was right about.* Jack raised his face to the showerhead and he heard Kate's scathing voice again: *That's why she left you, right?*

That part was true. Or at least that's what *she* said time and time again in the days leading up to her departure. She had said a lot of things. *You never have time for us. You never help out anymore. You're not really here. This isn't working.*

Jack wondered if their marriage was ever meant to work. He considered himself the easy going, take-it-as-it-comes sort. She was anything but. He was born to a pair of mid-level corporate executives. She was from the typical broken home— mother who drank, father who drank and then disappeared. She had a vision of the ideal family life—the opposite of the one she grew up in—and she would make it happen for her kids or die trying, killing her husband in the process.

He saw the first signs of foreboding doom when real life started deviating from the path she mapped out. He had an exciting new hobby—one that could lead to an exciting new career. Around the same time, she discovered a new hobby of her own: bitching. Initially, she displayed a window dressing of support for her husband in front of family and friends. Though, behind closed doors the message was quite different: *Go back to your day job.*

That's why she left you, right?

Jack turned off the water. He stood dripping for a few moments, surveying the sodden bandage around his knee and the now very colourful bruise on his hip. Plumb-purple at the center, pea-green on the edges. His near-fall from the bluff felt like a distant memory, though both wounds were fresh enough to hurt when prodded. He collected his small bottle of body wash from the soap dish and made his way out of the shower area.

The air in the locker room was a good deal cooler and he shivered upon entry. He grabbed his towel off its wall hook and began drying his hair. Half a dozen lockers lined the wall of the long, windowless room. Across from him a cheap countertop cradled two sinks. Over them hung a large mirror, a crack running through one end like the limb of a tree. Three toilet stalls grouped at the other end of the room. He had developed a preference for the middle stall—the others had doors that either didn't lock or even close completely.

Jack dried off then tied the towel around his waist. He went to the left side sink where his shaving kit waited. He gave his reflection a passing glance as he reached for the travel sized shaving foam. What he saw in the mirror forced a double take. At first, he thought he glimpsed his father's face. Then he wished he did. Dark, bloated sacks underlined his eyes. His lips were thin, his brow like corduroy. The few strands of grey he'd kept as a rather proud sign of maturity had multiplied and spread throughout the rest of his hair. No pride to be seen.

The same white tile as the shower covered the floor of the locker area. The dingy walls were mint green. The décor coupled with unflattering lighting gave everything in the room a brassy tint. Jack's skinned appeared jaundiced. He looked down at his hands then back to his reflection.

Something—a mere smudge in his periphery—caught his eye and threatened to stop his heart cold. Bright red blood could not be missed. Jack slowly turned to his right, his gaze drifting across the cracked mirror and down to the other sink. He saw one red teardrop on the rim of the white basin, and then another, and another. Streaks down the insides of the bowl gathered in a ruby pool at the bottom.

A knife.

His body went taught. His shoulders remained square, as he had to force himself to turn toward the gore. He made himself regard the knife, blade a quarter submerged, handle exposed. He felt the room shift and he grabbed the edge of the counter to steady himself. He didn't need to inspect the knife. He knew the handle would be wooden. He knew it would be black. The blade would be long, serrated, but he had to make sure.

Make sure it is Jonathan Dunn's knife, he told himself.

Make sure you have gone completely insane.

He stared at the knife.

His gaze lingered on the sink. He found himself willing the knife and the blood to disappear. Surely, they would. Like all psychotic delusions, this one had a shelf life. He waited for it to expire. When it didn't, he turned back to his reflection. His weather-beaten face peered back. He didn't know which sight was worse, and in an instant, the question no longer mattered.

Someone walked behind him.

A blur moved through the mirror's reflection. Jack saw nothing more, but he knew it was a man. He could feel his presence. He whipped his body around. The locker area was empty, but he wasn't alone. Whoever was in there with him couldn't have left. He would have had to pass by Jack to get to the door. That left only the shower room.

"I know you're in there—." Jack caught himself before he said *Warren* and instead said, "—asshole!" *After all*, he thought, *it could be Frasier. Or Pierre. Hell, it could be any of them.*

He cinched his towel and started for the showers, moving slowly, ears tuned to his surroundings. The fog in the room hung on the air like mustard gas. It obscured the other side of the room. The water going down the floor drain had slowed to a drip and it gave a persistent *gulk, gulk, gulk*. The fog made the sound very close, like it was in Jack's ears. He stepped inside.

"I got you cornered," he said as he went deeper into the haze.

The intruder didn't answer. He stopped. Clad only in a towel, he stood over the drain and peered at the corner of the room where the mist was thickest. "You may as well come out."

Silence returned, broken only by the *gulk* of the drain. Jack took a baby step forward, fearing someone waited for him in the shadow, poised to strike.

Somewhere behind him footsteps slapped the floor. A heavy thump followed as the shower house door flew open. Jack turned and raced to the locker area. He arrived in time to see the door fall closed again. He hurried to it and pushed it wide. Daylight stung his eyes. Squinting, he battled it as he tried to locate the intruder. He skipped down the steps and searched around the corner of the shower house. He scoured the bushes alongside the building for half a dozen yards before giving up the hopeless chase. There were too many places to hide—bushes, trees, and the neighbouring mess hall.

Jack's nerves threatened to run wild as he stood there, helplessly, in his towel. He felt eyes on him. It prompted a quick return to the shower house. The soles of his feet were now filmed with dirt and pine needles. He muttered curses as he went to retrieve his body wash so he could clean his feet. He reached the sinks and stopped in his tracks.

The knife was gone.

The blood was gone.

Every drop.

Jack stood motionless and prayed for sanity. He prayed that he wasn't delusional, that he was the victim of an elaborate ruse and that this was all a game. If that were the case, his opponents grossly overmatched him. Bleakly, he considered *that* the best case scenario. His gaze drifted up from the now spotless sink, over the cracked mirror and to his slightly older, slightly sicker self. He didn't have any answers, either.

Jack dressed in fresh socks and underwear, a clean T-shirt and jeans. In the shower, he had felt days' worth of dirt sluice off his body. He should have been refreshed, ready to face the day, but instead he felt defeated. He made himself shave only so Kate wouldn't ask why he didn't. He left his kit behind in the shower house. Somehow, he felt he wouldn't it again.

He stepped up to the mess hall door, and before entering, looked out over Wabasso. The sky had become crowded with cloud, some of it gunmetal grey. Still, the lake gathered enough sunlight to shimmer. Jack paused to take it in. Mere days ago, the lively waters enchanted him. Now, the sight stirred a tempest in his stomach.

Inside, he found Kate in the kitchen, clattering dishes and

utensils. Every cabinet door along the kitchen's back wall hung open. A thin line of blue smoke clung to the ceiling. Kate saw Jack enter and wafted the smoke with a dish towel.

"Oh, hi," she said as she attempted to lean casually against the counter. She tucked disheveled hair behind her ears. "I had a little trouble reheating Kubby's meatloaf." On the range a blackened skillet still smoked. It held what appeared to be a charcoal briquette at its centre. A large pot had replaced it on the burner. "I hope mac and cheese is okay."

Jack sat at the table nearest the kitchen counter. "That sounds good."

Kate smiled and fanned the smoke again. "Sorry, I'm not much of a domestic."

"I couldn't tell."

Kate laughed.

Jack didn't. He saw humor in the situation, but he couldn't feel it, like the system in his machinery responsible for smiling and laughing had suffered a critical breakdown.

Kate went to the range, checked the contents of the pot and stirred. Her every movement—lifting the lid, using the long handled spoon, replacing the lid—was measured, careful. Cooking for Jack took her out of her comfort zone. He thought her effort was endearing, but he couldn't honestly *feel* that, either. Perhaps that system had broken down, too.

He deliberately looked the other way as Kate finished making his lunch. Hushed swear words drifted from the kitchen as she drained the noodles. More came as she dumped in the packet of evaporated cheese. A few minutes later, she set a steaming bowl in front of him, along with a fork and a spoon. Jack took up the fork and tasted the dish while Kate watched hopefully. He chewed the too-firm noodles and swallowed.

"Very good." He forced a content grin that made his face feel like it might be the next thing to break. "This is just what the doctor ordered."

Kate poured a tall glass of water from a pitcher on the counter and set it next to his bowl before sitting across from him. "I had you pegged for a spoon man," she said, squinting and wearing a wry smile.

"Close," Jack said between mouthfuls. "Both of my boys eat their mac and cheese with a spoon."

"You should have some water. You look a little dehydrated."

Jack wondered if that was code for *you look like hell*. He eyed the glass. A fine film of condensation formed on the outside. Inside, tiny air bubbles still swirled round and round. He figured they should have settled this long after pouring. "Is that bottled water?"

"No, it's from the tap. Lake water."

Jack picked up the glass and peered into it from the top.

"What's wrong?" Kate said. "You're not going native are you?"

Jack shifted focus to her. "*Native?* I don't get your meaning."

"Just a joke. I thought you'd have heard by now—Kubby likes to talk about it so much. You see, the indigenous people who lived here two hundred years ago claimed that the lake water was tainted. Actually, what they said was that it was full of evil spirits." She made her eyes bulge when she said the last bit. "They believed it to the point that they happily gave it over to the government in one of their infamous land deals."

Jack swirled the contents of the glass. "Evil water, huh?"

"Well, they weren't completely wrong, just misinformed. Wabasso's water does contain bacteria. If you drink enough of it, it can make you really sick, even kill you, but we have a filtration system here that removes the bacteria so it's perfectly safe to drink." She winked. "We take out the evil spirits."

"Yeah, I saw that filtration equipment in the office basement," Jack said, watching the tiny bubbles swirling in his glass again. "Impressive." With Kate watching him now, he felt a sudden pressure to drink. He did and set the glass down, half empty.

"Thanks for making lunch," he said, seeking a subject change.

"No sweat," she said, and for a moment, held a serious demeanor. Then she started to giggle. "I suck at cooking."

"No. This is good. Really."

"And you suck at lying."

Jack and Kate strolled lazily past the office and toward the parking lot. She had a spare lifejacket in her car. It had belonged to her ex-husband and she claimed it would fit Jack nicely.

"Our paddle may be cut short," she said, eyeing the pregnant clouds overhead.

Jack's mind was back in the shower house, staring at the bloody knife in the bloody sink. He kept going over the event, step by step, seeking any angle that could prove it was a trick. Nothing added up. Once more, he counted the seconds he was away from the sink. There simply wasn't enough time to remove the knife and clean up the blood.

If Warren had staged the scene in the cabin, he would have needed a team of men to return it to normal before I could bring witnesses—Ralph, Kubby, Warren himself—their whereabouts were all accounted for. That left only Frasier and Pierre as the two possible cleaners. Two men could not have straightened up so fast. Oh, and Kate. She potentially could have had a hand in it also.

He watched her cheerfully going on about her joy of canoeing, her love of drifting on Wabasso's gentle sway.

No, she couldn't be that cruel. It doesn't matter anyway. Three people couldn't possibly clean up all the blood in Cabin Five and then put all the furniture back. That still doesn't explain the shower house. Even if someone managed to plant the knife, how did they get by me unseen? How did they manage to hide? They would have to be superhuman...or not real. If it wasn't a trick, that left only one possibility...

Kate rested a hand on Jack's shoulder. It jarred him back to the here and now. "Oh Jack, that dream really got to you, eh?"

Jack nearly asked what she was talking about then remembered the excuse he gave for attacking Warren. "Yeah, it did." He recalled the nightmare—his confrontation with Jonathan Dunn on the bluff. He pictured the ax. An involuntary shudder ran through his body.

Kate detected it and stopped walking. She stood in front of him, taking one of his hands in both of hers. "It might be good for you to tell me about it. It might help to flush it out of your system."

Jack couldn't look her in the eye. His gaze drifted across the grasses bordering the path to the scrub brush beyond. "Umm, okay. I don't remember a whole lot about it anymore. It's just that Warren was poking fun and it really kind of got me—"

Kate didn't let him finish. "You said something about a fire."

"Oh yeah. The entire retreat was burning."

"Just wondering, did the retreat seem different somehow, maybe bigger?" Their eyes met. Kate's were full of expectation as she waited for Jack's response.

He pressed his lips together. "Bigger? No. There were the same six cabins, the same office, same mess hall."

Kate nodded and started walking again.

"Why do you ask?" Jack said, catching up.

Kate wrung her hands together. "It's nothing. It's just when you told me about the fire, it gave me déjà vu. It reminded me of, well, did you know Wabasso Lake wasn't always a writer's retreat?"

Jack shook his head.

"Well, back in the thirties I think, it was the largest Boy Scout retreat on the east coast. Apparently, troops came from all over the country to camp here. Back then, there were closer to twenty cabins here. Actually the mess hall and the shower house are original. So are the six cabins we stay in. The rest burned."

Jack balked. "Everything else burned? It would have been an inferno."

"It was. At least that's what I saw in *my* dream." She said, thoughtfully.

Jack stopped and regarded her. "You had the same dream?"

Kate raised her hands, motioned for him to slow down. "No, Jack. We dreamed about different fires, different times."

Jack grasped her by the shoulders. "But, both of our dreams were about Wabasso burning down. That has to mean something."

She tilted her head, dismissively. "It's a coincidence, really, nothing else."

Jack released her. He turned away and rubbed hard at his brow. "Kate, don't you get the feeling like there is something else happening here. Like something that's just beyond the reach of our understanding?"

"You *have* gone native." Kate pinched the bridge of her nose and shook her head.

"No, you said yourself, Wabasso has a way of...speaking to us."

Kate dropped her hands to her sides. "Jack, I meant this place lets us speak to *ourselves*. Don't put a supernatural spin on it. It's quiet here. It's so quiet that people can think clearly for a change. It allows us to reconnect with ourselves. It allows us to do our best work, and we sometimes have vivid dreams because we can have really deep sleep here. There are no distractions. At least there aren't supposed to be."

Jack felt very small. He realised Kate had far better things to do with her time than waste it on him. She could have been at her desk, banging out a thousand words an hour. Instead, she made him lunch and was taking him canoeing. She did her best to help a fellow writer who she saw unraveling. Jack saw it, too. "You're right," he said. "I'm sorry."

"It's okay. It is." Kate drew a deep breath and as she released it, and with some effort, found her smile again. She turned and started for her car. She produced a set of keys from her pocket and a sporty, red car in the lot gave an electronic chirp.

Kate opened the passenger door and pulled out a yellow

lifejacket with black banding. She held it up. "Oh yeah, this should fit you just fine."

Jack stood at the back of the car, mentally purging his system of all insane ideas. He shoved his mindset into a happier place that would allow him to give Kate pleasant company for the rest of the afternoon. He owed her that much.

He was taking his own deep breaths, steeling his nerves, girding his bowels, and when his gaze fell upon Kate's license plate, his newfound resolve fell-in like a house of cards. The plate read,

DUNDREMN

Jack stared at it, trying to speak, his voice hitching once, twice. Finally, he said, in an almost too low tone, "What's that?"

"What? The bumper sticker?" Kate said circling to the rear of the car. "That's from Hampton High—my old high school. I donated a foolish amount of money to their library and they gave me a lousy sticker in return. Funny how the world works, right?"

"No...the plate."

"*Ugh*. The *plate*. Nobody ever gets it. It was always my dream to own a little red convertible sports car, and when I got my first good royalty check, I could finally afford one. Anyway, here it is and that stupid vanity plate is supposed to mean, *done dreaming*. You know, like, I finally realised my dream? Nobody ever gets it. It's dumb."

Jack stared at the plate while Kate continued on, complaining about the Department of Motor Vehicles not providing enough letters for her vanity plate to make sense. He pictured Big Red's bold letters at the top of a manuscript page. DUNDREMN. He pictured an arched sign over the roadway to a big white farmhouse. He pictured Jonathan Dunn and blood and death.

His gaze drifted away and lit upon his black Buick parked further down the lot —the old behemoth with the disagreeable trunk latch. He thought about getting in it and leaving Wabasso Lake. He could drive until he arrived at the office of the power commission, go inside and beg for his old job back. He could apologize to his wife, to his boys, to God, forever thinking he should pursue a career in writing.

He wondered if escape was still possible. Somehow it felt like the time to flee had passed him by. He was already on the farm. He had been for days.

"I have to go back to my cabin," he said flatly.

Kate read his face, the turmoil in his eyes. "What?"

Backing away, he said, "I have to check on something. I'm sorry."

"No, Jack, no! This has to stop!" Kate lunged for him and grabbed him by the wrist. So fierce was her grip, her knuckles whitened. "You need to get a hold of yourself. Whatever you saw just now, whatever you *think* you saw, just fucking forget it. I know you had another freak-out in the shower house. I saw you run outside in a towel, for Christ's sake. Now listen to me. There is nothing bad happening here. There is nothing happening to *you*."

Jack worked loose of her grip. "It's not safe here, Kate. I want you to go back to your cabin and stay there until I come for you."

She folded her arms, stood defiantly straight. "No. I'm not doing that."

"Please. Just 'til I figure out what happens next."

"*What happens next?*" Her jaw went slack. "What are you talking about, Jack? You're not making any sense."

"Just bear with me. I have to finish reading the—" He caught himself before he said *rest of the manuscript*, but, it was too late. He knew Kate was already piecing the story together. In seconds she formed a theory to his madness. She backed away from him.

"Kate, please." Jack reached for her hand. She yanked it away.

"Don't touch me, Jack."

The disappointment in her eyes hit home in the centre of Jack's chest. He did as she asked. He started away from her, turning after a few yards to beg her once more to keep to her cabin. The lifejacket on the ground, Kate leaned against the car, head hung, hands over her eyes. Jack couldn't bring himself to speak.

He ran.

As he hit the path leading to his cabin, the powerful sense that he was watched fell upon him. He focused on the trail for fear that if he looked into the woods, he would glimpse an observer. He feared it would not be Warren or Ralph or one of the other guests watching him. Jack could feel the emergence of a foreign intelligence. He gasped for air and it tasted like ashes.

Jack reached the shelter of his cabin, but felt little security once he shut the door behind him. The space was dark, too much so for the middle of afternoon, clouded skies or not. He switched on the light and found everything as he'd left it: the unmade cot, the cluttered table, the manuscript atop it.

He paced the floor and wrung his hands. Confronted with the time-yellowed pages, he wasn't sure he could read another word. If he continued to read, he wondered, would events from the manuscript keep coming true? Was it possible, that by reading it, he gave it life?

He pictured Kate tucking her fiery hair behind an ear and smiling at him the way she did on the beach. *She's the only one who hasn't given up on me. The only one who tried to help me. My family has already walked out. Teddy will turn his back next.*

Jack clenched his jaw and stepped to the writing table.

I have to do this. For Kate.

She doesn't understand the danger in the things I have seen. She won't leave Wabasso, but maybe, if I can learn the risk, I can do something about it. Maybe I can stop it before it happens.

Past the theory of elaborate hoaxes and practical jokes, Jack felt a shard of truth slip into the soft tissue of his brain. The realization threatened to bring tears to his eyes. Just as he had once allowed himself to believe, he found that fiction *did* have a strong connection to reality. He figured as much all along, but there was absolutely no solace in that. This story, this life, had an author and it was not him.

Together, Dead waited on the table. Jack eyed Big Red, poised beside the stack of pages. He gathered up the pen—his prized editing companion throughout his many drafts—and tossed it across the room. He sat down. He read .

Together, Dead

IV

Jill woke to darkness. She lay on musty blankets. The rest of her senses told little else. Her vision was awash with sparks of red against a black canvas. Slowly, she regained control of her limbs and brushed her hands over her body to search for various hurts. She felt nothing until she touched the side of her head. The lump under her hair began to throb. She gritted her teeth until the agony abated.

In the intervening moments, Jill relived her failed escape from the farm; the shovel twirling toward her, knocking her to the ground, her brother leisurely strolling after her while she crawled in the dirt, still trying to reach the road. He took his time, the hateful bastard. When he was good and ready, he took up the shovel and clubbed her like a prone seal.

A cold rush of urgency flooded her chest.

Where is he now?
Where am I?

It took all of her strength to roll to her side. The room swirled. As she moved, she heard the familiar squeak of mattress springs compressing and uncoiling. She did not need a clear head or even sight to figure out where she was. Like the scent of her mother's perfume, the squeaking transported her to childhood. She dropped her feet to the floor and sat up on the edge of her old bed. Her head pulsed with pain. When it passed, she was able to puzzle together her surroundings, half from her returning senses, half from memory. Across from her was the tall chest of drawers, beside it, a small writing desk, all tinted red by the dipping sun beyond the window.

Night is falling.

Jill wobbled badly when she stood. Her head throbbed, her movements encumbered by strange garments. Somehow she wore a sweater too snug across the chest and shoulders, with sleeves so tight they hardly allowed her to lift her arms.

Turning toward the blazing light from the window, she looked down at the big green *H* on her chest. *H* as in Hampton, as in High school, as in Huskies. She took in the matching pleated miniskirt and wanted to scream.

On some level, Jill could understand her brother's penchant for violence. Even murder, despicable as it was, was a concept she could grasp, but she could not fathom how deranged one had to be to undress their unconscious adult sister and put her in her high school cheerleader uniform.

She filed away her revulsion for now.

The only thing that mattered at this point was getting off the farm. She went to the window and squinted against the brilliance rimming the horizon. Outside, there was no sign of her car. The barn door was closed. Jonathan was nowhere to be seen.

Having been caught trying to get to the road, Jill guessed her best bet was to head in the other direction, behind the house. The woods were nearest there. If she could get amidst the trees without detection, she would be home free, and if Jonathan should give chase, the trees would provide some much needed coverage.

In under an hour, it would be dark and the time to make her move would be optimal. Could she wait that long? She could not guess what her brother intended to do next.

Her heart sank as she thought about the paperboy's final moments, how he must have felt as Jonathan loomed over him, knife in hand. He must have been terrified. The thought rankled Jill and her head throbbed in reaction. I'm no little boy. I won't roll over for this madman.

She went to the bedroom door, moving slowly, somewhat to maintain stealth, somewhat to keep her balance. The room continued to spin. She inhaled a long fortifying breath before opening the door, and stepped into the hallway.

East-facing, it was darker than her old bedroom. Jill was glad for it, but her relief faded fast. The radio softly murmured in the parlor below. The voice she heard belonged to Bill Jeffries, host of Down East Jamboree, her father's favorite

show. Mr. Jeffries' presence in the farmhouse was as commonplace as that of any
Dunn. There was a time she would have
been comforted by his familiar voice, but
hearing him now only served to remind her
of how far from normal her family had
gone. For the first time, she felt grate-
ful that her parents did not live long
enough to see how monstrous their son had
become.

Jill crouched at the top of stairs and
slid soundlessly down the top tread,
peeking between the railing's balusters
at the hallway below. She crept down another stair and now could see the floor
of the parlor. Bill Jeffries announced
that the Mayberry Boys were up next and a
fiddle started to whine to the dull
strumming of guitars. Jill eased down another step, on high alert for her brother. She got a better view of the parlor
and what she saw, purged the air from her
lungs.

Her husband slouched in a kitchen
chair, mouth gagged, arms and legs bound
with rope.

Shear panic constricted every muscle in
her body. She rushed down the stairs to
Luke's side. Only when she raised his
head in her hands did he rouse. His head
lolled and shook as he fought to clear
the cobwebs. When Jill pulled her hands
away to loosen his gag, her palms were
streaked with blood. It seeped freely
from the left side of Luke's head. The
sight of the injury triggered Jill's
tears as she struggled to loosen the gag.

"Run," he whispered as soon as she got
the rag out of his mouth. "Run, Jill. Get

help."

Jill moved behind the chair and started undoing the rope at his wrists.

"There's no time."

"Shhh." Jill continued working the knot.

"Jill, it's worse than you think. He's…"

She looked up for Jonathan, and as she did, she saw the other two people sitting in the parlor. She stopped loosening the ropes and raised a hand to clutch her mouth. She stepped tentatively toward the chesterfield and armchair.

"Jill," said Luke. "Don't look at that, please. You have to go now."

Jill could not wrest her gaze from the bloated remains of her mother and father.

Mom slumped at the end of the sofa, needlework resting on her lap, and Dad in his armchair, an open newspaper spread over his chest. Both were swollen and colourless in the Sunday best she had them buried in a week ago. Their heads sagged. Their faces drawn. Had they not been sewn shut, their eyes would have bulged and their mouths would have hung open.

Jill's mouth did hang open.

She felt something break inside her chest. This will hurt. She knew that. Long after her and Luke get to safety, after they have Jonathan taken into custody, after they get back to raising their normal kids in their normal house; this sight would hurt. There would never come a time when it did not.

Utter hopelessness on her face, she turned to Luke, but her eye caught on

Jonathan, standing in the hallway. Numbed by the sight of her dead parents posed in their favorite chairs, listening to their favorite show, she was not frightened by Jonathan's presence in the slightest. Maybe that's what broke inside me, she thought. Maybe my fear was broken.

"Why?" she managed. It came out child-like.

Jonathan did not answer. He simply walked past her, padding softly on the rug in his sock-feet, what Mom had always called his indoor feet. He sat at the vacant end of the chesterfield and attentively stared across the room at his father as though the two were in silent conversation.

"Jill, run," pleaded Luke.

Visibly trembling, Jill glared at her brother. "Why?" she screamed. "Jon, why did you do this?"

The Mayberry Boys filled the silence with their fiddlin' and pickin'.

"Answer me!"

"Because this is home," said Jonathan frankly. "This is where they belong. It's where you belong, too. Even him." He gestured Luke's way. "He married-in and that makes him family, too. And, this is what family does. They stay together."

Jill looked down at herself with tear soaked eyes. In some twisted way the Huskies uniform made sense. It harkened back to the last time the Dunn's were all together, before she had left for university in the city. She eyed Jonathan, the young man who wanted more than anything to keep his family together, the young man who was failing to do so. "Jon, this is wrong. Mom and Dad were at rest."

Jonathan pursed his lips together. He pointed his finger and thrust it downward as he made his point. "I couldn't leave them in that field with all them others. This is their house. They should be here."

"Save your breath, Jill," said Luke. "He's fucking nuts."

Jonathan was out of his seat, grabbing a fistful of Luke's hair in the blink of an eye. "You don't say that!" he roared in Luke's face. "Mom said you don't ever call me that!"

The display of purest rage urged Jill to back up.

"You're sick," said Luke. "You hear me? Sick!"

Jonathan released him and dug into his pocket. Jill could not see exactly what he pulled out, but it had a metallic sheen.

Luke's wide eyes told her it was a knife. His expression, one of utter dread, locked on her.

"Run!" he yelled again, and it rose to a scream as Jonathan plunged the blade into his abdomen.

She could not fully grasp the image of her brother inflicting a mortal wound on the man she loved. A moment later, she realised that she was on the move, in full sprint to the front door, and as she fled, she screamed from the bottom of her very being.

"You stay put," she heard Jonathan call after her.

Jill turned the doorknob and pulled.

The door did not budge.

"Don't you go out there," said Jonathan.

She glimpsed him enter the hallway, wielding the blade, bloody to the wrist. She gave the door another yank. It only rattled in the jamb. Then she saw the engaged deadbolt. She fumbled the lever with panicked fingers. Jonathan was nearly within arm's reach. In another stride he would be able to grab her hair, drag her back to the parlor to watch her husband die to the score of the Down East Jamboree.

Fear robbed her of dexterity. Her hands were all knuckles as she wrestled the lock. She could smell Luke's blood as Jonathan reached for her. She pulled the door open and almost tumbled down the front steps, putting precious distance between herself and her brother.

She ran blindly, hysterically, away from the house, scarcely feeling the ground beneath her as she crossed the yard. She skidded to a stop at the barn door.

A clunk sounded off behind her; the front door closing.

Jonathan descended the porch steps.

He took the time to put on his boots and now he came for her. Jill pulled on the tall door. Stiff from too many years of freezing and thawing, the door put up a fight. Only when Jill used all her weight, did it open wide enough to permit entry.

Luke's car was parked inside. The sight of it evoked a sharp pain in her chest. Her husband had come here to save her from Jonathan and she could not even say if he was alive or dying or dead already. She covered her mouth again and battled for control of her emotions. She forced herself to keep moving.

Her father kept yard tools on the far wall. She focused on getting to one tool in particular, the rusty sickle that hung among them. She hurried around Luke's car and past her Honda, parked in front of it. She eyed the windshield Jonathan had shattered when he had thwarted her last escape attempt.

The barn was more given to darkness here. Jill feared that finding her weapon in the black void would be no easy task. Would she be able to use if she found it? Would Jonathan find her first?

All of Jill's concerns vanished in an instant as the ground beneath her gave way. She fell. Her arms flailed for something to hold on to. Her leg caught on something and twisted her around. Before she could let out a screech, she hit solid ground.

Fresh pain flared in her ankle and she grabbed it, half expecting to find her foot disjointed from her leg. She saw nothing in the deep, black void. Blindly groping about the foreign place, she first felt an earthen wall to her right side and another to her left. She shifted on her hip so she could feel whatever was in front of her and the movement sparked a fire in her ankle. Reaching out again, she touched something wooden. Her hand played over it. An image began to form in her mind; two long, vertical pieces of wood braced together by shorter, lateral pieces. A ladder. A way out.

Jill's hand fell upon something else. She felt cool, box-shaped metal in her grasp. The discovery nearly brought a smile to her face when she realised that it was a flashlight. Her hands shook as she fumbled with the switch. A golden globe materialized on the dirt wall.

Jill shone the light in front of her, illuminating the crude wooden ladder she had felt. It climbed some eight feet before reaching the square opening in the barn floor that had swallowed her. She played the light over the walls, exploring the space. It seemed to stretch on in a narrow passageway back toward the front of the barn. She ruminated over how she had not known about this place, this root cellar under the barn. How, in all her years on the farm, had she never stumbled upon it? Why had her father never made mention of it? Had her brother known about it?

The last question stoked the terrible fire in her belly. He was coming for her. He was close. He may have been standing above her right now. Jill gritted her teeth and struggled to her feet. Her twisted ankle burned with every slight motion.

She suspended it off the ground, and for a moment, considered the ladder. She shone the flashlight down the long, narrow space. The light was overtaken by darkness a few yards in. Jill contemplated the ladder again then opted to move further into the cellar, hanging her last hope on the chance she would find another way out. She hopped on her good foot, holding the wall for balance. Every step she took drew a yelp of pain from her ankle.

Jill considered again how far the cellar might go. Might it have connected to the house and open into the basement? As Jill pondered this, the flashlight revealed a slight widening in the space. She saw shelves against either side, strewn with webs. At first, she assumed jars of preserves and pickled vegetables would occupy the shelves. When she got a little closer, what she saw baffled her.

On the nearest shelf rested a golden pocket watch. Jill stopped to examine it. Its presence here did not make any sense. A filthy root cellar was no place to keep such a valuable item. Beside it was a set of car keys. Further down she found a hank of blonde hair tied with string. She held the light on it. It took a few moments to fully grasp what the odd sight represented, and when she did, her bones turned to rubber.

This was not her father's place or her mother's. She understood that now. This was Jonathan's place and these were his things. She covered her mouth to stifle her disgust. She turned her head, but as though witnessing a train wreck, she could not look away. She aimed the light over the watch, the keys, the lock of hair, wanting so badly to scream.

Further down, the flashlight revealed more items on more shelves; the rest of her brother's keepsakes. There was a backpack. Next to it rested an old leather glove. Before moving on, Jill returned the light to the glove for a second take.

That's no glove, she thought.

Oh. My. God.

Her legs buckled and she fell to the dirt. Tears overflowed and she erupted into heavy sobs. Everything in here is a life. He's been at this so long. Killing.

Jill wiped the sweat from her brow with the back of her hand. She raised the flashlight, perfectly aware that she had to keep going or something of hers would end up on one of these shelves. She shone the light over the opposite wall. There was more shelving there, but she could not bear to see any of the items on it. Her only interest was in finding a way out of this hellish museum.

She got to her feet and worked her way further down between the shelves, focusing on the floor ahead and the ceiling, anything to avoid the macabre collection on either side of her. The air seemed to grow fouler the deeper into the cellar she went. She managed to dry her tears, but only for a few seconds before a new batch threatened to refresh the flow.

Jill saw the wall in front of her. She raised the light up, hoping that it would show a way around that led to an exit. She almost dropped the flashlight when she saw a bovine skull.

It was not so much the skull that held Jill's attention. It was the elaborate tangle of dried leaves and dead flowers arranged in a wreath around the skull that transfixed her. It horrified her. The idea that Jonathan had arranged the skull like a pagan altar, a place of worship sapped the remains of her strength. Her muscles went slack.

She lowered herself to the dirt and slumped against a shelf. Images of Luke came to her as she closed her eyes. She saw her parents decaying bodies in the parlor. She saw her boys playing in their backyard and knew she would never see them again.

Opening her eyes, she scanned the shelf nearest her. Pieces of jewelry glistened in the flashlight glow. She leaned in and recognized them at once.

Her parent's wedding rings.

For as far back as she could remember, the rings had adorned her parents' hands. She pictured them on the hands that had wrapped around hers, hands that had presented her with flowers and plates of home-cooked food. Now the rings were the trophies of a mad man. Jill loosed deep sobs from the bottom of her being. Her shoulders heaved and her mouth twisted and not a sound came out.

Jill dragged herself to the ladder. She started to climb, fully expecting to find Jonathan waiting above. He'll grab me the moment I climb out. The ghastly thought hardly registered with her. There was no spike in heart rate, no sudden burst of sweat on her neck. Jill was frozen inside. Jonathan's trophy room had seen to that.

There was no sign of her brother as she pulled herself out of the hatchway. Nor was there sign of him as she stumbled over to her car and leaned against it for support. Pain smoldered in her ankle.

He'll strike now, come rushing around

the car at me, bloodlust in his eyes.

Several seconds ticked away. Jonathan did not appear.

Jill slid her way down the car, toward the barn doors, expecting him to reach from under the car and catch her by the foot. That did not happen either, and when she reached the tall double doors she began to flirt with another idea. Maybe she had eluded him somehow, and maybe, just maybe, escape was a possibility once more. With this thought came a tingling sensation in her chest. The feeling threatened to blossom in to full-blown hope.

Moving with purpose, she pushed on the door. It gaped open a reluctant inch or two before falling closed again. Jill pressed her shoulder against it and shoved with all her less-than-perfect legs could muster.

The door sprung open.

She let out a squeal as she lost balance. She fell outward and landed heavily at the feet of her brother.

The sight of him shot an electric current throughout her body. Jill lost any regard for her injured leg as she kicked wildly at the dirt to put distance between them. She scrambled backward until she slammed into the side of the barn.

Jonathan did not move a muscle. He merely watched. His stony face made all the more grim in the furnace glow of the setting sun. Jill struggled to her feet. She spotted the ax hanging at Jonathan's side and a scream erupted from her throat.

"Stay back, you monster!"

Jonathan stood statue-still, unblinking.

"I saw your _things_. How could you? All those people?" Jill wiped her runny nose. "How could you keep those things here? This is our parent's home. _Say something, damn it!_"

"I had help."

Jill stopped fighting to get to her feet. Jonathan's cool monotone froze her joints in place. Her heart beat twice, three times, as she tried to decipher what he meant.

"Dad. He helped me build the cellar," said Jonathan.

Jill's mouth came unhinged. Her heart seemed to stop beating for several long seconds while her gaze drifted across the farmhouse as though seeking an explanation to Jonathan's ludicrous claim. She settled on the front door. Part of her, the tiny part that still believed wishes and dreams could come true, longed to see her father step out of the house with the answers she so desperately needed. Another part of her told her that no answer would do. This was uncharted territory. She did not know her brother. Perhaps she did not know her parents as well as she thought, either.

"Mom and Dad, they helped me keep it secret," added Jonathan.

Jill's lips quivered. "Jon? Did you kill them?"

He fixed his sights on her. His eyes widened as though he was hearing news of their parent's death for the first time. To Jill, the expression was both heartbreaking and sickening at the same time.

It answered her question more directly than words ever could. New tears streaked her dirty cheeks.

She got up, teetering on her good foot and used the barn wall at her back for support. She watched Jonathan all the while with a new-found contempt. His under-nourished face was no longer cause for pity. It was skeletal, hideous. This creature who used to be her brother did not deserve the slightest compassion. He had killed Luke. If her boys had been here, he would have killed them, too. Her gaze shifted to the ax.

"You need help, Jonathan." You need to be put down like an animal with rabies. "Please, give me the ax." So I can sink it in your skull. "You're my brother. I love you." Now let me kill you. "Mom and Dad loved you."

Jonathan's eyes narrowed. He tightened his grip.

Jill tensed. She had struck a raw nerve.

"They wanted to get rid of me, ya know," said Jonathan. There was venom in his voice now. "They said they were gettin' too old to watch over me. They wanted to put me in some kinda home, just like you do."

Jill swallowed the film on her tongue. She began working her way down the side of the barn, widening the gap between them. She hazarded a peek at the field beyond the farmhouse and the trees she had earlier hoped would offer safe haven. They were impossibly far.

"Mom and Dad forgot that family stays together." Jonathan lifted the ax blade to inspect its edge. Satisfied, he looked past it to Jill and took a step forward. "I had to remind 'em of that."

She felt a scream building in her core. Her knee double clutched and she nearly collapsed. The motion pushed her forward. She knew that if she fell, she would die. Instead, she threw her twisted ankle in front of her and it took the brunt of her weight. The scream escaped her now. It was the most loathsome noise she had ever heard and she could hardly believe it had come from her.

Jonathan closed in.

Jill glimpsed his face. A placidity had returned to his eyes. Any emotion had bled out of them. She had seen dead bodies and she had witnessed her husband's gruesome assault, but the sight of Jonathan's calm demeanor frightened her more than any of it. There was a blankness about him as he came for her. There was no soul behind those eyes, only a driving urge to kill.

The intense fear pumped blood down to her legs. She bolted for the pines and, in her delirium, she no longer felt her banged-up ankle. The pain had become a distant beacon, blinking dully with each footfall. More treacherous was the pitted turf. She could not read it in the weak light of the dying sun. She could only pray she did not catch her foot on a raised root or roll her ankle in a divot. The trees lined up before her, awash in scarlet. Jill pushed all caution aside. It came easily when she heard Jonathan's call behind her.

Jonathan looked up at the coming dark. The first stars looked back, bearing witness. He strode into the field after his sister, watching her hobbled flight. He tasted the air. The grass smelled minutely sweeter this evening. It'll be rainin' come morning, he reckoned.

Jill had taken quite a lead, but Jonathan did not rush. He knew the trees would slow her down good and plenty. She'll be easy pickin's.

He ambled on and allowed himself to picture that green and white Hampton High sweater on a shelf in his trophy room. The thought made the corner of his mouth twitch a little. A smile threatened.

He made himself concentrate on the task at hand. It was something Dad would have said to do. He had a bunch of them rules. Jonathan remembered one of his own rules now: always give 'em a reason. Even if it ain't the truth, you always give 'em a reason. He called out to Jill just as she reached the woods.

"Hey Jill, if you want to leave this family, there's only one way out!"

The blood ran out of the sky. Full dark came and he raised the ax in both hands.

Chapter Thirteen

A t some point, Jack became aware of the pattering of rain drops on the cabin roof. The persistent sound roused him from his trance. He stared at the page in front of him on the table—the final page of the *Together, Dead* manuscript. Too many thoughts ran through his head, making it impossible to focus on any particular one. He stood up, paced the floor once and returned to the table. He picked up the page and read the last paragraph again.

```
The blood ran out of the sky. Full dark
came and he raised the ax in both hands.
```

Jack turned the page over in search of more text. Blank.

"Is this all?" he whispered. He thought for a moment then turned and got down on his knees. He uncovered the ragged hole in the floorboards and reached down inside. After blindly feeling around in the cavity for more pages, he came up empty. He got up and considered the story again, its open ending. It left him feeling sick to his stomach. He had hoped for a definitive conclusion to this nightmare—something that had the damsel escaping the monster, something involving a happily-ever-after sentiment. Instead, a new idea had taken hold. It was one Jack didn't want to recognize, but it was getting harder and harder to ignore. Once he had read the words *Hampton High School*, it stared him in the face.

Kate was in danger.

But, how am I to articulate that? he thought. *I don't have any proof. Kate will think I'm nuts if I bring this to her. I'll sound like a stark-raving lunatic.* Then it occurred to him. *It needs to come from someone else—someone she trusts. I need Kubby's help.*

How the hell do I get that? I already cried wolf once.

Jack attempted to build his case. There were too many intangibles in his argument, too many wild claims that required blind faith to be believed. He paced the floor again, drumming on his cheeks as he narrowed down his story to the irrefutable facts. He stopped, hands frozen to either side of his face, and regarded the stack of pages. He arrived at two certainties that rendered all other arguments moot. One, he had in his possession a story, a horror story, no one knew existed, and two, horror stories always get violent before the end.

He scooped up his duffle and tossed it on the cot. He gathered and armful of clothing off the floor and stuffed it in the bag. His plans came together in an instant. He would show Kubby the manuscript. He would show the parts of the story that he had witnessed in the shower house and in Cabin Five. Perhaps most importantly, he would come clean. He would admit that he found the manuscript and planned to pass it off as his own.

Jack paused in his hurried packing and surveyed his gut for feelings. He actually felt a burgeoning sense of relief and it surprised him. Yesterday, admitting to stealing another's work was the last thing he would have done. That rather grand confession brought with it minor, yet no less poignant admissions. *I don't belong here, it's true. I am not a writer. I had no business trying to be. In trying, I lost so much of myself. I lost everyone.*

He exhaled and felt as though his body had expelled some kind of poisonous gas. It was liberating. He savoured the sensation for a moment then resumed his packing with greater fervor. He went to the closet to get the few articles he had hung up the day he'd arrived. He pulled open the bi-fold door. What he found inside sent him reeling backward.

A soiled pair of green work trousers hung in the closet, and beside them, a red plaid shirt.

The room started to spin. Bile climbed Jack's esophagus. Poison seeped into his lungs. He stood, fixed on Jonathan Dunn's clothing, his chin starting to tremble.

What the hell is happening here? The thought played on a loop in his head, again and again. Packing no longer mattered. He didn't want to keep anything from this cabin. It was all tainted. He went to the writing table and gathered the manuscript under his arm, gave the place one last look, and stepped into the rain.

Jack hunched under the small roof of the three sided phone booth outside the mess hall. Rain had soaked though his shirt and nearly through his jeans as well. Heavy drops pelted his back as he waited, on hold. Finally, Ted Marsh picked up and cheerfully said, "Jackie-baby, how's tricks?"

During his sprint from the cabin, Jack decided on exactly what he would tell his agent. I'll make it short and sweet, he had promised himself. Now that he heard Ted's voice, his tongue tied in knots. "Ted, I, umm…"

"Hey, you getting any sun up that way? It's been raining cats and dogs here all week. I've had the roof on the car for way too long. I'm starting to wonder why I bought a convertible." Ted gave his customary proud-of-himself chuckle.

This is going to be harder than I thought.

As always, Jack had difficulty fitting his words into the conversation while Ted freely babbled on in all different tangents. This time around, Jack had something to say that required a little tact. Ted didn't leave much room for tact.

"So you'll never guess who I ran into yesterday," Ted went on. "Artie McCall. Can you believe it? I said, 'Hey you old duffer, you still taking Mulligans every time you pick up a club?' Jack, you remember that time we played Rockwood with him? He was losing tee shots in the rhubarb all afternoon and he still finished the day under par."

Jack raised his voice. "Ted, listen—"

"Can you believe that lousy cheat?" Ted sputtered with more laughter.

"—I have to tell you something."

"I mean, I'll never play another round with him again as long as I live, I swear."

Hot steam gathered in Jack's belly. He could no longer suppress it. He yelled, "*Ted, I can't deliver the draft.*"

That got through. Dead air followed. For several seconds the only sound Jack heard was that of raindrops smacking the phone booth walls.

When Ted came back, there was no trace of cheer in his voice. "What do you mean, Jackie?"

Jack made a fist and rapped his forehead lightly. "I don't have anything to send you."

"Jack, I don't get it...*aww wait.*" Ted's tone changed again. It sounded to Jack like he was grinning on the other end, like he figured it was time once more to massage his flighty client's ego to get him back on task. "*Come on,* Jack. You must have *something* to give me. I mean, I know you're under pressure and maybe it's not your best work, but you still have to give it to me. The publisher is waiting." The agent said in a sing-song voice, "We've been over this already."

Jack looked down at the bundle of pages he sheltered against his chest. He couldn't let the manuscript see the light of day. He was never so certain of anything. It belonged buried under a cabin, deep in the country. He drew a breath to compose himself and answered in his most sincere voice. "Ted, I'm sorry, but I really don't have anything to give you. For real."

Another long pause ensued. When Ted came back, his voice nearly cracked. "Jack, I don't understand. What the hell happened? I mean, you had the time you needed. You went to that retreat for a private place to work. Was there a problem up there? Is someone fucking around?"

Jack didn't know how to answer that. He didn't have enough time to answer that accurately. "Wabasso Lake is... umm...the place is not to blame. This is all on me, Ted."

The temperature rose in Ted's words. "What the hell am I supposed to do now? Can you tell me that?"

Jack pulled the receiver from his ear. He considered hanging up, but there was one other thing he had to say. "Ted, I want to thank you for everything you have done for me."

Ted no longer listened. "What am I supposed to tell the publisher, *your* publisher? They took a chance on you. They paid you a huge advance." He groaned as he reminded himself of the contract. "They're going to sue you for breach of contract. You know that, right?"

While Ted's emotions geared up, Jack's became placid. Maybe it was side effect of letting go of the things he had fought so desperately to keep. The contract, the money, those things were gone and they were no longer worth fretting over. "I can't do anything about that right now," Jack said plainly.

"Oh, that's just great. You don't even care. I stuck my neck out for you and you don't even care." From Ted's end, Jack heard what sounded like a desk chair toppling over. He pictured Ted flinging it aside as he jumped to his feet. He pounded a fist on his desk. Jack was sure of it. "I got you into that fucking retreat and *that* wasn't easy. I fought with the publisher to get you more time. *That* was even fucking harder. All you had to do was finish some stupid fucking ghost story and you couldn't even do that. I mean, what happened? You had peace. You had quiet. You had privacy—no kids to distract you, no ex-wife. I know she hasn't been harassing you because she's been calling here, harassing *me*!"

Ted panted like a rabid dog, waiting for Jack to speak, so he could cut him off with more screaming. He granted Jack all the time in the world to respond. Jack didn't have to cram his words edgewise into the conversation any longer. He took advantage of the rare occasion to ask a question that had been on his mind. "Why did you send me here, Ted?"

"Fuck, what?" Ted seethed into the phone.

"Why Wabasso Lake? Why here?"

Ted's tone dropped a gear. "What in the hell are you talking about? You stood here in my office, pointed at that goddamned magazine article and told me you just *had* to go there."

Jack felt his lungs deflate as the wind went out of him. He tried to recall those days back in the city when the deadlines flew by, one after the other. All he saw was the big black wall that was his block. Dazed, he lowered the receiver and he could still hear his agent on the other end, yelling at the very top of his range.

"Sending you to that fucking retreat wasn't my idea! If it was up to me, I would've sat you at my desk and held a gun to your fucking head until you finished your book. You hear me, you *fuck*? Do you know what this is going to do to my reputation? You screwed me, man, you really scr—"

Jack hung up. He considered the pages under his arm and what might have happened to Ted if he had sent them. *Would Ted start seeing Jonathan Dunn in the corner of his eye? Would he discover his murder weapon in the bathroom sink one morning? Would he see blood?* Jack peered out over the lake, a slate grey mat under the weeping sky. Somehow, he knew that, away from Wabasso, *Together, Dead* would be nothing more than a pile of paper.

Kubby grinned when Jack pushed through the office door. "Ah, man, I was just thinking about you. I must have the sick sense...*sixth* sense, I mean." He stood behind the front counter, *Ziploc* bag in front of him, rolling what he would call a *fatty*.

He did a double take when he noticed the water running off Jack. "Shit, dude. Didn't you pack a rain coat? No matter," he said, raising the joint between his fingers. "This bad boy will dry you right out."

"I didn't come for that," Jack said.

"No? Time to freshen up your bandages, then?"

Jack walked to the counter and plunked the papers down on it. "No."

Kubby set the joint down. "Oh, I see." He seemed to brace himself like a patient expecting bad news from a doctor. Then his mood brightened instantly. "Oh yeah! I heard from Frasier. Yeah, he called from the road, said the drive home was going well. Made it all the way to Portland, Maine. And I saw Pierre at lunchtime, too. He's cool. I know you were concerned about 'em, you know…since this morning."

Jack didn't respond to the news. His gaze lingered on the pages in front of him. That Pierre and Frasier's whereabouts were accounted for only confirmed Jack's worst case scenario. He had little doubt now. There were other forces at play here, and this bunch of paper possessed a power he couldn't hope to comprehend.

He regarded Kubby.

The caretaker looked back, clueless.

"Kubby," Jack said. "I haven't been entirely honest with you."

Kubby smiled, uncomfortably. "Oh, that's not good."

Jack didn't humor Kubby with a smile of his own. He straightened and scanned the interior of the office, the book-shelf near the doorway. The bestsellers of Wabasso lined up there to rub salt in his wounds. The sight squeezed a sigh out of him. No words could sum up what he was feeling better than that. At that point, he wouldn't have been surprised if he laughed or cried. "I haven't been working on my book since I got here."

"No?"

"I haven't written a page, or even a word."

Kubby looked from Jack to the pages between them and back to Jack.

Jack could see Kubby's confusion piling up. He drew a breath and forged ahead. "The thing is, I have writer's block. I've *had* writer's block for a while now. I've had it ever since my wife left and took my boys with her."

Kubby's eyebrows knitted an expression of remorse coupled with puzzlement. He shook his head and picked up the joint from the counter. "Why don't I light this? We'll have a toke and we can talk this out."

Jack grabbed his hand. "I'm not finished."

Kubby locked eyes with him. He set the joint down.

Jack rested both hands on the counter and nodded at the pages. "I found this story. It's not mine." He took another steadying breath. "I was going to use it. No, I was going to *steal* it."

Kubby squinted at the pages then he abruptly turned from the counter. He stroked his beard and in solemn reflection. "Okay. Yeah. Okay. Umm, I didn't just hear that. I didn't hear that, and Jack, you just take this back to wherever you, umm, *borrowed* it from. Just put it back and we'll just pretend we never talked about it."

Jack clenched his jaw. His temper flared and he battled to smother it. He wondered if Kubby actually thought there was a manuscript store in town where he managed to shoplift the story. "I can't put it back," he said, flatly. "I *found* it."

"Come again?" Kubby said.

"I found it in my cabin," Jack said. He thumbed the pages of the manuscript and continued his confession. "I've missed so many deadlines. I had absolutely nothing to show my publisher. I was at the end of my rope. Then I found *this*."

For the first time Jack saw something like anger in the caretaker's expression. Kubby stepped around the counter and went to look out the front window.

"At first, I wondered if it was some kind of gift from God. I mean, it seemed to answer all my prayers. Here was this manuscript just when I needed something to submit. I was pretty sure it was unpublished. It seems old, so I figured, if it had gone to print, it was likely years ago. The reading public had likely forgotten about it by now."

Jack pushed the manuscript across the counter, away from him. He turned toward Kubby who stared intently at the beach. "I started to read it, edit it, change it, you know, so I wouldn't get caught. That's when...that's when things started getting a little weird." Jack waited for Kubby to show a reaction. He didn't.

Kubby stroked his beard again and continued to peer out the rain distorted window. Several seconds passed before he spoke. "You're wrong." Kubby regarded Jack. He appeared depleted, overwhelmed. "That's not a gift from God." He turned back to the view of the beach as though he hoped it would inspire him to a course of action. "Okay," he said, finally. "We can deal with this." He returned to the counter and tried to give Jack a reassuring smile, but there was something broken about it. "It's good you brought this to me. We'll destroy it, burn it in the woodstove, before things start getting out of hand, and you and me, we'll act like this never happened."

"I don't know if burning this will help." Jack shifted uncomfortably. "There's more."

Kubby raised his brow.

"The things I read about in this manuscript...I have seen them happen here at Wabasso. I can show you examples right out of these pages—things I've seen, things that no one should see." When Kubby kept silent, he added, "Of course, maybe I'm going straight out of my mind."

"What sort of story is this, Jack?"

"It's about a guy who murders his family. Straight up horror."

The caretaker closed his eyes and muttered something under his breath.

"What are you not telling me?" Jack demanded. "What do you mean about things getting out of hand?"

Kubby picked up his joint, lit it and took a long, deep haul. "You know, I warned the ownership about you," he said once his lungs were empty. "I warned them not to let a horror writer come here. You guys always carry bad mojo around." He inhaled again, held his breath. "Do you think they'd listen to me? Why would they? I'm just the guy who's given them several years of peaceful service—years without incident. If we kept records around here, mine would be, like, perfect."

"Why? Why shouldn't I be here?"

Kubby looked at the manuscript. He peeled several pages off the top and silently read a few lines of it. He shook his head and let the pages fall. "I gotta sit down," he said, walking away.

Jack followed him into his room. Kubby flopped on the cot and propped his back against the wall. Jack sat in his roller chair, pulled it close. "Please tell me, what the hell is going on here?"

Kubby smoked again and offered the joint to Jack.

Jack waved it off. "Talk to me."

Kubby sat back and loosed a long sigh. "Okay, Jack. You want to know what's wrong with Wabasso Lake. Well, you'll have to get in line for that answer. I've been here a long, long time and I'm still trying to figure it out, myself. Hell, the Maliseet Indians never learned the secret. At least they were smart enough to cut ties with this place two hundred years ago. *Iontoqwahant*, they called it. The devil's water. Shit, they couldn't give it over to the Whiteman fast enough."

Jack ran a hand through his hair and grabbed a fistful of it. "That's fascinating, but why don't you tell me where that manuscript came from, and why I'm seeing parts of it happening all around me?"

Kubby took a few moments to process the question. "It's hard to say. It's not an exact science or anything. That kind of weird stuff doesn't happen all the time. Sometimes we don't get any strangeness for long stretches. Sometimes years. It's like the place goes dormant or something. You can forget just how weird things can be around here at times. Makes you doubt it ever really happens. Other times, when it gets active, it's like it wants to make up for lost time."

Throwing his palms up, Jack said, "Am I supposed to understand a fucking word of that? Come on, man. Help me out here. I mean, I'd just as soon get in my car and leave this bullshit for you to sort out on your own."

"Okay. Hold on." Kubby took in a long breath. His cheeks puffed as he slowly exhaled. "Okay, the best way I can describe it is, you know when you go to sleep? Sometimes you dream about the most recent thing that was on your mind? Let's just say, here at Wabasso, you'd probably want to be thinking about a hot blonde with a rocket bod when you go to bed." Kubby sucked on the joint in a few quick bursts and held his breath.

Jack tapped his toes as he waited for Kubby to start making sense.

"The point is we see our share of dreams come true around here. And that's all well and good when biographers and romance writers are the dreamers. Nobody seems to mind when they catch a fleeting glimpse of Gandhi walking through the woods or two lovers playing in the water." He exhaled as he spoke, letting the smoke billow from his mouth. "But, it's a different story when Wabasso has other energy to draw from. *Darker* energy. And something tells me you know exactly what I mean, don't you Jack?" He watched Jack closely now with judgment in his eyes. "You brought the darkness here with you."

Jack silently conceded the point. He knew it was true. Every nerve ending in his body told him as much.

"These things you've seen. These dreams, they're just getting started. They'll feed off you, get stronger, more real. Soon, you won't be able to tell the difference between them and reality."

"I've never had dreams like these," Jack said solemnly.

"Oh, they're not *your* dreams. They're Wabasso's. You just put the place in a dreaming mood. Come to think of it, it might be best if you *did* leave."

Jack's gaze fell to the floor. "I can't."

He was a little surprised that Kubby called his bluff. There was a subtle shift in the caretaker's bearing—a hint of newfound intensity. Jack guessed the subject matter brought it out in him. He went on, opting to take the honest approach. "I'm worried about Kate. I have reason to believe she may be in danger. She has certain *ties* to one of the characters in the story, this woman named Jill. The way Jill is described, she looks like Kate. They're about the same age. Their high schools have the same name. There's other stuff, too." *Like, they both try to help a lost cause and they both suffer for it.* "I'm afraid, if this goes on much longer, something is going to happen to her."

"What happens to this Jill person in the story?"

Jack reached out and took the joint from Kubby. He let his silence answer the question as he inhaled deeply.

Kubby understood. "We have to do something about this. But, you already have a plan, don't you?"

He surprised Jack again. Good old Kubby, who would get lost in the most elementary conversation, was now reasoning, calculating. Jack was sure he made the right decision in seeking his help. "We have to evacuate the retreat," he said as forcibly as he could.

"Whoa dude." Kubby got up and went to the window, shaking his head and shedding a mirthless laugh as he went. "We can't just go ahead and tell everyone they have to leave."

"I really don't see the problem, considering the situation."

Kubby turned and pointed his thumb in the rough direction of the guest cabins. "Well, these writers, they're here to finish projects. They have deadlines, obligations."

Jack tilted his head. "Do you really want me to tell you what I think about deadlines?"

"And the ownership—they'd freak if I closed the retreat. It's just not done. Wabasso hasn't been closed for one day in over seventy years. Hell, I can't be the first caretaker to do it."

"What do you think the ownership would say if someone got killed here?" Jack pressed. "That wouldn't be very good for the retreat's reputation in the writer's community." He stood up, pointed a finger in the caretaker's chest. "That's not to mention *your* reputation. Think about what would happen if a guest was murdered during your watch."

Kubby rubbed his eyes with thumb and forefinger. "This story…the stuff that happens, is it really that bad?"

"It's a horror story, Kubby." Jack went to stand in the doorway. "If things are progressing, getting worse like you say, it will get bloody before it's over. I've already seen the killer, Jonathan Dunn. He was strolling along the path like he belonged here as much as me or you."

Kubby regarded Jack. The colour went out of his cheeks. "Jonathan Dunn?"

"What?" Jack braced himself. Somehow he knew the situation had just gotten worse.

Kubby scratched the back of his head. "Umm, did you know, Kate's maiden name was Dunn?"

"Don't tell me she has a brother named Jonathan."

"*Had,*" Kubby corrected. He gazed out the window at the rain drenched trees. "We have to close the retreat."

Jack hurried up the steps to Kate's cabin. He was poised to knock before reconsidering. He looked over his shoulder at Kubby. "Maybe you should tell her. I think it will be more convincing coming from the caretaker."

Kubby nodded. He had thrown on his poncho before leaving the office and the downpour had already soaked it at his shoulders. He went to the door and knocked.

Jack stepped back and a wave of nervousness came over him. He wasn't sure he was ready to face Kate. She had an ability to shame him like no one else ever could. All she need do was give him a look, tilt her head just so, wince just right. When she opened the door, she would assuredly set those shamrock eyes on him and they would cut him to the bone. He waited in the rain for his dose of admonishment.

Kubby knocked again. He called for Kate through the door. "I'm sorry to bother you, but it's really important. It's an *emergency.*" He eyed Jack as if seeking approval for classifying the situation as so.

Jack gave his assent and urged Kubby to knock again. He thought Kate must have been sleeping. Then after more silent seconds went by, he *hoped* she was sleeping.

No response.

"Open it," Jack said.

Kubby nearly voiced a protest. He thought twice and reached for the doorknob. He turned it and it gave a tinny squeak. The door clunked as it slid out of its jamb. The aged hinges sang as Kubby pushed the door open a few inches. "Kate?" he said again, more softly. Jack tried to peek inside, over Kubby's shoulder.

He heard the caretaker gasp.

"What is it?" Jack said.

Kubby cautiously pushed his way inside. "I don't know," he said. "You tell me."

Jack went in and found the furniture pushed against the walls, like he'd found Cabin Five. Kate's clothes and office supplies heaped in the corner. Her laptop had been tossed aside. It all seemed to be done to make room for the odd hatchway in the middle of the cabin floor.

Kubby stared at it, his long hair matted and dripping. Jack stood beside him. The only sound for several long seconds was of the rain pelting the roof. "This shouldn't be here. These cabins don't have cellars. They're built on blocks." He broke his focus on the hatch to search Jack. "Why is it here?"

Jack knelt for a closer look. Constructed of roughhewn pine planks, the hatch had two large wrought iron hinges at one end and a yellow rope handle at the other. "This is the door to Jonathan Dunn's trophy room," he said, almost under his breath.

"Jack?" Kubby said, his hushed voice marked with astonishment.

"It's from the story I found. Dunn kept a souvenir from everyone he killed and put them in his trophy room." Jack stood up never taking his eyes of the hatchway. "This is the way in."

"*Shit.* What's it doing *here?*" Kubby protested. "Why is it in Kate's cabin?"

"Kubby, I told you this kind of thing has been showing up around here."

"Yeah, but, this isn't a quick glimpse of someone who shouldn't be here—something you'd see one second and it's gone the next. I've never seen anything like this before. I mean, this fucking thing is *real*." As if to prove his point, Kubby stepped up to the hatch and stomped his bare foot on it. A hollow thud issued.

"Don't do that!" Jack hissed. He grabbed a handful of Kubby's poncho and pulled him back. Both men lost balance and came close to falling over. They braced each other to keep upright.

"Kubby, forget we ever saw this thing," Jack said when he recovered his bearing. "Kate's obviously not here. Let's just move on, tell the others to get out."

"I can't just walk away from this thing," Kubby said, pointing at the floor. "I need an explanation or something. We can't…"

Jack heard a noise, some kind of *thud*. He raised his hand to silence Kubby and froze in place, straining to listen. The noise returned. Dull and distant, it sounded as though it came from under the floorboards.

It sounded again, this time more distinct. Kubby heard it, too. His mouth dropped open and he dropped his awestruck gaze to the hatchway.

Another *thud* issued. Then another.

Jack thought he might vomit when he determined the nature of the sound: workboots climbing the rungs of a wooden ladder. The footfalls stopped. Jack stole a glance at Kubby. The caretaker's eyes stuck on the hatch. He swallowed hard.

The hatch rattled slightly. Its hinges creaked. It started to open.

Jack dove for the hatch. He landed heavily on top of it, knees first, slamming it shut.

"Holy shit," wheezed Kubby. He pointed at the hatch with a trembling finger, his face awash with panic. "Dunn?"

Jack shook his head. "I don't want to find out." Fear made his muscles go to mush. He begged his bladder not to let go. The hatch started to shudder under him. He felt his body lift. "Kubby, help me," he yelled.

"What do I do?"

251

"Move the cot over here."

Kubby did. His movements were spastic and awkward. Jack could see that terror hobbled the caretaker, though he managed to slide the cot across the floor. Jack centred one of its legs on the hatch. He told Kubby to pile the dresser on the cot along with anything that wasn't nailed down.

The hatch shook without relent as the pile grew. Whoever was on the other side, they sorely wanted out. Kubby worked his way around the cabin, heaping Kate's things on the cot. He piled on her laptop, her books, and her luggage. He even made the effort of piling on tops and shorts that could not have weighed more than a few ounces. The task had taken over. He no longer thought with any sort of rational.

"That's it," Jack said, soberly. There was nothing left to add. He took one foot off the hatch. "Get ready to run."

Kubby went to the front door and opened it to the downpour. He nodded.

Jack took his foot off and the hatch sprang up a couple of inches and trembled in place. Jack loosed a pathetic yelp. The hatch held open briefly before falling shut again under the weight of the furniture.

Jack exhaled, the air sputtering out of him. He walked softly over to Kubby and followed him outside. Before they closed the door, Jack watched the hatch, rising one or two inches before banging shut again and again. Each time the hatch opened, he tried to catch a glimpse inside. He could see only darkness, so deep and all-consuming that it seemed to spill out across the floor each time the hatch lifted.

Kubby pulled Jack out of the way by the arm and closed the cabin door. He dug into his jeans pocket, produced a key and locked the cabin with it.

Jack was never so glad to be in the pouring rain. He turned his face to the sky and savoured the cool deluge.

Kubby went down the steps and crouched to look under the cabin. He yelled, "Jesus Christ!"

Jack rushed to join him.

"There's nothing," Kubby said, standing up. "There's

nothing under there. You can see clear through to the other side. *Fuck!* What the fuck was that?" Kubby bent at the waist as though he was going to retch and rubbed at his face. Jack presumed he was clearing tears. He patted Kubby's back and averted his eyes.

Kubby recovered a measure of composure and straightened up. "This is bad, Jack. We have to get out of here *now*."

"You're right. We should split up. We can cover more ground that way."

Kubby scanned the trees around them, wringing his hands as he did. "I don't know, dude."

"You round-up the guests from the other the cabins. I'll check the mess hall and the shower house. We'll meet in the parking lot in ten minutes." Jack shifted into the caretaker's sight line to meet his gaze. "Kubby, we're leaving regardless of who's with us."

Kubby considered the plan. Jack expected him to complain about the hazard in parting ways. Instead, he said, "This place, Wabasso, it's evil right through to the core, isn't it? I mean, that stuff I said about seeing things, nice things, nice people, around here, it's like Wabasso isn't satisfied with that. It wants to show us stuff like this." He nodded at Kate's cabin. "It wants to show us darkness. It's so much better at it." Kubby's face twisted with grief as the impact of his revelation hit home.

Jack laid a hand on his shoulder. Kubby had been here so long. Wabasso was his entire world and, before today, he likely never entertained the idea of leaving. Jack didn't even think Kubby had his own car in which to leave. Now, he wore the defeat of a man who just learned the love of his life didn't share the same feelings.

"Are you going to be okay on your own, Kubby?" Jack asked.

"I wish…I wish we could torch the place, burn it right to the ground. All of it," he said, turning to Jack. "Then no one will make the mistake of coming here again."

Jack recalled what Kate told him about the Boy Scout retreat, how it went up in flames. He figured Kubby wasn't the first person to have that idea.

"It's a little wet for fires," Jack said, cracking the faintest grin.

Kubby mustered a halfhearted smile on his own. "Okay, man. Ten minutes."

Entering the shower house, Jack felt as though he had inadvertently stepped into an alien dimension. A detectable charge filled the air and tickled his skin. The small hairs on his neck prickled. A deathly silence took hold. The shower house became a vacuum where sound failed to propagate. The rain didn't tap the roof. The wind didn't rattle the door and windows. Jack inched his way further inside. His footsteps, muted as well.

He stopped and raised a hand before his face. Rain water coated his skin. It pooled in his palm and tracked down his fingers. But the water did not drip off him. It clung to his flesh. Jack watched this phenomenon as he tilted his arm side to side.

A distinct drop of water hit the tiles in the shower room. It echoed off the porcelain, loud and clear.

Another drop echoed. Jack held still. Eyes glued to the floor, he took a pensive step forward.

"Kate?" he called.

It echoed back at him.

"Anyone in here?"

The water drip answered.

Jack took another step. He saw the blood in his periphery. It was hard to miss. The walls of the shower room to his left, the sinks and mirror to his right, the toilet stalls straight ahead, all of it glistened ruby red.

The drip sounded again.

It was the sound of blood dripping into a puddle.

Bile rose in his throat.

To hell with this. He turned on his heel and bolted for the exit.

The sky had been a dreary, milky grey when he last saw it, and where it had been raining only to adhere to the rules of nature, it now rained like it meant to. The sky had inked over. Its roiling clouds were coal-smoke black. Larger ones were infected with pale yellow and orange cores. Jack remembered pointing similar clouds out to his sons and playfully referring to them as thunder-boomers. He felt none of that jovial wonderment as he took in this sky—ominously dark with floral blotches of rage.

Jack pushed on. He had only the mess hall left to check. If he found it empty, he'd get to the parking lot on the double and wait for Kubby and the others. He hoped Kate would be among them. He tried to concentrate on that outcome. Or perhaps he'd find her in the mess, drinking coffee to warm up on the stormy afternoon, drying out in the perpetual warmth of the kitchen. Or maybe she had simply left in her car after he'd so rudely abandoned her in the parking lot. She had been so upset. Maybe she had intended to never see him again. Jack could find a way to accept that, too. Anything was better than her remaining at Wabasso and coming face to face with its spreading horror.

As Jack made his way to the mess hall, he tried to stay positive. *Everyone is leaving the retreat,* he thought. *Kubby is on board with the decision. We're doing the right thing. And who knows? Maybe we can all get out of here before any real harm is done.*

As he rounded the side of the mess hall, his fragile hopes took a nose dive. Propped against the front steps was a bicycle, parked so casually that it suggested its owner simply rode it here for lunch. Only this bike couldn't be ridden. The spokes of its rear wheel were mangled.

Like someone jammed something into it while it spun.

Jack knew who owned the bike even before he read the lettering on the newspaper bag slung over the handlebars.

He exhaled sharply, disgusted by the sight. He'd had his fill of Wabasso's displays and vowed to ignore this one, like a person out for a stroll would purposefully look away from road kill as they passed by. The bicycle proved difficult for Jack to ignore. Maybe it was because it was a young boy's bike, the sort Brian and Thomas would covet for its ape-hanger handle bars and its banana seat, so ideal for doubling. Jack paused by the mess hall steps and watched the rain running off the bicycle in steady streams. The same rain that ran off his nose and chin. It was as much a part of the world as he was. This bicycle, from the imagination of a writer he'd never met, sent a shudder through his bones.

He climbed the steps, intent on throwing open the door, and in the shortest possible order, determine the place void of humanity so he could move on to rendezvous with Kubby. Before opening the door, he took a second to prepare himself for another gruesome sight. He lowered his eyes and vowed that no matter what ghastly scene unfolded inside, he would keep them trained on the floor.

He opened the door, already calling aloud for Kate. Her name died on his lips. His gaze fell upon a body a few paces inside the door.

The man lay on his side, bound to a toppled chair. A river of blood ran from his midsection. Jack's feared he had discovered Wabasso's first victim. The stakes in this diabolical game had risen. Jack couldn't identify the man. He lay with his back to the door, but from his shoulder length, dirty-blonde hair, Jack could tell he wasn't one of the guests. Then it hit him. He wasn't looking at a person. He was looking at a character. This was Jill's husband. This was Luke.

This is how he died, Jack thought. *This is what happened minutes after Jonathan stabbed him. Jonathan went after Jill and left Luke alone in the farmhouse to bleed to death.* He stumbled backward out of the doorway and started to close the door.

Luke stirred.

Jack halted, his body stiff.

He's still alive.

Luke raised his head off the floor in a jerky, labored motion. "Wh-who's there?"

Jack held his breath.

"I know…someone's there," Luke said, his voice scratchy, dried out. "I need help."

Jack's mouth opened, but he lacked the air to make a sound.

Luke sputtered, "He stabbed me…and…he went after my wife. Please…we have to help her." His head dropped to the floor with a dull thump. He wiggled his fingers as though to challenge the knots that bound him.

Jack watched in petrified silence. The pathetic sight of Luke struggling turned his blood cold. Jack assured himself that Luke wasn't real. He had never existed. The wife he feared for now had never existed. His killer never existed. Still, Jack could not deny the sympathy he felt, watching the dying man spend his last reserves to free himself so he could help his wife to escape.

Jack found his voice. "I—I can't do anything to help you."

Luke's fingers stopped their fidgeting.

"I'm sorry for what happened to you," Jack said. He began to wonder if he had never found the manuscript, would this character have been made to suffer like this. *Whatever powers are at work at Wabasso, they gave this story life. Did they also give Luke life? Would they give him death as well?* Jack contemplated his responsibility in that. "I'm sorry for all of this," he said as much to himself as to Luke.

Luke fought to raise his head again. His neck jittered like old machinery as he turned his head to look over his shoulder at Jack.

An icy chill climbed Jack's spine and bunched the muscles in his shoulders. He started to breathe hard as Luke's eyes rolled in their sockets to meet his. The dying man's eyes widened with recognition. "*You…*" he said.

Jack's heartbeat fluttered. He thought for a second this is how it must feel to communicate with a ghost. He started to assure Luke that they had never met, but the searing hatred in Luke's eyes made Jack swallow the words. Luke clearly thought he knew him. So strong was Luke's familiar loathing that Jack started to second guess their connection.

"You stay away from my wife!" Luke bellowed, impossibly loud. "You leave her alone!"

Jack winced and covered his ears as Luke roared again. He nearly slid down the steps as he got out of the path of the door to slam it shut. Jack put his shoulder to the door for fear that Luke would try to push it open in pursuit. From within, the yelling continued, "You let her go, you hear me? You let her go!"

Why? Jack thought. *Why is this happening to me?* He couldn't remember when a case of mistaken identity hurt as much as that. He contemplated the years of psychotherapy it would take to get over it.

First things, first, he told himself. *I'm getting the hell out of here.*

Jack hurried along the path where it curved close to the beach. The further he got from the mess hall, the more he felt the strain in his shoulders alleviate. He told himself he had witnessed Wabasso's final trick. Soon this horrid experience would be behind him. He wasn't certain, however, how long it would take to fully recover from it. The total damages were, as yet, untallied. This much he knew: he was now unemployed. He owed his publisher more than a hundred thousand dollars and his ex-wife would say she wanted just as much. Jack could see himself turning into one of those solitary drinkers who took up corner stools at the neighbourhood bar, aged beyond his years, emotionally scarred and too far behind in the race to ever hope to catch up. He felt a new, but milder sort of fear spread throughout his system—fear of the future.

He was sure of one other thing. He would never be so glad to climb into his old Buick. He would offer Kubby a ride, too. Hell, he'd offer him a place to stay. Then they could both take some time to figure out what to do with the rest of their lives. They would be the new odd couple—pot-smoking, barefoot Kubby and straight-laced, liberal Jack. He would teach Kubby the merit of refinement and socks. Kubby would teach him to be a little more laid back. It made for an interesting book idea. That mere thought made him groan aloud.

Jack didn't want to so much as see another book let alone attempt writing one. He had learned his lesson, and like the difficult lessons of his childhood that were often times punctuated with spankings he would not forget it anytime soon. That's what he would take away from Wabasso. *It gives us what we need most*, he thought. *Maybe I needed Wabasso to teach me that.* If there was any sort of intelligence behind that lesson, it was not only well beyond Jack's reckoning. It was also a malignant one.

The office was straight ahead. The parking lot, off the long driveway leading to the retreat's exit, came up on Jack's left. To his right, the rain packed sands of the beach, and beyond it, the haunted lake. Jack didn't know why he stopped. The parking lot was a short jog away. Kubby and the other guests would be there soon, if they weren't already. In a few short minutes, they could all be outside the gates, putting the retreat in the rearview.

He turned to the right. He looked upon Wabasso one last time. When he first saw it, he'd felt an immediate disdain for the word *lake*. It was a weak and loathsome word to describe such an awe-inspiring spectacle. The water was a jewel in the middle of the wild, northern woods. Jack had thought he had found a piece of the heavens, a slice of the celestial body dragged down to Earth. He could think of other words to describe Wabasso now, none of them relating to beauty in any way. It had lost all of its charm.

Jack watched the bland expanse of matte grey. The driving rain turned its surface to gooseflesh. In the distance, Jack saw a spot of colour in the gloom. He squinted and took a few steps toward the beach. Rubbing rain water from his eyes, he strained his vision across Wabasso to its north shore, some two hundred yards from where he stood.

The red object was easy to pick it out against the cold landscape. Jack rubbed his eyes again and looked back to the distant shore in hopes he was seeing things. The answer was as much on this shore as it was on the adjacent. Here, laying next to the stone ringed fire pit, was the overturned green canoe. Its red mate was absent.

Jack ran to the edge of Wabasso, stopping short only so it wouldn't touch his feet. Across its breadth, he could see the red canoe, beached with purpose and overturned to keep out rainwater. Jack's anguish overcame him. He grabbed handfuls of his hair and tugged them. He wanted to scream. After he had left Kate in the parking lot, she hadn't gone back to her cabin, nor did she go to the mess hall. She had gone ahead with her planned canoe trip, and when the downpour became too much, she put ashore to seek shelter until it abated. As if to give confirmation, Wabasso lapped further up the beach and doused Jack's shoes. He backed up, turned to seek out Kubby amid the retreat's buildings. Jack was alone. And, across the water, so was Kate.

His body moved before his mind was made up, a reflexive action that sent him rushing to the green canoe. The mental image of Jonathan Dunn stalking Kate as she crouched under the sheltering boughs of a pine tree, spurred him to action. Jack saw him slinking closer like a woodland predator, from behind one tree trunk to the next. Jonathan cradled his knife, planning out how he would turn it loose on Kate.

On his sister, Jack thought. *That is what Kubby said.*

Jack turned the canoe over and revealed two wooden paddles on the dry sand beneath. He grabbed one of them and dragged the canoe to the water's edge. He pushed it in and waded in after it, no longer timid of making physical contact with the eerie body of water. Jack knew there wasn't a nook or cranny in his being that Wabasso hadn't already touched in some way. When the water was knee deep, he climbed in the canoe and started to paddle.

From the personal journal of William Jessop:

7 September, 2012.

After failing to question Mr. K with any sort of success, I decided to take a break from my Tanner Black story. I shoved the file to the corner of my desk. A few more days went by and I closed it in a drawer. I was dangerously close to forgetting it, altogether. Until tonight. Until I got the call.

I tried to get this transcript down quickly so I didn't forget anything.

At first, I thought it was one of my friends prank-calling me. Everyone gets those calls from time to time—heavy breathing, incoherent mumbling. I listened to this act for nearly a minute and was on the point of hanging up when the caller finally said something I could comprehend: "I know you're not a member of the following, asshole."

I knew this voice and it did not belong to one of my immature acquaintances. I had to cut through the caller's slurred speech before my memory could place it. Then I realised I was once again speaking with the senior editor at Lightning Storm Press.

Mr. Hustwick was obviously drunk. He panted on the line while waiting for me to respond.

"I may have misled you," I said, measuring every word of my answer carefully in hopes of avoiding any legal snares. Maybe it was too late for that. "I *was* a member of The Tanner Black Following when I was in high school, but I was never an officer."

"Why did you lie to me?"

"I needed information for my story on Black and I thought you'd be more forthcoming with a representative of his fan club."

"Whassit about?"

"My story? It's about the reason he retired from writing—the real reason—not some song and dance about family issues."

Hustwick's panting resumed. Finally, he said, "Good. That's the only reason I didn't call security about you. Howssit coming?"

"Not great. I hit a dead end."

"Then, you're lucky I called, 'cause what I'm about to tell you will give your project a boost."

I waited and wondered what Hustwick could tell me now that he couldn't before. Was the publisher releasing some newly discovered work of Black's? Yours for the low, low price of thirty five bucks a pop?

"Tanner Black isn't dead."

I nearly dropped my phone. "What did you just say?"

"He isn't. His agent cooked the whole thing up to hide the truth—him and those people who own the retreat he attended."

It took a few minutes to fully absorb Hustwick's news. As it sunk in, I told him everything I knew about the retreat, ending with my meeting Mr. K. Hustwick had plenty to say and went on to make bold claims about the vast influence of Wabasso's ownership, that they're more than capable of pulling off such a cover up.

"I must admit, it's not quite the Herculean task it sounds like," Hustwick added. "Because Tanner Black was never really alive in the first place."

After thinking for a moment, I said, "It's a penname. *God*, I never knew that."

"*Ha*. Indeed. I guess there is *some* truth in saying that Tanner

Black is dead. Although, his alter-ego, Reggie LeMay, is still very much alive. Tonight, I opened a single-malt scotch I'd been saving to toast that fact. I suppose I got a little carried away."

"Why the cover up, Hustwick?"

"You'll know why as soon as you see him. In his current, er, *state*, he constitutes something of an embarrassment—for the memory of his career and for the retreat that last hosted him."

"What happened to him?"

"Just go see him. And write your damn article. Tell the truth. For my part in this, it would be the only fitting end. There's a little town down the coast. You'll find him there in a place called Saint Michael's. It's a hospital for the mentally ill."

From the personal journal of William Jessop:

8 September, 2012.

I just met Tanner Black.

I suppose it is only right to refer to him by his real name, but old habits die hard.

Finding Saint Michael's was easy in this little berg. It is the only mental health facility in town, and when I asked the attendant at the gas station for directions, all he had to do was point. The place is run down, but I don't imagine its guests complain much. I went inside and was first met by a rather intimidating orderly named Klewes. I gave my name and said I was there to see my wife's uncle, Reggie LeMay. Jim Croce's *Leroy Brown* played in my head as Klewes stared me down. Using the details I'd learned about Black's family, I told him that I had travelled from the west coast and wouldn't be in town long. It was enough to convince the orderly. He led me to a lounge off the main corridor and nodded toward a man seated in the corner and wrapped in a light blue robe.

I crossed the large room and took the chair beside Black, saying loud enough for the orderly to hear, "Hello Uncle Reg. How are you feeling?"

I almost couldn't finish my sentence when Black raised his head and his eyes met mine. His appearance more than gave me pause. I was stunned. This looked nothing like the man I had met just a few years ago while he was on book tour. This man was haggard, old. Stringy grey hair, left long to accommodate a comb over, hung down the side of his face. White stubble frosted his chin. It seemed that patient grooming was a low priority among the Saint Michael's staff. At least the residents were oblivious to the fact. They lounged about the room in their various stupors, basking in the infiltrating sunlight. As for Black, his half lidded eyes studied my face while his lower lip quivered. Most troubling, he wore that beleaguered mask only illness can account for. It slackened his face, making for significant bags under his eyes and jowls about his mouth.

In his watery eyes, I read a complete lack of recognition, but he did nothing to blow my cover story. He nodded slightly and gave a grunt. I took that to mean he was accepting of my company. For his part, Klewes got seated on the other side of the lounge and took up a *Sports Illustrated*, the pages of which he occasionally peeked over in our direction.

Black pulled the collar of his robe tightly closed and as he did, I caught a glimpse of the cross he wore around his neck. No rudimentary thing, it was gold and included a finely detailed corpus. My grandmother, a staunch Catholic in her own right, told me once of the significance in wearing the likeness of Christ's body on the cross. She held that it offered the wearer the Lord's protection. Whether or not Black's original reason for donning the cross was to ward off evil, I am quite certain he no longer knows. Within seconds of sitting down with him, it became painfully clear that he was not in full possession of his faculties. He gave no answer to my questions regarding his comfort at the hospital, his enjoyment of the food. Everything I had to say was met with an expression of utter confusion.

Until I mentioned Wabasso Lake.

As soon as I broached the subject, a firmness entered his visage. His mouth became a thin line and his half lidded eyes peeled back. He leaned in close to me with some effort and whispered, "Are you one of them?"

"One of who?"

"Are you from the lake? Are you one of them?"
I tried to assure him that I had no affiliation with the retreat.

Black was skeptical and now he eyeballed me with intensity. The orderly, with his periodic peeking over his magazine, seemed all the more watchful as well. I lowered my voice and told Black about the story I was working on. He listened intently as I explained my interest in his career and in the retreat he'd attended.

265

"They're devils," he said, cutting me off. "At Wabasso... they're not people like us. They're devils."

To say that the manic conviction that accompanied Black's outrageous claim was dismaying is an understatement. I held out hope that he wasn't being literal in his description of the people at Wabasso, but as he expanded on his experience there, it became plain that his sanity was in shreds. He grew more and more animated as he reported his time at the lake. He spoke of the vivid nightmares he'd had of the retreat going up in flames. He claimed he was taken by force across the lake and on these trips he saw alien lights deep under the water.

The whole thing filled me with sorrow. I could scarcely believe this was the same man who wrote *Rumor in the Night*, one of my all-time favorite novels. As he spoke, I wondered how the man who had woven such a complex mystery could end up so devoid of rationale. And the worst was yet to come. He said, "They're watching me, you know."

It was clear from his scowl that he wasn't referring to the orderly across the lounge.

"They want to take me back there."

"Back to Wabasso?"

"They thought they could take my story from me," he whispered sharply. "They tried, but I hid it."

"What did you hide?" I asked, but he ran off on a different tangent.

"I saw the damned lights in the water. I saw them. They deny it, but I saw them." His voice rose and I cast a look across the lounge.

The orderly had put his magazine down. "Everything okay out there?" he said, staring as he awaited response.

"Yes. We're fine," I said, unconvincingly, I'm sure.

Black was indeed not fine. He clutched my arm then and I almost howled. He pulled me in close and said, "Don't let them take me back there."

From there, he started into a rambling fit about these underwater lights. His agitation continued to build during his tirade. It was enough to bring Klewes over and a second broad-shouldered orderly appeared from the hall. Klewes told me that visiting hours were over and I didn't offer any complaint. I was eager to end this painful encounter, myself. I apologized to the staff and got up to leave.

Black shouted to me before I reached the corridor. "Young man!"

I turned and found him straining against the orderly, who did his best to calm the patient down.

"If you go there, don't let them take you across the lake. They're devils!"

What I saw in Black's eyes is going to haunt me. One might expect that his expression hinted at mania or dementia as he yelled to me. More troubling than either of those, his eyes conveyed a true sense of pleading. Whether or not there was anything extraordinary happening at that lake, he believed in his heart of hearts there was. His conviction was not enough to sell me on the existence of light phenomena or any wrong-doing on behalf of the retreat staff, but it did pique my curiosity all the more. I have to admit, I have already had feelings of foreboding about the place based purely on the secrecy surrounding it.

Mr. K had provided little useful information during our conversation and I have since come to think that it was no accident that his office was empty for our meeting. It seemed he desired total privacy for any discussion concerning the retreat. His specious behavior aside, I can't let myself lose sight of why I started this project. I need to know what happened to Tanner Black at that lake.

Somewhere along the line, a career writer who was unanimously seen as a consummate professional and artisan of his craft broke character and failed to finish a book. What's worse, during this time, his mental health suffered a serious blow. While the strange lights he claims to have seen at the retreat are not likely to blame, I believe that is where his breakdown occurred.

Too many questions about the place have gone unanswered. But of one thing, I am certain. I have to see Wabasso Lake for myself. I rented a car for my visit with Black. It shouldn't be much trouble to extend my lease by a couple of days. Mr. K, himself, recommended I visit Wabasso. There is no reason why I can't depart for the lake immediately.

Chapter Fourteen

J ack fought to keep the canoe travelling straight. He made Jill's red boat on the adjacent shore his target and followed it like a homing beacon. One moment, it was left in relation to the canoe's bow. He corrected his course and it moved to the right. He corrected again. He figured from a vantage on dry land, he would appear to be zigzagging his way across the lake.

He counted one blessing. The waters were still. For all the rushing wind, no waves resulted. The passage across was relatively safe and as Jack fumbled the paddle from port to starboard, he was thankful for it. He looked down at the small wake peeling from the boat as it cut the water, pleased that he gained speed.

A flash overhead drew his focus skyward. He saw a branch of lightning reach across the sky and fray into fine threads in the distance. The sound of the detonation came as soon as the fire faded. The blast rattled Jack's teeth and he dropped the paddle in the boat so he could cover his ears. The canoe pitched. Jack seized the rails to steady it. For a moment, he pictured rolling over, dumping into Wabasso. He imagined struggling to swim in his sodden jeans and he tightened his grip on the boat.

The rambling thunder trailed off and he took up his paddle again. He guessed he neared the halfway point and he put his back into paddling. He couldn't get off the water fast enough. That lightning bolt shot through the sky, instead of striking the ground. Jack wondered if his luck would hold out next time or if he would get fricasseed in the middle of the lake. Maybe Kubby would find his charred remains adrift in the canoe or maybe he would sink to the bottom with no trace of him ever to be found.

Jack could not dwell on that thought for long. He cried out as the canoe heaved under him. The boat leveled out as it passed over a solitary wave. He looked behind him as the swell in the water travelled several feet before it dissipated. He watched to his left where a new wave gathered some thirty yards out. Jack turned the bow toward it so it wouldn't upset the canoe, but the wave seemed to change direction. It cut across in front of him.

Jack went as stiff as the wooden paddle in his hands. Under the surface, at the leading edge of that wave, he saw a shadow. His face slackened and his eyes bulged. He tracked the dark mass, close in size to his Buick, to his right side and lost sight of it.

School of fish, he thought. *That's all. Or a sturgeon. They can get pretty big. That's it*, he promised himself.

Jack's sturgeon left a large wake and when it reached him, the canoe bobbed. Jack spurred into motion. Keeping an eye trained behind the boat, he dug the paddle into the water and shoveled for his life. Fear fuelled his muscles. Another flash lit the sky. Jack found another gear. The waters around him remained, for the moment, relatively calm, still Jack couldn't shake the feeling that he was being followed.

Thunder boomed.

Jack figured the deafening grumble from the heavens was the worst noise ever made. Then he heard a dreadful scraping on the underbelly of his canoe. Worse yet, he *felt* it. Something coarse rubbed the bottom of the boat and the sensation travelled right up his backbone. His imagination conjured images of curved claws at the end of a long, scaly appendage grasping for the boat. More scraping issued from below. Despite his fevered paddling, the canoe's forward momentum ground to a halt. The claws had him.

He gripped his paddle, ready to defend himself. He whipped his head around in search for his assailant and saw that he had run the canoe aground. The claws he heard scraping the bottom of the canoe were stones on the lakebed. He loosed an exasperated sigh and dropped the paddle in the boat. He awkwardly got out and waded through shin deep water to the shore. He dragged the canoe to a stop alongside Kate's. Under her overturned boat, he could see her lifejacket and paddle, sheltered from the rain.

Jack searched the lake for sign of other rogue waves. He puzzled over what he had witnessed on the water. It didn't fit with the other phenomena happening around the retreat in that it wasn't a recreation from the pages of *Together, Dead*. Jack considered the shadow cutting through the water mere feet below the surface. Whatever it was, it knew he was there—it responded to his change in course. It was intelligent. Given the choice, Jack would take a run-in with Jonathan Dunn any day.

Jack turned to scan the landscape for a sign of Kate. Cedars and firs crowded together, their branches entwined in an unruly mesh. A few feet from the rocky shore, spiny shrubs grew in earnest. They consumed all available space between the taller trees. The slippery stones would prove treacherous. This was no beach for visitors to enjoy. This was a wild place.

Jack expected Kate would be nearby. Passage through the trees would prove too difficult for her to make it very far. He looked further down the shoreline in each direction and found nothing but more rough terrain at the water's edge skirted by encroaching vegetation.

He called Kate's name and waited. He called again, louder.

Rain slapped the canoes, the water and stones.

Jack wrung his hands. He got the dismal feeling that his attempt to rescue Kate was too late. Surely, she would have stayed within ear shot of her canoe. Surely she would have answered him…if she was able.

He called her name, louder again.

No answer.

He moved cautiously along the shore, scanning the trees as he went, searching for an entry point. Again, he tried to picture Kate penetrating the intertwining branches and he couldn't fathom it. There was no trace of her entry—a broken branch or a trampled shrub. She simply could not have gone into those woods. Regardless of that reasoning, he pushed his way in.

With his hands shielding his face, Jack plowed between two brambly pines. Their fine limbs, sharp as blades, scraped across his exposed arms. He heard the snapping of a thousand matchsticks as he worked his way through. Here another spiny pine blocked his path and he shoved his way around it as well. More scrapes marked his arms and one especially nasty branch dragged across his ear, drawing a line of blood. Jack paused to apply pressure to the cut and he yelled for Kate again. His plea went unanswered and he continued on.

Either it had stopped raining or the growth here was too dense to permit so much as a water drop. Jack couldn't tell which. All he could do was push his way through as though he were shoulder to shoulder in a mob of people. Only these people raked him with their nails as he went by. He stopped again to rub the sting out of his arms.

He looked back the way he had come and was dismayed to find he'd only gone about ten feet. They were the hardest earned ten feet of his life—painful ones. When he held up his hands they were blood smeared from all his fresh scratches. Ahead, the next jagged obstacles stood in his way and beyond them, there were more, and beyond them, more still.

He yelled Kate's name, not expecting an answer. The slight venting of frustration felt good enough to make him yell again. And again. And after his brief tirade, he stopped to catch his breath. He closed his eyes and stood perfectly still among razor sharp branches, pawing at his every side.

He heard a call, distant and weak.

"*I'm here.*"

Jack's eyes sprung opened. They shot toward the source of the cry, further into the dense forest.

"Kate?" he called, praying what he'd heard wasn't his mind playing tricks.

He waited. His body locked up for fear his slightest movement would drown out her faint response. Two seconds passed, four, six, while he refrained from taking a breath or blinking an eye.

Her response reached him again.

"*Help me.*"

Jack gasped. *She's here.* The epiphany summoned a strength to his voice he did not know he possessed. "*I'm coming!*"

He threw himself into the thicket of ruthless pines. He raised his forearms and ducked his head behind them like a prize fighter taking heavy blows. The trees slashed as he fought his way through. They sliced into him, more seriously than the cut to his ear this time. His arms took the brunt of the assault. Lines gouged into them that at first felt cool then quickly warmed as the blood flowed to the surface. One limb snagged his shirt and he heard it rip as he marched onward. He shoved past another tree, suffered another raking, and nearly fell forward as he stumbled into a clearing.

The break amid the forest was only a half dozen yards wide and more soldier pines bordered it, threatening more cuts and scrapes. Moss and low ferns covered the ground. Jack savoured the reprieve the clearing offered from the punishing forest. He brushed the carpet of needles out of his hair and off his shoulders and he braced himself as he started toward the trees at the far side of the break.

His footsteps sounded hollow on the forest floor. He stopped and kicked at the moss. A patch of it lifted to reveal wooden planks beneath. He had discovered the remnants of a building. The planks were blackened. As he moved on, he recognized more wooden beams jutting up from the greenery, black and charred.

Jack wondered if it was part of the lost Boy Scout retreat or evidence of some other forgotten incarnation of Wabasso.

"Jack!"

Kate's call came from the trees across the clearing. A waver in her voice suggested she was injured and it spurred him onward. He thrust himself into the pines. "Stay where you are, Kate," Jack yelled. "I'm coming."

The branches whipped him without mercy, but he didn't slow. All he could think of was Kate hobbled and hurt, needing his help. She cried out, giving her position to whoever else might be listening.

He pictured Jonathan Dunn stalking amid the trees, his ax making short work of the limbs in his way. The image redlined Jack's heart rate. He yelled aloud to tell Kate he was close. Daylight penetrated the wall of trees. In a few yards he would be out of the woods and he would find her. He could *feel* her presence. So strong was the sensation, he no longer felt the need to yell. Between labored breaths, he said, "Kate. I'm here. It's okay. I'm here."

He could see tall grasses beyond the trees. Ducking under the bough of one last evergreen, he pushed out of the dense woods and into a wide field of knee-high, golden grass.

Kate wasn't there.

Jack paused to slow his racing heart. He tried to harness his wild breathing long enough to call Kate's name. He drew a breath, but before he could summon his voice, he realised calling her would be pointless. She wasn't close. He knew it. That sure feeling of being in her presence had slipped away. A bleak isolation replaced it. It served a bitter mouthful that Jack couldn't swallow.

He jogged along the tree line, searching the grasses for sign of her. The long blades bent and flattened as he went through, leaving a clear line in his wake. He could make out no other indication—no depression where Kate might have sat, no trampled grasses showing which way she may have walked. Jack stopped, wiped the sweat from his brow and gazed across the field. All thoughts of Kate's whereabouts evaporated from his mind as he stood staring dumbly at a large white building.

His mind grappled with the sight of the structure—the *house*, he decided—that jutted up from the field like the lone tooth in a broken smile. It appeared so out of place, he couldn't fathom what in the world it was doing there. Yet, it was eerily familiar. Its long black shingled roof was sectioned by three dormers, each with French paneled windows. Decorative black shutters bookended each window in the two storey house, but there was little appealing about the place. Dry rot and flaking paint mottled the white plank siding. Some of the boards were missing here and there, likely blown down in a high wind and never repaired. None of the windows that Jack could see shed light or any other sign of inhabitants. Neither of the red brick chimneys at either end of the house hinted at fires within.

Jack's eyes began to sting and he realised he hadn't blinked in some time. He closed them and was mildly surprised that the house hadn't vanished when he opened them again. He started toward it, slowly at first, and broke into a run, never taking his eye off of the place. Like a desert oasis, he expected it to fade into the evergreen background before he got anywhere near. He wondered if Kate had seen it, too. Did she go there seeking help? Would he find her there?

For the first time, he took account that it was no longer raining. The sun was an orange blaze as it dipped toward the distant hills. It tinged the few remaining clouds in the otherwise clear evening sky. He didn't question how the day faded so quickly into night. His mind had completely seized on the house. As Jack drew closer, he saw another structure peeking out from behind it. He changed his angle of approach for a better view of this other building. He stopped running. It stood as tall as the house, built from roughly finished boards with two wide doors on its front side.

No. Oh God, no. It can't be.

He lunged forward and ran to the house, screaming for all he was worth, *"Kate! Get out of there!"*

He knew this place—the big white house with the old adjacent barn. Around the corner of the house, he'd find the mud room entrance that led to the kitchen. From there, he knew the hallway would take him to the parlor on the right, the stairs on the left, and the front door dead ahead. He knew the cellar and he knew the bedrooms. He even knew which one belonged to Jonathan Dunn.

Jack rounded the corner of the house. He found the mud room open and went in. Throwing all caution aside, he again yelled for Kate. His voice bounced off the walls and the space fell silent again. All Jack heard was his pulse thundering in his ears.

He stood in the Dunn's house as it was imagined by *Together, Dead's* author. Idea made print, made real, and Jack couldn't care less. Any astonishment to do with fiction becoming reality had left him. All he wanted was to find Kate and get her away from Wabasso Lake—back to the real world, if there still existed such a place.

He entered the kitchen filled with evidence of mundane, everyday life. Dirty dishes piled high beside the large steel sink. Blotches of dried food speckled the range. An empty milk bottle stood solemnly on the counter beside the refrigerator. Jack scanned all this with little interest, but he froze on sight of the kitchen table.

Three places were set with napkins and flatware. On the middle placemat sat an old-fashioned type writer. A sheet of paper drooped on the reel. More papers were stacked face down beside it. Jack recognized the pages. They bore the same yellowy tint as the rest of the *Together, Dead* manuscript. It dawned on Jack that he stood over a work station—*the* work station. His heartbeat revved.

This is where it was written. He gathered the pages up with tremulous hands. *And, this must be the ending.*

He battled the overwhelming urge to flee the farmhouse.

A run-in with Jonathan Dunn no longer frightened him. The prospect of meeting the story's true author, on the other hand, infused him with a dread he was unaccustomed to.

"Does this place look familiar to you?"

Jack spun around to find Kubby standing in the kitchen doorway. Once he recognized the caretaker, relief flooded in. "Kubby? How did you get here?" he asked, tripping over his own words.

Kubby's lips bent in a secretive grin. Jack's relief began to fade. There was something *off* about Kubby's appearance. He was different. His beard, usually a bird nest of tangled whiskers, was squarely trimmed. His normally unruly hair was greased and tied back. In place of his dirty t-shirt and torn jeans, he wore a form fitting black sweater and slender burgundy trousers. His feet, though, were as bare and as black as ever. That was the extent of the traces of old Kubby. The doughty, stoned retreat caretaker was gone, replaced by a man with calculating eyes.

Kubby walked past him and snatched the pages out of his hands. He glanced at the top page then let them dangle at his side. "The better question is how did *you* come to be here?"

"Well…I came looking for Kate."

"I don't think she's here."

"What's going on, Kubby?" Jack nodded at the pages. "Did you write that?"

"*Me?* No, I told you before, I'm no author. I'm just an observer." Kubby sauntered across the kitchen and into the hallway. Jack followed, allowing some distance between them. He caught the faint smell of rotten eggs in his Kubby's wake.

"I don't understand." Jack scowled. "What is this place? Whose house is this?"

Kubby smiled over his shoulder at Jack. "I honestly don't know. This is your world, my friend. I'm just visiting." He stopped and leaned against the wide doorway to the parlor. His brow furrowed as though what he saw did not impress him.

"What kind of an answer is that? Where are the people

who live here?" Even as he posed the question, Jack knew the truth. They were dead. At least, that is how the story went. He looked around the parlor, to the folded newspaper on Mr. Dunn's armchair, to Mrs. Dunn's needlepoint waiting on the chesterfield. Kubby watched Jack reach his own conclusions. His new, smug grin played on his lips again. Jack didn't like it. He roared, "*Answer me.*"

Kubby broke into laughter, so soft it sounded like a dry clicking in his throat. An exaggerated pout came over his face, like he was disappointed in Jack's powers of deduction. "Jack, why do you think you were invited to Wabasso Lake?"

Jack's gaze drifted in search of an answer.

"I'm sorry to say it wasn't based on your talents as a writer."

A little rouge crept into Jack's cheeks, as he regarded the caretaker.

"Nevertheless, you were chosen to be here. You were *meant* to be here." Kubby turned from the parlor and went to the front door. He pushed it open and the scarlet brilliance of the evening sky wreathed his form. "Wabasso wants you as much as you *need* it."

"You're wrong," Jack said. He stood defiantly in the hallway. "I don't want anything to do with it. I'm leaving."

"Come now, Jack. Must you be so dramatic? You and Wabasso reached out to each other. You were drawn here. You two have been communicating for a very long time." Kubby read the lost look in Jack's face and laughed again. "You didn't believe you were really at a writer's retreat, did you Jack? Did you think real writers actually worked this way—in tiny cabins around a lake?"

"What the hell is it, then?"

"Good question, Jack. Honestly, we're not even sure anymore. All I know is books are written here and we help them reach the public. So long as we get to add a few choice messages into the text, we really don't care who the writer is. So many countless souls have been summoned here over the years. There have been more Warren Hellicksons and Ralph

Deakins than I can shake a stick at—every single one of them, unfit. They have all failed to hear Wabasso's true voice."

Kubby pointed his index fingers at Jack like they were pistols. "But, not you, Jack. Those others, they're weak. Then again, commandment-breakers so often are, but we all have to work with what we're given, right? But, there's a fortitude about you, Jack. I see it. Wabasso has seen it. It likes you. It deems you fit. You two have formed a bond that is stronger than you can begin to imagine—stronger than the one it shares with me, perhaps."

"Who are you?" Jack said, his defiant stance starting to waver.

"Well, I'm the caretaker, at least for the next few hours." Kubby folded his arms across his chest. "Then you will replace me."

Jack's jaw went slack.

"I'm old, Jack," Kubby continued. "In fact, my age likely far exceeds your ability to reckon. In short, I am retiring— going someplace *warmer*, you might say. And Wabasso has chosen you to replace me, Jack. By morning, Wabasso Lake will be entrusted to you."

Jack shook his head, unable to speak.

Kubby stepped back into the hallway, closed in on Jack. "Yes," he said evenly. "There must be a sort of give and take in any successful relationship, and you must give something back since you have already received Wabasso's gift."

"Gift?"

Kubby shoved the pages at Jack. "It gave you your story."

Jack clutched the papers to his chest then held them at arm's length, examined them briefly. "No," he said, a rattle in his voice. He cleared his throat and spoke more forcefully. "No. I don't want this. I don't need it anymore. I'm done with publishers."

Kubby's lips peeled back to reveal his gnashed teeth. Jack flinched. "I didn't say it was the *publisher's* story," The caretaker grumbled, and just as quickly, restored his composure. He smiled warmly. "I said it was *your* story, and because it is *your*

279

story, you are the only one who can finish it. Give it the end-ing it needs. The ending *you* need. Finish it and cement your bond with Wabasso. Take your place here and you will never want for anything again."

"I can't! I told you before. I can't write anymore."

"Jack, please, haven't you been paying attention? Words don't count for much in these parts. It is the *show* that truly matters." With that, Kubby grinned again and went to the front door. He looked outside expectantly as though the train he waited for was due any moment.

Jack eyed the top page in the bunch. It contained only nonsensical typing. The name of the story, *Together, Dead*, repeated again and again, in capital letters, populating the en-tire page. The next page was the same. So was the one after that. Jack shot a confused look at Kubby while he thumbed to the final page. As the name of the story repeated over and over in succession, spaces were introduced in the text in dif-ferent places, breaking the title down, separating the words. Jack first thought the text had deteriorated into gibberish, but he seized on the final line and he saw the words take on new meaning.

He read it aloud, "'To get her dead...'" He raised his head. "What does this mean?"

"Come," Kubby said with a wave of his hand.

Jack crossed the floor to join Kubby, apprehension slowing his steps. The words, *to get her dead*, echoed in his head. The message stirred revolting feelings. He held up the bunch of papers, peeled back to the final page, and turned it toward Kubby as if to get his opinion on the matter.

Kubby didn't offer so much as a glance at it. His stare aimed outside, in the direction of the barn. When Jack sidled up to him, he saw the barn doors standing wide open. Inside it, he saw the back of the silver minivan.

Jack let the pages drop as he went out the door. They fell in a heap on the porch. He stumbled down the steps, never taking his eyes off the vehicle. He stared at it, willing it to dis-appear like Wabasso's other cruel illusions. The van remained.

In the rear windshield, the ghosts of Brian and Thomas waved goodbye as they did on moving day. Jack inhaled sharply. He turned to Kubby, pleading for an explanation.

Kubby, lingering in the doorway, rubbed his hands together and shrugged. He nodded at the barn. Jack turned back to the gaping doors just in time to see his ex-wife come tripping outside.

She hopped on one leg, her other, bent at the knee. A line of blood snaked from under the leg of her Capri's and ran down her sandaled foot. Her good leg could not handle her forward momentum. She spilled in the dirt.

"Oh my God!" Jack yelled. He rushed toward her to offer help.

She screamed at his advance, "*Stay back*," and scrambled to her feet. "Stay the hell away from me!"

Jack stopped in his tracks and held out his palms in a placating gesture. His mouth hung open to speak, but his dozens of questions log-jammed and nothing came out.

"What are you doing here, Jack?" she demanded. "What is this place? You said you were going to a resort to work on your book." It seemed she registered the blood on Jack's arms and face for the first time. She screamed again. "What have you done?"

A mix of dread and disgust twisted her face, all the more dire in the red tint of the setting sun. Jack released a desperate, nervous laugh. He was about to tell her that he could explain everything when she cut him off.

"I saw the cellar, Jack," she said as evenly as she could, but emotion cracked her voice again. "I saw those *things* in the cellar. What have you been doing here?"

"No, no, those aren't my things," Jack said. He turned to Kubby and threw out his hands. "Tell her, Kubby, please. Tell her those aren't my things. They're from the story. Tell her."

Kubby casually stepped down from the porch. "I don't think she can be reasoned with right now."

"Why is she here?"

"This is *your* story, Jack," Kubby said, forcefully. "And she has a rather large role to play in it."

"Who in the fuck are you talking to?" she screeched. "You're out of your fucking mind!"

Jack pointed to his right. "It's okay, he's the caretaker."

She looked briefly where he indicated and started to sob. "What happened to you?"

Kubby stopped a few feet from Jack. "This is it. You're in the final chapter, on the last page. This is where you write your ending and start a new life for yourself. This woman took everything from you. She took your sons. She took your craft. And she didn't think twice about what it would do to you."

Jack faced the caretaker. "What are you suggesting I do?" he asked, but even as he said it, he pictured the title of his story in bold, black ink.

To Get Her Dead.

That was Wabasso's gift.

It has a way of giving you what you need most.

Kubby extended his arm. He held an ax and he offered Jack the handle.

Jack looked at his ex-wife and back to Kubby. "Whoa, I can't do that. I won't." Jack shuffled back from Kubby as though the ax was radioactive. "I can't. I'm no killer."

She seized on the word, *killer*. A scream erupted from her core: "Who are you talking to?" She bent at the waist as if to spit the words at him. "Stay away from me. You leave me alone!"

"Sorry, Jack," Kubby said, resting the ax on his shoulder. "There is no other way to finish this."

"What?" Jack slapped a hand over his face. "God help me."

The caretaker's face turned beet red in an instant. Thick veins swelled on his neck and webbed up the sides of his head. "*He* can't help you. *He* stood by while your life came undone." Kubby exhaled out his mouth and his complexion blanched. He thrust the ax handle toward Jack. "Now take this. Wabasso is waiting. It has so much more to give you than that fat, old bastard ever could. It can give you a new life. With Kate.

With your sons. Whatever you want."

Jack regarded Kubby, his eyes wide and wet. "It can? M-my boys?"

Kubby held the ax out to him. "I don't know if it's guilt or what, but without them, you're nothing. Your inkwell is dry. That dismal block rose up at your feet and now it towers over your head. Without them, you will never write another word."

Jack gaped at the caretaker. In Kubby's eyes he saw infinite depth, infinite wisdom. His words cut through the meat of Jack's heart like only the truth could. Jack pressed a hand to his chest, half expecting to find a physical wound.

She took one tentative step toward him, holding her hands out in a gesture meant to calm both of them. "Jack, you used to be a good man. You can still *be* a good man. Whatever is happening here, you need to get help. Let me leave, please, and get yourself some help."

Kubby circled close behind Jack, his mouth inches from Jack's ear. "Do it for your sons, Jack. Do it for you *and* your sons."

Jack bit his lip hard enough to draw blood.

"Listen to me, Jack," she said, taking another jittery step forward. If a nurturing tone was her target, she missed the mark. Terror left jagged edges on all her words now. "Brian and Thomas need a father. They need you to be healthy. Please, go home, get yourself cleaned up and get some help."

An easy breeze sent a few of the fallen manuscript pages dancing across the yard.

At Jack's shoulder, Kubby urged, "Accept Wabasso's gift. Take your place here."

Jack wiped his eyes, stepped back and regarded Kubby, met his knowing gaze. He looked back to his ex and read the wild fear in her bulging orbs. "Why did you leave me?"

Her slow advance ceased. She bunched her hands and held them to her chest. "Jack, just let me go home. I promise we'll talk about everything later."

"I don't want to talk about it later. Tell me now."

"Maybe in a few days, maybe next week, we can all go out

for dinner like we used to and we can talk—"

"*Tell me now!*"

Her whole body quaked like a bomb went off inside her. She shut her eyes briefly and hunted for resolve. "Jack, I didn't leave you," she said finally. "You left *us*. Remember? You shut yourself up in your office for days on end." As she spoke, her brow went rigid, her shoulders tensed. Anger heated her words. "It was like you weren't even there. Like we were living with your ghost. I couldn't let our boys live like that any longer."

"Live like what? I was *working*."

"You were *gone*...mentally, emotionally. You know, you missed Brian's birthday? You spent the whole day at your desk while we had a party. And I made excuses for you when everybody asked where you were. That was the last straw for me. You left us, Jack, and for what? Your stories? Your stupid fucking *stories*?"

A stray page did a pirouette as it blew past Jack's feet. "They're not stupid," Jack said, watching it go. "There was a time I might have agreed with you, but not today, not in this place."

Kubby sidled him. The calm determination in his dark eyes reeled Jack in. "It's okay, Jack," he said in a whisper. "Allow yourself some happiness. You have earned it."

Jack reached for the ax, pulled his hand back. He bent at the waist and something like a growl escaped him.

Kubby, rested a tender hand on the small of his back. "You *have* earned this. So has she. She took your life away from you and I'll bet...I'll bet she didn't even look back."

Jack stood straight, his cheeks streaked with tears.

"Take the ax," Kubby said. "Do it for your sons." He squared his shoulders and stood tall and resolute.

"Jack, I'm sorry I came here," she said, now taking guarded steps back. "I shouldn't have asked Ted for the directions. I'm sorry. I should have left you alone. I'm sorry. Just, *please*, let me leave. You can stay here. Do whatever you want. I won't say a word to anyone. I promise."

Kubby whistled in disbelief. "Ooh, bad idea. If you let her leave now, everything will be jeopardized." He stood at Jack's back. He spoke softly into his ear. "She will talk to the authorities. She will tell them about you. They will come for you and I doubt if they will like what they find here. She certainly didn't. I'm afraid, if she is allowed to leave, Wabasso may suffer the consequences. And, of course, our deal will be off."

Jack turned to his ex-wife and raised a finger. "Wait. You can't leave."

She staggered toward the van.

Kubby said, "Stop her, Jack. Don't let her leave."

She opened the driver's door.

"The clock is ticking, Jack. You're about to lose it all—a life at Wabasso with Kate, with your boys—it's all going down the drain."

She lifted her injured leg into the van and began to drag herself inside.

"Stop her, Jack," Kubby whispered. "She's taking your boys all over again. I wonder if she will spare you a look in the rear view when she leaves you this time."

Jack dropped to his knees. He clutched the sides of his head and released an animal scream. When he raised his face to the darkening sky, a placidity returned to his eyes. Any emotion bled out of them. He slowly got to his feet.

Kubby stepped back. His lips parted with expectation as Jack stood straight and stretched his neck from side to side.

Barely loud enough to be heard, Jack said, "If you want to leave this family there's only one way out."

She heard him perfectly. Half in the van, she ceased her fevered climb to share some parting words. "You're sick! You're a monster! I swear to God you'll never see your sons again."

Kubby's eyes became slits as he watched her. "Is she right about that, Jackie-boy? Are you really going to let that happen?"

Jack sneered at Kubby and snatched the ax from him.

The caretaker couldn't hide his glee. His lips wriggled

apart, displaying his stained teeth.

She saw the ax in Jack's grip. Bewilderment swept across her face. It seemed she was about to ask where it came from. In the intervening seconds, she reached another decision. She gave up on the van. She ran. Out of the barn and past the farmhouse, she ran, taking several strides before resorting to a desperate hobble as she reached the tall grass.

Jack held up the ax and eyed its nasty edge. He winced and bit his lip again as he searched for the strength he needed. He shook off nagging pleas from his conscience for sober thought. Instead, he forced himself to relive a sour moment: moving day. He saw his boys waving from the back of the van. She never looked back.

"Finish the story," Kubby whispered at his shoulder.

Jack's brow stiffened. His eyes darkened. He watched her flee. The blood ran out of the sky. Full dark came and he raised the ax in both hands.

Epilogue

Jack stood behind the counter, finalizing his shopping list for his impending trip to town. Eric Fisher in Cabin One had requested prime rib for dinner again. Jack had gotten quite chummy with the butcher at Tommy's Market and was glad another visit was in the offing. He would also stop at the corner gas and shoot the breeze with Gordy while topping up the company truck. Then he planned to swing by Sears parcel pickup for the wool blankets he'd ordered. Autumn winds had started to blow and the comfort of his guests was his paramount concern.

He stared off into space as he tried to remember the day's other elusive errand. Outside the front window, he caught sight of William Jessop hurriedly approaching, a bundle of papers tucked under his arm.

William had arrived at Wabasso three weeks ago under invitation from the retreat's previous management. He came without a bag, without a shaving kit, but what he lacked in personal belongings he more than made up for with his stubbornly inquisitive nature. Jack had signed him in to a guest cabin without asking many questions of his own. The reason for William's invitation may have been unclear to him, but he could be certain of one thing—no one arrived at Wabasso Lake by accident.

William claimed to be working on a journalistic piece, but Jack saw little evidence of that in the writer's daily routine. What he saw plenty of was William questioning the other guests in the mess hall or outside the shower house or on the beach or anywhere he could corner them on their own. Judging by the determined countenance William now wore, Jack figured he was in for another barrage of questions regarding the history of the retreat.

William pushed inside the office cabin and went to the counter. His one T shirt was past due for its weekly wash. Dark patches ringed his armpits and neck. A film of sweat glued his brown hair to his brow. William said hello and smiled at Jack, but there was something in his eyes that rendered the expression less than genuine.

"How is your day going, Mr. Bishop?" William asked.

"Every day is a gift, my friend. I'm still unwrapping this one, and please, call me Jack. I go by Jackie-baby in some circles, too. Use whatever floats your boat."

William hunted unsuccessfully for an apt response to Jack's folksy manner. He simply laid the stack of pages on the counter between them.

"Oh shit," Jack said looking down at them. "I didn't get anything for you." He laughed.

William tried to join in, but his laughter smacked of angst.

Jack tucked a long strand of hair behind his ear. "What is this, the first draft of your article? I should have told you, I don't really proofread."

The journalist puzzled momentarily over Jack's reaction before getting himself back on track. "Mr. B—*Jack*—I think I might need your help with something," he said, delicately.

"You have it, my friend." Jack straightened.

"The thing is…how should I put this? Something has come into my possession that another party may…I don't know…find valuable."

Jack leaned in, and in a hushed tone, said, "You find a wallet?"

"No, Jack." William winced slightly—the first chink in the

armor of his patience. He slid the pages across the counter toward him. "I found *this*."

Jack nodded and scratched his stubbly chin. "What is it?"

William became rather fidgety. He shifted from foot to foot. "It's a manuscript. A first draft, from what I can gather. He placed his hands on his hips then folded his arms, failing to find a comfortable stance. "

"I see."

Jack stepped around the counter and went to the front window. He stowed his hands in the pockets of his grey hoodie. The pull-over sweater coupled with the olive camouflage shorts he wore had become his uniform of choice. When he wasn't working the mess hall or heading into town he, preferred to go shirtless. It allowed him a readiness to swim the lake whenever the mood struck him. It struck often. So much so that he'd given up on footwear, altogether. Also, he liked the feeling of Wabasso's sand between his toes, although its perfumed breeze fanning his long hair was his favorite sensation.

"Where did you find it, exactly?" Jack asked.

"It was in my cabin, under the cot." A fault line ran through William's voice.

Jack grinned at the journalist's reluctance to divulge the whole truth. Outside, Jack could see Brian and Thomas on the beach. They ran, kicking up sand as they threw the Frisbee around with Kate. She saw him watching and waved. Then she was off again, sprinting to catch the disc, her hair flowing behind her, almost surreal.

"Listen to this," William said. He turned the text to face him and began to recite the story. "'The old man laid a wide farmer's mitt on the boy's head. It had swelled knuckles that had been broken and rebroken in countless wars waged with other hard men.

""'Son," the man said. The boy looked up at him, his lower lip showing the slightest of tremors. "You're old enough to know," the man started. "The true measure of a man don't come in inches and feet or pounds and ounces." He stared at the boy. "It don't even come in battles won and lost. It comes—""'"

Jack focused on the lake while William read. The sun hung lower in the sky these days, but the brilliance of the waters didn't suffer for it. A million twinkling lights filled Jack's vision, each of them a voice whispering the oldest secrets of the world.

""'"—it comes in how he manages fear. Does he master fear or does he let it cripple him? Does fear make him stronger or does it get the better of him? I decided a long time ago, I wasn't gonna be a man who lived in fear. I was gonna be a man *to* fear."'"" William turned to Jack for his take. "So, what do you think?"

Jack remained focused on the lake, hands in his pockets. A stray laugh from the Frisbee game reached them.

William pressed. "Do you think it sounds familiar? I mean, do you think you may have read this before? Because I was thinking, you know, if it hasn't been published, that maybe somebody is missing it."

Jack glanced over his shoulder at him before returned his gaze to the window.

"I just thought that since you're the caretaker you might know who wrote it, and maybe we could ask them if they wanted it back." William cleared his throat into his fist. "And maybe they would offer a reward for it."

From his vantage, the journalist couldn't see Jack's smirk.

"You didn't by chance read the whole story, did you William?"

"Well, umm." He gave up a humorless laugh. Jack thought it sounded more like a sneeze. "Yeah, I sort of did. Yes."

Jack didn't look back. He said, "William, how well do *you* manage fear?"

About the Author

Todd Allen lives on the East Coast of Canada with his wife, Michelle, and daughter, Maya.

No Greater Agony is his second novel.

http://toddallenbooks.com